Praise for
Blood Oranges

"A pedal-to-the-metal, balls-to-the-wall female antihero who doesn't give a damn if you like her or not . . . which totally made me love her."
—Amber Benson

"A memorably exhilarating and engaging experience. Sly, sardonically nasty, and amusingly clever."
—*Kirkus Reviews*

"[Kiernan] brings an engagingly fresh perspective to well-trod territory. . . . Colorful side characters and a fully realized setting make this a fast-paced series opener well worth checking out."
—*Publishers Weekly*

"Kiernan . . . has made it her business to turn the comfortable genres of imaginative fiction inside out. Now writing as Kathleen Tierney, she introduces a heroine as fascinating and compelling as she is foul-mouthed and impatient."
—*Library Journal*

"[A] fast-paced, profane, and combustive little thriller."
—The Black Letters

"A strange (and unmistakably fun) project, a parodic urban fantasy that at once vivisects the tropes of the genre as it currently stands and also employs them with vigor and a backhanded, wild immersion."
—Tor.com

"A lot of fun."
—*Locus*

"A dark, twisted ride through the seedier side of life, but it's peppered with enough humor to make it enjoyable."—*RT Book Reviews*

"A mesmerizing exploration of magic without certainty . . . a must read for anyone drawn to the darker edges of urban fantasy."
—All Things Urban Fantasy

continued . . .

Praise for the Novels of
Caitlín R. Kiernan

The Drowning Girl

**WINNER OF THE BRAM STOKER AND
JAMES TIPTREE, JR., AWARDS**

**NOMINATED FOR THE WORLD FANTASY, NEBULA,
BRITISH FANTASY, SHIRLEY JACKSON, *LOCUS*, AND
MYTHOPOEIC FANTASY AWARDS**

"This subtle, dark, in-folded novel, through which flickers a weird insistent genius, is like nothing I've ever read before. . . . A stunning work of literature."　　　　　　　　　　　　　　—Peter Straub

"A prose style of wondrous luminosity, an atmosphere of languorous melancholy, and an inexplicable mixture of aching beauty and clutching terror."

　　　　　　　　　　　　—S. T. Joshi, author of *I Am Providence:
The Life and Times of H. P. Lovecraft*

"A masterpiece. It deserves to be read in and out of genre for a long, long time."　　　　　　　—Elizabeth Bear, author of *Range of Ghosts*

"Wholly different and achingly familiar, more alien, more difficult, more beautiful, and more true."
　　—Catherynne M. Valente, *New York Times* bestselling author of
*The Girl Who Circumnavigated Fairyland
in a Ship of Her Own Making*

"Incisive, beautiful, and as perfectly crafted as a puzzle box, *The Drowning Girl* took my breath away."
　　—Holly Black, *New York Times* bestselling author of *Black Heart*

"A beautifully written, startlingly original novel that rings the changes upon classics by the likes of Shirley Jackson, H. P. Lovecraft, and Peter Straub . . . chilling and unforgettable, with a narrator whose voice will linger in your head long after midnight."
　　　　　　　　　　—Elizabeth Hand, author of *Available Dark*

The Red Tree

"A strange and vastly compelling take on a New England haunting. . . . Kiernan's still-developing talent makes this gloriously atmospheric tale a fabulous piece of work." —*Booklist*

Daughter of Hounds

"A hell-raising dark fantasy replete with ghouls, changelings, and eerie intimations of a macabre otherworld . . . an effective mix of atmosphere and action." —*Publishers Weekly*

Murder of Angels

"Lyrical and earthy, *Murder of Angels* is that rare book that gets everything right." —Charles de Lint

Low Red Moon

"Eerie and breathtaking . . . [a novel] of sustained dread punctuated by explosions of unmitigated terror." —*Irish Literary Review*

Threshold

"*Threshold* is a bonfire proclaiming Caitlín Kiernan's elevated position in the annals of contemporary literature. It is an exceptional novel you mustn't miss. Highly recommended." —*Cemetery Dance*

Silk

"A remarkable novel." —Neil Gaiman

BOOKS BY CAITLÍN R. KIERNAN

Novels

Silk
Threshold
Low Red Moon
Murder of Angels
Daughter of Hounds
The Red Tree
The Drowning Girl: A Memoir

Writing as Kathleen Tierney

Blood Oranges
Red Delicious

Caitlín R. Kiernan
Writing as Kathleen Tierney

RED
DELICIOUS

A ROC BOOK

ROC
Published by the Penguin Group
Penguin Group (USA) LLC, 375 Hudson Street,
New York, New York 10014

USA | Canada | UK | Ireland | Australia | New Zealand | India | South Africa | China
penguin.com
A Penguin Random House Company

First published by Roc, an imprint of New American Library,
a division of Penguin Group (USA) LLC

First Printing, February 2014

 REGISTERED TRADEMARK—MARCA REGISTRADA

LIBRARY OF CONGRESS CATALOGING-IN-PUBLICATION DATA:

Tierney, Kathleen, 1964–
    Red delicious: a Siobhan Quinn novel/Caitlín R. Kiernan writing
as Kathleen Tierney.
      pages cm
    ISBN 978-0-451-41653-7 (pbk.)
    1. Werewolves—Fiction. 2. Vampires—Fiction. I. Title.
    PS3561.I358R42 2014
    813'.54—dc23   2013038068

Printed in the United States of America
10 9 8 7 6 5 4 3 2 1

Set in ITC Galliard
Designed by Sabrina Bowers

If your ears, eyes, and sensibilities are easily offended, this book is not for you. If you want a romance novel, this book is not for you. And if it strikes you odd that vampires, werewolves, demons, ghouls, and the people who spend time in their company would be a foul-mouthed, unpleasant lot, this book is not for you. In fact, if you're the sort who believes books should come with warning labels, this book's not for you. Fair notice. Also, high-school dropouts are not necessarily illiterate idiots who don't know "big words." I speak from experience.

To paraphrase Ursula K. LeGuin, this is me once more taking back the language of the night. If only for myself.

The Author

A wiser man than myself once said, "Sometimes you eat the b'ar, and sometimes, well, he eats you."

—THE STRANGER

You're dumb. You'll die and leave a dumb corpse.

—OLD ASURA PROVERB

RED
DELICIOUS

CHAPTER ONE

A GHOST OF MYSELF

Hello. My name is Siobhan Quinn, and I'm a murderer. It's been three days since my last homicide.

See? You like me already.

Not that everyone and her mother considers vampires and werewolves—or some poor shit like me who lucks out and gets the best of both worlds—a murderer. Most everyone is too busy either painting us nasties as this or that stripe of demon or monster, or (and this truly does get my goat) they've managed to romanticize the fiends we are into tortured Byronic figures who sparkle in sunlight or pretentiously haunt the streets of, say, New Orleans.

1

The heroes and heroines of lurid "shifter" romances and self-proclaimed "otherkin" and "therianthropes" who'd shit themselves silly if they ever got so much as a peep at a genuine *loup.* Or we get to solve paranormal crimes in an attempt to redeem our damned souls. Or we seek to regain our lost mortality. Or, so say various Academic sorts, serve as metaphors for mankind's fear of the Other. Or . . .

You get the picture.

And John Wayne Gacy was just some misunderstood candy-colored clown. Jeffrey Dahmer, guy just had an eating disorder. Sure thing. Anyway, we'll no doubt come back to all this falderal later on, repeatedly, because it never ceases to amuse me.

I hate recaps. With a passion do I hate recaps. But I suppose—for all you folks just tuning in—I should at least make a half-assed, token effort at something of the sort. Here goes:

Once upon a time there was a girl ran away from home to live on the hard streets of Providence, Rhode Island. Before long, she discovered the joys of heroin, or they discovered her, and she took to junk like a fly to horse poop. Then, lo and behold, a series of highly unlikely events transpired during which she accidentally killed a ghoul and then a vampire—in the process discovering, hey, guess what, *monsters are real.* Whee. Now, homeless junkies who kill two nasties without even trying, they tend to attract attention. Mostly, not the good sort of attention. Which is how it went for me. This dude calling himself B, he shows up. B's sort of a middleman for all sorts of dealings between things what go bump in the night, which makes him as many enemies as friends. More, actually. So, he shows up and gives me one of those offers you can't refuse: I go to work as a sort of body- guard, and he protects me from the baddies want me dead, and he gives me a place to live. Plus, generous soul that he is, he'll supply me with all the free smack I can shoot into my veins. Well, as long as I can balance being high and getting the job done. I accept, and he pins a rep on me, tall tales of his own invention, how I'm absolute and certain doom to anyone dares fuck with him, and . . . Jesus, I'm boring myself already.

Shorter version: I screw up. And I mean I screw up bad. The same night I get sloppy and get bitten by a werewolf, I'm also bitten by a very, very formidable vam- pire child called herself the Bride of Quiet. Or Mercy Brown, depending on her mood. B, who sees no shame in cowardice, he takes a powder, leaving me to fend for myself, because, turns out, I'd become some sort of pawn in a decades-old labyrinthine intrigue of revenge and bitch-slapping between the Bride and this even scarier she vamp down in Brooklyn, a firebug of thermonuclear proportions known as Evangelista Penderghast. Events unfold. Wham, bam, thank you, ma'am. Folks die, most of whom have it coming. Most of whom I ate. Finally, I make a deal with Penderghast, and she loans me a magi- cal doodad—real eldritch voodoo stuff—that allows me to bump off the Bride (and a church bus full of were- wolves in the bargain).

B comes back, and all is forgiven.

Cue exit music. Close curtain.

Fast-forward six months or so.

Which brings us, constant reader, to the here and now, and the fact that *this* story needs a beginning, and I think a good place to start would be the freezing, snowy mid-February morning I was strolling along College Hill, minding my own business. Sky the color of lead, as they say, battleship gray, as they say, and fat, fluffy flakes spiraling lazily down to cover up the frozen mix of ice, sand, and salt from the last week's snowfall. Providence—something else I don't generally romanticize—isn't so bad on a day like that. All the hard, ugly winter edges get smoothed away, you know.

So, I was coming around the corner at Fones Alley and Hope Street, basking in the afterglow of a good feed, free of the hunger for a while—and, even though it had to be eleven a.m. by then, there's not a soul in sight—not a pedestrian, not a car, not a bus. What the fuck was with that? Sometimes oddly peculiar shit just happens. Like accidentally killing a ghoul. I'd smoked a Camel down to the filter, and I flicked the butt into the gutter, when here comes this cocksucker barreling out of the bushes by the sidewalk. I know right off who it is. Remember the notorious Bobby Ng, wannabe demon slayer and all around ass clown? You know, he who was the brunt of many a joke and had the misfortune of becoming first meal as a *loup*?

Well, shortly after Bobby's demise, this *other* dude had shown up. Nature abhors a void, right? Natura abhorreta vacuum or something like that. However, whereas Ng had been the worst sort of fuckup—at best, good for the occasional belly laugh among the demonkin, too ridiculous to even bother killing—the new guy, he was a defrocked Catholic priest with at least a few brain cells still in working order. Father Bertrand "Burt" Rizzo, who'd been ousted from a parish somewhere in New Jersey for having his way with twenty years' worth of altar boys. He'd started out with dreams of taking a place among the lofty order of the *Societas Iesu*, or the Jesuits (if you've never suffered the joys of Catholicism). But he washed out, and had to settle for a plain old priesthood. Maybe that left him a little unhinged. Me, I didn't know, and I didn't care. What mattered was, whereas Ng's antics had been pretty much harmless (until he caused me to take out the blood daughter of the Bride of Quiet), Father Rizzo had his act together, and in only a few months had somehow become Providence's own Abraham Van Helsing.

Lucky us.

This shitbird had a price on his head, but somehow had eluded the bounty for three months. During that time, his body count included four ghouls, a night gaunt, a baby vamp of no particular renown, and, during a field trip to Woonsocket, three *loups*. Like I said, dude sorta had his shit together. There were suspicions he'd traded the Holy Trinity for darker gods, and that's how he was keeping his ass covered. Maybe so. Maybe not so.

Rizzo was a big man—lucha libre big—almost a foot taller than me, say six foot six, and at least two hundred and fifty pounds. Most of that was muscle and bullshit. He was fast. Worse, he was well armed. That morning, all I had was the Glock 17 9mm I always carry, and I was nowhere near on my toes. I was walking in a winter wonderland, not braced for an ambush by Rizzo. He hit me hard from behind, knocking me off my feet. I've gotten pretty good at taking a spill without breaking anything, and I rolled to my left, ending up half in the dirty mound of slush burying the edge of the sidewalk. I looked up, and there he was, standing over me. The cold morning sun glinting off his bald head, the long, scraggly beard that always made me think of Rasputin. His breath fogged like a steam engine.

This was, as it happened, the first time he'd dared take a swipe at me, the one soul in all Rhode Island who also happened to be his competition. Honestly, I hadn't thought the dude was that stupid or that ballsy.

Wrong. Wicked wrong.

There he stood, aiming his crossbow at my chest. Oh, yeah. He was armed with the same make and model crossbow B had given me back in August—self-cocking, pistol-grip mini with that lightweight aluminum frame and fifty-pound draw. I could see the fiberglass bolts had silver tips. Rizzo had carved little crosses on the bolts. Cute. Silly, but cute.

"Siobhan Quinn," he said, and grinned.

"No one fucking calls me Siobhan," I growled.

This is a true fact. People have died for calling me Siobhan. People who didn't mean to do me mischief on snowy February mornings. Now, I'm sure he knew this. He smirked and kicked me in the ribs. It hurt, but you can't knock the breath outta something doesn't breathe.

"Tough titties," said Father Rizzo. No, seriously. With dog as my witness, I shit you not. Here, this guy who used to be a man of the cloth, trusted to place the transubstantiated flesh of Christ on the tongues of his flock, outs with *tough titties*. How was I *not* supposed to laugh? I guess getting yourself booted outta the priesthood for buggering young boys really does a number on your sense of propriety.

"You did *not* just say that," I said, doing my best not to giggle.

"You gonna lie there and waste your last moments before I send you to Hell worrying about dirty language?"

Lots of time since the summer before, the July night when I'd died, I had considered shuffling off this immortal coil. Murderer or not, monster or not, I couldn't seem to shake my conscience, no matter how good it felt. Turning my mosquito trick on some unsuspecting soul or letting the Beast run wild beneath a full moon, they beat sex, beat heroin, beat everything I'd known before, but it's a pretty shitty existence. And usually a pain in the ass.

Still, I was not gonna become just another notch in Rizzo's holy crossbow of Jesus doom.

Sometimes the oldest and dumbest tricks are the best.

"Dude, your fly's unzipped," I laughed. When he checked (and yes, he *did* check), I kneed him in the balls hard enough I figure they must have collided with his spleen. At least, he howled like I had. Rizzo staggered backwards a few steps, then slipped on a patch of ice and landed on his ass. I was on my feet in one of those heartbeats I didn't have to bother with anymore. He'd dropped his crossbow, and I kicked it into the street. Finally, traffic! Right on fucking cue! A RIPTA bus sped past and crushed the weapon pretty much flat. Shit like that makes me wonder if what we call reality is nothing more than a movie someone's filming in an alternate universe Hollywood. Because . . . damn.

But! Not so fast, Quinn!

While I'd been distracted by the bus and my reflections on the possible existence of a cosmic screenwriter, Father Rizzo had drawn one hell of a hunting knife from his work boot (yeah, cassock, white collar, and work boots), and it whizzed past my right ear close enough I figure he'd surely sliced off the upper half inch or so of skin. Then he drew an identical knife from his other boot.

"Okay," I told him. "Enough fun and games." I pounced, and he lost his grip on the knife; it went spinning away across the sidewalk into another muddy slush bank of last week's snow.

Both my knees came down hard on his biceps, the toes of my Chucks slamming into his rib cage, one hand gripping each side of his hairy face. I politely waited until he was drawing breath again and had stopped gasping like a beached cod. I leaned close and whispered, my lips so near he could feel my icy breath in his ear.

"Back in seminary, how much pain they teach you to endure in the name of the Lord?"

Then there was this kid's voice behind me. "Hey, you're beating up on a priest," it said. I looked over my shoulder to find this Asian guy, maybe nineteen, all earbuds and one of those colorful hats they ship in from Tibet or Ecuador or wherever. You know, dongley things, earflaps, hanging down on either side and the pom-pom on top?

I bared my shiny piranha teeth.

"So, go find a cop," I told him. "Or get in line. Take your pick."

Needless to say, the kid did not get in line. I turned back to Rizzo, who was hurting plenty enough now he'd stopped struggling. I had an instant of satisfaction, thinking on how this scene was gonna look on the evening news, and splashed across the front page of the *ProJo*. B would go pale as a sheet, sure as shit, and that never gets old, watching him freak. This public dustup would be another mess he'd have to find a way to cover up.

Sweet. No, double sweet. With a cherry on top.

I stared down at Rizzo, who—gotta give the bastard credit—was staring straight right back at me.

"Do your worst, hellhound," he said.

Is there a how-to manual aspiring "demon slayers" get these quips from? Maybe so, published by Pentecostals down in Mississippi or Georgia or somewhere equally vile, distributed like those ridiculous Jack Chick pamphlets.

"I know I'm a few days early," I said, smiling wide enough I hoped it was ear to fucking ear. "But Happy fucking Valentine's Day, Father." And then I kissed him. A big, sloppy kiss, tongue and all. He tasted like donuts and bad teeth, but it was worth it and back again.

And then I stood up and walked away, leaving Rizzo retching on the frozen sidewalk. I'm betting he spent days after that gargling with holy water and chrism, saying Hail Marys because I'd *felt* his hard-on under me during that long and blasphemous kiss. So, hey, sure I *could* have killed him, but the continued existence of other nasties had never been high on my list of priorities, since most of my work for B involved their undoing (for everything but noble reasons). Let someone else deal with Rizzo.

In retrospect, leaving him alive was merely the latest boneheaded move in *Quinn's Little Golden Book of Boneheaded Moves*.

Returning now to the subject of Mr. B, or, as I tend to think of him, Mean Mr. B. Trust me. The moniker fits. See, some might aspire to be a son of a bitch; I'm pretty sure B was born that way. I imagine he popped out of his mama's womb and immediately began trying to suss out the percentage in screwing over every single solitary soul in the delivery room. Hello. What can you do for me? Still, B, he's nothing half so lowlife as a grifter. Maybe he *was*, long time back. Every now and then, I sit staring at him and wondering if he began his career as just another confidence fuck, hustling the short cons—pigeon drops, the looky-loo, pig in a poke, rocks in a box, et cetera and et cetera. If so, I gotta wonder when he fell in with the nasties and figured there was better money to be made as a more or less honest businessman brokering and mediating deals where few mortals had ever feared to tread.

I ask myself those questions, but he's never volunteered an answer, and I ain't about to ask out loud. B frequently reminds everyone around him they're disposable: *I found you, made you, and you give me too much shit, I can find another tout de suite. Don't you ever fool yourself into thinking any different.*

Which I don't.

Work for me, kitten, you'll make enemies of a sort even the likes of a Mr. John Milton and a Mr. H. P. Lovecraft didn't dare conjure up in their blackest, most fevery dreams. You fuck me over, little girl, or cock up a transaction more than I'm in the mood to get it sorted, I'll feed you to the lot of them, arse and tits and all.

Sweet guy, right? Real charmer.

But, on the other hand, I've a feeling I've caused B more headaches and inconvenience than most of his lackeys. For my transgressions, I get scoldings, slaps on the wrists, threats, and extra shitty jobs, but he hasn't yet cut me loose. And that's another question I'll never ask aloud. I figure the motherfucker's got his reasons, and that's good enough for me.

Want me to paint you a picture of the man goes beyond his lovable personality? Fine. There he is, on the rough side of fifty, some stripe of Londoner or someone only affecting the accent and mannerisms. He's sort of a shrimp, but I suspect if he ever has to he could hold his own in a brawl. Probably, he's had to do that quite a lot over the years, but he also strikes me as one of those badasses who's let himself get soft and a little complacent. These days, he's got other folks to fight his battles. Mean Mr. B, he dresses like he's a gangster in a 1930s or 1940s gangster flick. There is an effete and practiced dapperness about him. A proper dandy, is B, with his slicked-back hair the color and sheen of coal, the sharp edges of his suits, shiny wing tips, his fedoras, and the carefully folded breast-pocket handkerchiefs. And he's a smooth talker. He could have put the *s* in suave. Could sell celery to a vampire. Hell, he probably has. More important, he's ace at talking himself outta the tight spots that are an occupational hazard in his line of work. You deal with demons, dissatisfied customers and unreasonable clients abound. Folks decide they're above (or below) paying his fee, once the task is done. So you have to give him the due in that respect.

And he's queer as they come, with an especially keen taste for jailbait drag queens and pre-op trannies. Hardly ever see the man without a cross-dressing morsel of top-shelf arm candy in tow. But I'm one to talk, unrepentant dyke that I am, she who has never once slept with a man in her life or undeath and never fucking will, thank you very much.

Which brings us to one last salient point. If B has a legal name printed on a birth certificate somewhere, I've never yet met anyone or anything knows what it is. He's B, except every night that B stands for *le nom de jour*. This would be funny, if it weren't so annoying, trying to keep up. Oh, and all his aliases? All of them begin with B, naturally enough: Basil, Blythe, Benjamin, Buckminster, Barlow, and on and on and on. That February, I'd known him for those aforementioned six months, so you figure that's close to two hundred names right there, and I'd never heard him use the same one twice.

So, B holds court in this bar up on Wickenden Street—Babe's on the Sunnyside. Not sure when Anthony "Babe" Silva first opened the doors and pulled that first pint of Guinness, but it had to have been half a century ago. The walls are crowded with black-and-white photos of Providence boxers—Rocky Marciano and Willie Pep, old-timers like that—and there's a faded needlepoint mural of John F. Kennedy strung up over the billiard table. A rheumy air conditioner chugs in the summer, and the color TV offers up an endless variety of sporting events. Local color out the wazoo. But it's the last place I'd expect to find this scary old queen with his pretty boys, sipping Cape Cods (and never anything else, mind you) in a booth at the very back of the joint. Likely, just to be contrary. Still, I've never seen anyone bat an eyelash at B. If anyone disapproves, they keep it to themselves, like here was a bona fide made wise guy from the Providence Cosa Nostra who'd taken up residence there in their midst.

Okay, so now you know as much as I do about Mean Mr. B, which will have to suffice.

Which brings us back to that snowy morning, me up to nothing more sinister than a walk home when I'm jumped by that defrocked pedophile priest motherfucker. So much for minding my own business and keeping my nose clean (both among Mean Mr. B's prescribed virtues). Having not delivered a much-deserved coup de grâce upon my attacker's person, I decided it was best I hunt down B. Always better he learn about this sort of shit from me than hear it through the proverbial grapevine. But Babe's didn't open until noon, and I had no idea what to do with myself for the intervening hour. There probably wasn't time to drop by home for a shower and a change of clothes. For that matter, there was no guarantee this was one of the days B would even turn up early. He might leave me dangling anxiously for hours, during which time he might learn of the thing with Rizzo before I had a chance to break the news myself.

But I had one option, a stopgap until the face-to-face. I sat down on the curb, reached into a pocket of my parka, and pulled out the iPhone he'd given me for Xmas. It was a bad joke. Probably, he'd given one of his mollies a credit card and sent the kid off to the mall. The backside of the phone's case was a glittering mosaic of diamond rhinestones, arranged into the six-whiskered, mouthless, macrocephalic face of Hello Kitty, with a pink diamond rhinestone flower set at each corner. Yeah, ha, ha, fucking ha. I should have thrown the case away, but you never know what's gonna piss the man off. What he's gonna interpret as a failure to appreciate his overwhelming generosity.

So there we were, me and Hello Kitty. I tapped in his number, and it rang eight times before anyone answered. Nothing unusual there. I was lucky when anyone bothered answering at all. It wasn't Mean Mr. B, of course. He never answers the phone himself. It was one of the boys; their voices were as interchangeable to me as their faces.

"Need to speak him," I said.

"Him?" the voice asked, drenched in indifference.

"Yeah, *him*. Put *him* on the line, and stop fucking around."

"I take it you mean Bosco. You're being very vague."

"Bosco? You're shitting me. *Bosco?*"

"Unless you mean someone else, Quinn," the boy sighed, his indifference changing over into mild exasperation. "Maybe you have the wrong number."

"Fine. Yeah, I mean Bosco."

"Well, he's not in at the moment. I can take a message, though. If you wish."

I wanted to punch the sidewalk. Sure, the cement would probably break my hand, but it'd have healed by the next day. I gritted my teeth.

"No," I said, as calmly as I could manage, 'cause B hates when anyone gets grumpy with one of his play pretties. "I don't want to leave a message. Do you know when he'll be back?"

"I haven't a clue. Call back later, or try Babe's."

Nine chances out of ten, *Bosco* (probably the worst name I'd heard him use yet) was sitting right next to the boy, silently chuckling to himself. I knew it wasn't beyond the realm of possibility that he'd already gotten wind of the altercation and had decided to savor my discomfort for a while.

He does shit like that, all the goddamn time.

"Tell him I called. Tell him I'll be around."

"That's very vague, Quinn."

"Yeah," I replied and hung up.

Fuck me.

So, as Willy Wonka said, strike that. Reverse it. I did have time to swing by home and clean up, after all. I stuck out my tongue and tasted the snow. The flakes take just a little longer to melt on the tongue of a dead girl. One flake, two flakes, three. Then I stood up, dusted snow off my jeans, and turned north up Hope Street. It was only four blocks to my apartment, the second floor of an old Victorian.

This isn't the dump I was living in when Mercy Brown and Jack Grumet the Werewolf made of me the pretty hate machine I am today, that shithole down at the south end of Gano that B rented for me just after he took me under his wing. By that February, I'd moved up in the world. Sure, the place was still a dump, but it was a way classier dump. There isn't even a hole in the kitchen floor. And the ugly Play-Doh blue carpet doesn't crunch when you walk on it, from all the roaches that are busy living and dying underneath. Nothing but the best for Mean Mr. B's red right hand. Can't have folks thinking he doesn't take care of his own, not a classy gent like him. Demons talk.

Walking those four blocks, I kept my head down, avoiding the casual glances of anyone else I passed. The night before, I hadn't felt like bothering with the contact lenses and dental prosthetics and the layers of makeup I usually used to hide my true face from the living, breathing world. B had given me the contacts a day or two after I died, to conceal my shark-black eyes—no distinguishing pupil from iris—behind a lie of hazel green. Before Mercy Brown, my eyes had been blue, but what the fuck? He'd sent me to a cosmetic dentist a month or so later, after that mess with the Bride and Penderghast was over and done with, this dude up in Pawtucket who practiced a smattering of half-assed Enochian magic on the side and could generally be counted on to keep a secret in order to stay in the good graces of the nasties. That, and I figured Mean Mr. B had some dirt on him, as well.

But the contacts hurt my eyes, the fake teeth made it difficult to talk, and the makeup . . . well, it was all just too much trouble, and I'd taken to forgoing all that subterfuge when I went out at nights. Especially the nights I went out to eat.

I was on my way up the front steps when a silver Buick

LaCrosse pulled up in front of the house and the driver honked its horn. I turned and stared at the car a moment, pretending I didn't know it was B come around to collect his troublesome hired gun. The horn honked a second time. Fortunately, my downstairs neighbors were out of town (a situation that would soon grow increasingly fortunate). I haven't mentioned how Mercy and Grumet had left me with the ability to hear a mouse fart from three states away, but they had, and I heard clearly the whir of electronics as the backseat window on the passenger side of the Buick descended, revealing the grinning face of B, smirking out at me. He was wearing a gray-and-white seersucker suit, as if he'd dressed to blend in with the weather. I rubbed my eyes another moment before walking over to the car.

"Wanna go for a ride?" he asked, all cordial as cordial can be. He patted the seat beside him.

"Not especially," I said. "More in the mood for a long hot shower."

He cocked an eyebrow. "That's not what you indicated just a few minutes ago."

"Yeah, well, you snooze, you lose."

These sudden, unexpected spells of pushing my luck? Just another wrinkle in the bottomless charisma of me that B has always—well, usually—let slide.

"You sound rather put out, kitten," he said, making an attempt at seeming concerned. "Whatever in the whole wide world has you in such an unpleasant disposition, this fine winter morning?"

I very briefly calculated the potential expense of punching the motherfucker in the face.

"Must have been sod all, to have you so at sixes and sevens. Climb in and tell me all about it."

I ignored the second invitation. Not as satisfying as punching him in the face, but infinitely less hazardous.

"Sure some little birdie or another hasn't already told you, *Bosco*?"

"Now, now. Bosco is a fine and noble name—"

"For chocolate syrup."

"—of Italian origin, from the Piemonte region. Have you truly never heard of Father Giovanni Melchiorre Bosco? Don Bosco, as he's more popularly known. Canonized in 1934 and, as it happens, the patron saint of magicians."

"See? You know it was Rizzo, and you're just fucking with me for shits and giggles."

"Be that as it may, I'd like to hear of this misadventure from you, Quinn, my sweet. Now, please stop wasting my time and get in the car."

Now, B almost never says *please*, not even when speaking to his more infernal, perfidious, and perilous clients. I shut up and got in the Buick. The inside of the car smelled of aftershave lotion, the rainbow-colored Nat Shermans B smokes, and black coffee. At least, those three formed the uppermost stratum of smells. I could list dozens of subtler odors. Like my hearing, Mercy Brown's ministrations had cranked up my nose to eleven. I glanced at the rearview mirror and the chauffeur, who was watching me with a mix of suspicion and boredom. He was Filipino, no more than nineteen, and, I have to admit, subtler and less garish in his gender bending that Mean Mr. B's usual bill of fare.

"He started it," I said, keeping my eyes on the driver (who was still sizing me up).

"I'm very sure that he did," B replied. "It was only a matter of time before the good father expanded his ambitions. Fancy a fag?" he asked, offering me my choice of a red, blue, or green cigarette.

"I'll pass."

The driver narrowed his eyes very slightly, as if he wasn't so keen on my having refused B's offer.

"She thinks she'll pass," B sighed, and the boy finally turned away from the rearview mirror. He shrugged and laughed very softly.

"Frankly," said B, "I don't entirely understand the silly git's problem with you. After all, in a sense, you're both in the same line of work. True, you're more discriminating, and less zealous—"

"And only kill what and who I'm told. I'm hardly on a goddamn holy crusade."

"I trust you do know the meaning of the word *zealous*, don't you?" he asked. Then he motioned at the driver, and the silver Buick pulled away from the curb.

"Maybe he's pissed about the competition," I said, ignoring the question.

"Possibly. But surely he's aware there's plenty of victims to go around. No, I fear it's more personal."

"You give the bastard too much credit."

"I'm only reminding you of the risks in underestimating your adversaries, and in jumping to conclusions as to their motivations."

I slumped back against the seat, wishing I were just about anywhere but in the company of Mean Mr. B(osco) and the Filipino kid. Preferably taking a hot shower to wash away the night's grime. I stared at the ceiling as we headed south down Hope Street.

"Did I mention he started it?"

"You did," B replied, and lit a Nat Sherman.

"I know I should have killed the fucker, okay? I know that. I just wasn't—"

"No, no, no," he interrupted, waving his cigarette about dismissively. Smoke oozed from his nostrils. "Truth be told, dear, I'm impressed by your restraint. Can't say, in your position, I'd have let the wanker off with nothing more than a kiss."

"Okay, *Bosco*, that's a relief. So, if you're not pissed at me for leaving Rizzo alive—"

"There's another matter."

Isn't there always?

I turned my head, staring at him instead of the ceiling. It was a pretty boring ceiling. He took a drag on his cigarette and blew a series of perfect smoke rings.

"Look, I'm tired. I need a shower and I need some sleep. So, can we talk about it tonight?"

"Afraid not, precious. The customers are rather insistent the matter in question be resolved quickly. I can't say I blame them, given the particulars. Also, they're hardly the sort we can afford to fob off because you need to freshen up and get some shut-eye. You've heard of the Maidstones, I trust?"

I had. Of course I fucking had. Anyone whose business involves the nasties and their hangers-on knows about Edgar Isaac Maidstone and his clan. The three Mayston brothers had arrived in the Colonies sometime in the early

1800s, having ditched England to avoid prosecution for a variety of ghoulish crimes: grave robbing, witchcraft, kidnapping, cannibalism, murder, and . . . well, it's a long list. At some point, they'd changed their names to Maidstone and prospered, which is a lot easier when you have the sort of otherworldly connections those three had. Some people, they might call themselves necromancers, and brag about once having made a cadaver twitch. Shit like that. But the Maidstones, *they* were the real goddamn deal. More than once, Maidstones had taken demon brides, and it showed, both in their prowess and their appearance. Edgar Maidstone had (still has) a big-ass house over in Newport, and from the outside it might be any stately Gilded Age mansion, but inside the place is rotten to the core.

"One of their daughters has gone missing," B continued. "Amity, the youngest."

"And . . . what?" I shook my head and went back to staring at the boring ceiling. "How's Edgar Maidstone's inability to keep tabs on his brats got anything to do with when I'm allowed to brush my fucking teeth?"

B whistled between his teeth, the way he sometimes does when he's impatient.

"Edgar Maidstone," he said, "isn't yet aware that his sweet-sixteen Amity is missing."

"Which brings me back around to what the fuck this has to do with me."

"Two nights ago, Quinn, I was approached by the elder daughter, Berenice—"

"I *know* her name," I said, and thumped the ceiling. The driver glared at me from the mirror, so I thumped it again, twice as hard, and smirked.

"—who, aside from her sisterly concern—"

"Fuck that, B. I've heard those two hate each other like cats and dogs."

"—wishes, and not unreasonably so, that Amity Maidstone be located before their father *discovers* she's missing. Ergo, Amity is forgoing the family's usual, and I will admit, considerably more effective, resources in tracking down her sister's whereabouts."

I thumped the ceiling again. When the driver ignored me, I considered kicking his seat.

"So, put what's his name—Shaker—put Shaker on it. I'm sure as hell no sort of detective."

"That's exactly what I did," B told me, "and now he's vanished, as well."

"What a shame. Send flowers to his widow."

Mean Mr. B scowled and exhaled a cloud of smoke. "Since when, kitten, have you acquired the privilege to pick and choose which assignments you will and will not accept from me?"

"Not a detective," I repeated.

The car rolled through a stop sign and someone blew their horn. I don't think B even noticed. Not like he had to give a shit about traffic laws. I'm pretty sure he was invisible so far as the Providence PD were concerned; too bad that invisibility has never rubbed off on me.

"As I recall, you did a fair enough job last summer."

He was referring to how I'd managed to unravel the mystery of my part in the squabble between the Bride and Evangelista Penderghast.

"That was stupid luck, and you know it," I told him. "Plus, it cost me a goddamn finger." I held up my left hand, minus its pinkie. I'd bartered the finger for information when I'd run out of leads in just who had set me up so it looked like I'd offed a vamp bitch named Cregan, which had put me on the Bride's radar to start with. It hadn't been much consolation when my inner wolf wound up eating the rat-bastard asshole who'd sold me the intel.

"And a toe," he reminded me. Because, you know, I might have forgotten.

"*And* a fucking toe. And fuck you, because there's enough on my plate without playing Nancy Drew."

"I'm not asking. You know that."

Yeah, I did. I knew that like I know the sun rises and sets. Like I know dead people get up and walk around if you ask 'em just right or pay off the right sort. Like I know *loups* have bad table manners.

Like I know a lot of stuff.

"So, no more fuss and nonsense," he said. "Be a good girl and find Shaker for me. I'd prefer to have him back. And please have a talk with Berenice. She's a student at Brown. Be polite. Wear clean clothes."

"I hate you."

"We all have our crosses to bear, precious."

The boy behind the wheel pulled over at the intersection with Wickenden.

"Stay in touch, Quinn. And take care not to disappoint me. It isn't necessary to stress how much is riding on this situation."

There was nothing left to say, and I didn't waste my breath not saying it. For the time being, I was still firmly under B's well-manicured thumb. The way things stood, if I dared walk, I wouldn't last twenty-four hours on my own. He'd seen to that, making sure I ticked off all the wrong bad guys so I'd need his protection for a long, long time. Without another word, I got out of the Buick. I stood there a moment, staring at the blood caked under my nine fingernails, then turned for home again.

CHAPTER TWO

THE GIRL

Most of what I knew about Berenice Maidstone and her wayward kid sister had been covered in the backseat of Mean Mr. B's silver Buick. I'd be going into this affair just shy of blind. He hadn't slipped me a hush-hush dossier filled with the deepest, darkest secrets of the two or a *Mission: Impossible*–style "this tape will self destruct in ten seconds" cassette. Yeah, I could undoubtedly have fished out a few more details if I'd had the presence of mind to speak up. But I didn't, and I wasn't about to call him back. "Oh, hey. I'm a dipshit and totally forgot to ask, but . . . ."

No. I'd had enough of his gloating for that particular day. So, could'a, should'a, would'a. Now move on.

She's a student at Brown. Her and about ten thousand other people. Thanks, dude. That's a lot to go on. Still, over the months since my death, I had cultivated a couple of contacts who, in turn, had a couple of snitches. It was a hit-and-miss, ragtag string of confidential informants who had to be compensated for tips that rarely panned out, but it was slightly better than nothing at all. Back home I made a couple of calls, the second to a back-alley dealer in pilfered karma and memories who went by Cutter. He occasionally fed me the lowdown on someone, and, in return, I mostly left him and his operation the fuck alone. Anyway, he promised to call me back as soon as he had time to see what he could dig up, as regards the specifics of Berenice's comings and goings at BU.

"It's important, Cutter."

"Gotta be *delicate* on this one," he sort of whined. If ferrets could talk, they'd sound like Cutter. "Prying into the Maidstones, that's some dangerous undertaking."

"No shit, but that's the score."

"You don't ask much, do you?"

I kicked an empty Narragansett beer bottle at the door. It didn't break. "Dude, you want me to go tellin' B you're being anything less than cooperative?"

"Quinn, you know it ain't like that. You know—"

"Shoulder to the wheel," I said. "That's all I'm asking. Come up with something good, it'll buy you a couple of months hassle free."

"Well, I know this hacker—"

"I don't care *how* you do it, just *do* it."

Jesus, I love talking shit to douche bags.

I tossed the ridiculous Hello Kitty iPhone onto my puke-colored sofa, undressed, and spent the next half hour or so standing under the showerhead, letting the hot, hot water hammer my back and shoulders, my face and chest. The morning's encounter with Rizzo kept playing over and over in my head, and despite B's insistence that all was cool and no damage had been done by leaving the son of a bitch alive, I was fairly certain it was only a matter of time before that act of "mercy" came back to take a chunk out of my ass. By the way, when the *loup* Jack Grumet bit me that July night out at the Scituate Reservoir, he'd bitten me in the ass, so there *was* a precedent. B had bigger fish to fry at present, and that's the only reason he hadn't reamed me for not putting Bert Rizzo down.

By the time I finally got out of the shower and dressed in the cleanest clothes I could scrounge from the dirty assortment of T-shirts and jeans scattered about my bedroom, it was early afternoon. There was a Radiohead shirt that didn't smell too bad. I sat down on the edge of my sagging mattress and stared longingly at the pillows. What possible difference did it make if I tracked down Ms. Maidstone today or tomorrow? As for Shaker, either he was dead or he wasn't, and a few hours' shut-eye wasn't gonna change that, either.

I lay down, blinking at the sunlight through the windowpane. The clouds had begun to break up. I'd just shut my eyes when the phone started ringing.

No peace to the wicked, right?

I rolled out of bed and made it back to the sofa by the

fourth ring. It was Cutter, and the extra-ferrety tremble in his voice was enough to tell me he was none too happy to be making this call.

"Senior year. Linguistics. I got her schedule and emailed it to you. Black hair, amber eyes—"

"Amber."

"That's what I said, ain't it? Tall, too. Almost six feet, so you shouldn't have too much trouble spotting her. Her address and phone number, they're in the email. But you might want to try watching the Front Green, along Prospect Street. Seems she and some pals have a habit of congregating near Carrie Tower, round about sunset."

"Sunset. In February?"

"Quinn, that's what I heard. And that's all I got for you. That and what's in the email. And you didn't hear *none* of this from me. I could go my whole life without so much as seeing one of the Maidstones, much less—"

"Cutter, how about you take a Valium and try to calm the fuck down?"

"Two months," he said. "Two months, free and clear."

"That's the deal, if this shit pans out."

He hung up first. So much for sleep and letting it all slide until the next day. If B found out I had a lead and didn't act on it right off, he'd go on the warpath, which I definitely didn't need. I went back to the bedroom and slid a heavy wool sweater on over the T-shirt. No, it's not as if vamps get cold—as I have said—but I knew I should make an effort at blending in. Lurking about at night, that's one thing; broad daylight at a crowded campus, that's another. So, mortal drag—the hazel-green contacts, the dental prosthetics, the heavy makeup to hide my waxy pale skin—my camouflage against detection from all those people who have no idea the nasties walk among them. And who are best off never learning otherwise. I used the phone to check my Gmail account, and Cutter's email was there, just like he'd said it would be. Pretty thorough, too. Probably a lot more than I needed.

On my way out the front door, I jammed a knit cap with a Slytherin House patch on my head. Maybe that *was* overplaying my hand, yeah, but fuck it. B wants me to pass for a fucking muggle, might as well hit it full tilt boogie.

You want history? Well, Providence is just stinko with it. Carrie Tower, for instance, at the corner of Prospect and Waterman, a looming marble and redbrick monolith, complete with a bronze clock face and topped off with a bronze dome, both stained verdigris by more than a hundred years of New England winters. The thing was erected back in 1904, a gift from some Italian dude in memory of his dead wife, granddaughter of this other dude who the university had been named after. All the names escape me. Well, except for Brown, which is obvious. Look the other two up. The internet is the goddamn friend of the curious and lazy. But on the foundation, chiseled into the stone, an inscription reads LOVE IS STRONGER THAN DEATH.

Well, maybe so. I'm gonna say I wouldn't know.

Way up tippy top of the tower, there's a bell, though it doesn't chime anymore, just like the clock no longer tells the time. Shit gets old. Shit breaks. No one bothers to fix it. Indifference. Budget concerns. Government cutbacks. Whatever. Regardless, must have been a big deal when that tower went up, but, really—who can be bothered to give a rat's ass these days? The last person who'd have gotten all sentimental over that dead granddaughter of the school's founder has probably been a corpse for half a century, stuck in some local boneyard, partying with the ghouls.

Still, there's an amusing anecdote about Carrie Tower, a bit of *secret* history only us nasties and our fellow travelers are privy to, that sort of anecdote. In 1950, see, the clock began to lose time, then speed up, then lose time again. At one point, it actually ran backwards. Whoever investigates such things—let's say a few maintenance guys—they investigated, and the official story was that some doodad or another inside the clock's innards had been tampered with by frat boys, but the truth of the matter, that *secret* truth, involved a Masonic Lodge over on Federal Hill and a demoness went by the name of Sulfurous Sal . . .

You know what? It's not nearly as amusing an anecdote as I remember, so forget it. Fuck it.

That afternoon, when I got to the tower, there was no sign of Berenice Maidstone. Just college students coming and going between those stately Ivy League buildings, along with the usual retinue of pigeons and sparrows hanging out in the snow. Of course, it was still a few hours until sunset, and Cutter had told me Maidstone tended to show up there around dusk. I sat down on a bench, chain-smoked (not like dead girls have to worry about the Big C), and stared out at the traffic beyond the tall black wrought-iron fence facing Prospect Street. I just sort of spaced out for a while, which I actually do quite a bit.

Don't think being me is all playing demon slayer when some uppity mope gets out of line, or doing Mean Mr. B's bidding, or finding myself in the crosshairs of nut jobs like ex-Father Rizzo. Mostly, it's boredom. Monotony. The same tedium set on endless repeat. Beer and TV Land, masturbation and video games. Waiting on my rumbling belly to remind me it's time for the next murder, the next fix—blood ain't nothing but heroin misspelled, after all—and waiting, too, for my "time of the month" to roll around, when I'd black out and wake up wondering what sort of trouble the Beast had landed me in. Why do you think so few vamps stick around for more than a couple of centuries? Why immortals aren't? Because immortality is damn dull, that's why, and you can damn well ignore all the pop-culture mumbo jumbo that would have you think anything to the contrary. Hell, the way our naughty parts atrophy after only a few decades and eventually wither away (I'm pretty sure I mentioned that in the *last* book), even masturbation ceases to be an option before too long, which will probably be the final nail in *my* coffin.

What joy remains in all this godsforsaken world when a lady can't even get off to Miss August or the *Sports Illustrated* swimsuit issue or that glorious, all-you-can-eat buffet of freakish Japanese porn on the internet?

So, that afternoon in February, I was sitting there, these pointless, depressing-ass thoughts going round and round in my head, when someone came up behind me and said, "I'd have taken you for a Hufflepuff myself."

I was up off the bench in an instant, startled from my reverie, a hand reaching inside my parka for the Glock because better safe than sorry. Shoot first, interrogate later, yada yada yada. I didn't actually draw the gun, but I had a firm grip on the pistol in its shoulder holster before I realized there was no one behind the bench but some goth chick, all done up in leather, pointy boots, big hair, obligatory facial piercings, and the excessive cosmetics of a counterfeit stiff.

"Jesus," I said. "Jesus, fuck me sideways."

"What's *your* problem?" the goth girl wanted to know. She glowered at me, and, in return, I wanted to smack her.

"Don't fucking sneak up on people, that's what my problem is."

She just stood there, staring at me.

"What?" I asked her (my turn), taking my hand off the butt of the gun and out of my coat.

"You're really her, aren't you?"

"Her who?"

"*Her* . . . Quinn. Siobhan Quinn. The vampire who put down Mercy Brown and—"

I wasn't exactly stunned she'd recognized me. Word gets out. There are those among our ranks who don't know when to shut up, whose tongues do waggle. They're often the sort it falls to me to deal with. Still, I'd been clocked by the mortal girl. Not good.

"Who the fuck told *you* that?" Then I added, "And no one calls me Siobhan. Do that again, and I'll—"

"But you *are* her. You're missing a pinkie."

I glanced around to be sure nobody was in earshot. "Kid, you tell me who the Sam Hell you are, or—"

"Thought you'd be taller," she interrupted, continuing to glower with those red, red lips. "Taller and paler."

"Has all that eyeliner affected your hearing?"

"And *way* less uptight. The way Berenice goes on, I was expecting something a little more, I don't know . . . Anita Blake. Or Sonya Blue. Or, hey, Kate Beckinsale in *Underworld*."

"Who?" Right about here, I was considering shooting her after all.

She rolled those black-lidded eyes. "Don't you read? Or see movies?"

"Are you physically incapable of shutting the fuck up for two seconds?"

"You keep asking me questions. I can't very well shut up if you keeping asking me questions. Not if you want answers."

I sat back down on the bench, turning my back to her, wondering when the hell I'd grown a fan club. Siobhan Quinn has a motherfucking posse.

"Chill, okay?" she said. "Berenice sent me, all right? After her baby sister went missing, she's sort of keeping a low profile."

I rubbed my eyes; the contacts always bug me. "And you're the best she can do in the way of lackeys."

"I'm a *messenger*," the girl said, sounding supremely offended. Which, of course, had been my intent. "Part of her coterie. Berenice doesn't have lackeys."

"Right," I sighed. "And the pope doesn't wear a dress and a funny hat."

She sat down next to me, uninvited.

"You want to talk to her, you're gonna have to talk to me first." She took out a BlackBerry and started texting.

"You gotta name?" I asked.

"Lenore," she replied, without looking away from the BlackBerry.

"Bullshit. I meant an actual *name*-type name. What-ever's on your driver's license, your birth certificate."

"So, I tell you that, I can call you 'Siobhan,'" she said, still pecking at her BlackBerry's tiny keys.

I changed the subject. "Who are you texting?"

"I'm letting Berenice know you showed up."

"How did she know I was coming? I didn't even know I was coming until a few hours ago."

Lenore looked at me then like I was the biggest idiot on earth.

"Right," I said. "She's a Maidstone. Never mind."

"Yeah, she's a Maidstone. She's special. She can do magic, and I mean *real* magic. Not that phony goddess worshipping, white-light Wicca crap."

"Well, la-di-fucking-da. And while you're talking to her, how about you ask where Shaker Lashly has gone?"

"Never heard of anyone called Shaker Lashly. You'll have to ask her that yourself. *If* she decides to see you."

"If? Hey, *she's* the one came to my employer for help finding this misplaced sister of hers. If she doesn't want to talk to me, I'll go back and tell B the client has had a change of heart. But she should know, whatever he asked for up front, he doesn't do refunds."

Lenore stared at the BlackBerry's screen a moment, typed in something else, then dropped that *mobile hand-*

held device back into the huge, shapeless chartreuse velvet bag she was carrying for a purse.

"You have to understand," she told me, "Berenice has good reason to be cautious. Besides, I expected a vampire to be more, I don't know. Like, patient? You are so not living up to your reputation."

I leaned close to her, wishing I wasn't wearing the hazel-green contacts. I did, however, reach into my mouth and pop out the molded porcelain grill hiding my real teeth. She drew back an inch or so and her eyes went wide.

At least she *looked* scared. Hence, I assumed she was.

"Girly," I said, "if I wipe that funeral paint off your face, swat some of that attitude out of you, I'm pretty sure I'd find nothing much hiding under there but another pampered white girl recovering from her high-school Justin Bieber fixation."

She pointed at my mouth. "Those are *real*," she said. It wasn't a question. "They're so sharp—"

"All the better to persuade you to stop jerking me around."

"—and they're wicked cool."

Which is when I socked her in the face. Not hard enough to do any real and lasting damage, mind you— just a firm poke—but plenty hard enough that her lower lip split open and her nose gushed. I won't lie. It felt good.

Lenore's head whipped back, and she sort of yelped.

I said, "Wanna play nice and try this one more time, Elvira? You won't get a third chance."

"Fuck you," she mumbled through the blood and the fingers hiding the bottom half of her face.

Just for effect, I licked her blood off my knuckles. You know, that kind of over the top, tough guy, unnerve your opponent shit. Most nasties would have laughed at me, but this malarkey does tend to make an impression on mundanes. I realized that my fake choppers were still lying on the bench between us, and with my free hand I slipped them back into my mouth.

I told her, "Seeing how we've moved past the 'We can do this the easy way, or . . .' part of our conversation, I want to make it absolutely fucking crystal clear that I do *not* need you to find Berenice Maidstone."

"She's gonna *kill* you," Lenore replied, that warm red gravy dripping between her fingers onto her black jeans.

"Fine. Let's cross that bridge when we come to it. Fact is, she'll probably be doing me a favor. Now, listen—"

"You think I'm *joking*?"

Every time she said something, her breath caused a fresh gout of that crimson junk surrogate to spurt towards me. The notion very briefly crossed my mind that I could probably do her, then and there, and most anybody passing by would just think we were a couple of lesbos making out. Wishful goddamn thinking.

"—we're going to stand up and walk to my car, which is parked about a block away. You'll lead, and if you go rabbit on me, I don't think your boss lady will approve."

"You're good as *dead*!" she said with enough force that blood actually spattered my T-shirt. Whee.

"No, honey, I'm way worse than dead." (Gotta admit, that cornball line was pure Hollywood gold. Or at least TV fool's gold. *True Blood*, eat your dippy, white-trash heart out.)

Lenore glared at me, but it was plain—whatever assurances Berenice Maidstone had offered—I'd sown some serious doubt as to Lenore's safety.

"Now, pretty please, get your poseur ass up and head for the gates. And, like I already said, do *not* run, little girl. I don't feel like chasing you." I motioned towards the tall iron gates, and she got up and did exactly as I'd instructed.

Turns out, the missing Ms. Maidstone was holed up in a deserted warehouse on Kinsley Avenue, other side of I-95, just across from the scrubby banks of the Woonasquatucket River. It was a part of Providence I knew all too well. The dirty green water flowing through a man-made desolation of concrete, the rusting heaps of scrap, and boarded up or broken windows. A few strip clubs, some buildings that have been converted into pricey lofts for trustafarians, train tracks, the occasional warehouse that hasn't yet been abandoned. You get the picture. Of course, there will undoubtedly be those who complain that this is a decidedly unfair portrayal of a neighborhood busy being all spruced up by urban renewal. Those people, they'll point to the newish strip mall less than a quarter mile to the west.

This is me totally not giving a shit.

See, back in my homeless days, before the patronage of Mean Mr. B, when I still drew breath, I'd been made all too familiar with those unforgiving streets. Me and my ever-changing cast-off compatriots—runaways, addicts, runaway addicts, the good, the bad, the ugly, the schizophrenics and panhandlers and petty thieves. All those disreputable ragtag nomads going nowhere except maybe farther down the laundry list of ne'er do wells society tries hard to ignore so it doesn't have to feel guilty about full bellies, warm homes, and plasma-screen televisions.

Once someone who'd called herself Lily and was just about the only person I'd ever come halfway near to being in love with, she'd died in a squat hardly a stone's throw from the industrial ruins Lenore led me to that evening. Lily was killed by that aforementioned ghoul motherfucker who'd been my first and, as I have already pointed out, accidental kill. She'd been the domino set all the rest to tumbling over. Needless to say, afterwards, I did my best to steer clear of that section of town. I only went there when ordered to do so. There was plenty of present-tense lousiness without going out of my way to dredge up bad memories and regret.

Lenore—who I'd made drive—parked in front of that warehouse and cut the engine. I peered out at it through the windshield. The shadows were getting long as twilight came on. The sun had turned the sky pink and indigo.

"Well," she said (pouting around a wad of Kleenex she'd found in her bag), "this is it."

"Cool beans," I said. "Lifestyles of the swank and infamous."

"Think your zookeeper would be pleased with how you've handled this?"

"Let me worry about him."

I took out my gun, checked and double-checked the

Glock to be sure it was shipshape. Yeah, I'm paranoid by both nature and experience, and I was beginning to get a weird vibe about this rendezvous. Sure, the goth chick in the car with me was a bad joke dressed up for all tomorrow's Halloweens, but fuck only knew what sort of unsightly surprises a well-heeled bitch from the Maidstone clan might have waiting in there to be sure Mean Mr. B's pit bull didn't get out of line. Plenty enough paranormal mercenary types plenty dumb enough to be swayed by someone offering them whatever the hell satisfies their appetites in return for a little protection.

"Any surprises waiting for me in there?"

"I'll let *you* worry about that," Lenore replied, and got out, slamming the door behind her.

I cursed and followed suit.

When we got to the reinforced steel door, Lenore rang a buzzer three times in quick succession. My vamp ears heard heavy footsteps approaching from the other side, and I gave myself the silent stay-the-fuck-cool speech I reserve for these occasions. Locks turned, tumblers tumbled, and the door creaked slowly open.

Eyes like those of a boiled fish stared out at us. Of course it was a zombie. What the fuck else would a Maidstone have as a butler but a goddamn resurrection job?

Lurch grunted and ushered us inside. We followed him down a very short, unlit hallway—one turn to the left, another to the right—and into the vast, barren interior of the warehouse. The only illumination came from a banker's lamp with the traditional green shade. It sat on a folding card table before which, in turn, sat Berenice Maidstone. She looked up at us from the Nora Roberts novel she was reading and leaned back in her folding metal chair.

"Classy digs," I said. "Guess Daddy isn't footing the tab." My voice echoed.

"It suffices," she said, laying her paperback down on the table and motioning me to sit in a second chair at the other end of the table.

"I'm fine standing," I replied.

"I really do insist," she smiled disarmingly. "Take off your coat, and, please, take off that ridiculous cap."

Two more zombies stepped out of the shadows behind her. The shamblers were big motherfuckers, and the last thing I was in the mood for was a tussle with mindless goons. One of them took my parka and green Slytherin cap; I walked over to the card table and sat down. Lenore lingered restlessly a few feet away.

Berenice raised an eyebrow and pointed at the shoulder holster and the Glock. "You brought a gun?" she asked me.

"Yeah," I replied. "I brought a gun. I do that."

She tapped the cover of her paperback once, twice, a couple more times; it was a nervous sort of gesture. "Very well," she said.

Here she was, the elder daughter of Edgar Maidstone, and I'd imagined, at the very least, to be confronted with a grim, unnatural beauty. But she was damn near to unremarkable. A looker, sure. No denying that. But nothing much out of the ordinary. Her mousy hair was pulled back into a long French braid. Her lips were a little too thin, and she was a little too skinny, sorta flat-chested. Her eyes were almost the same shade of brown as her hair. She had a slightly haggard air about her that made me think she was well acquainted with insomnia. Her voice was calm, with a certain unflappable quality to it. Only her hands struck me as in any way unusual; her fingers were just shy of conspicuously long and slender, and her unpolished nails were filed to sharp points. Oh, and she had a small red-and-black pentagram tattooed on her left palm. I guess a lot of mundanes would consider *that* unusual.

"Much better," she said as I took my seat. "Much, much better. I've heard a lot about you, Quinn."

"Mostly bullshit, I assure you."

"Yes, well. As they say, it's not the veracity of our reputations that keep us in one piece. Your left little finger and that toe you gave away not withstanding. Would you like something to drink?"

"So long as we're not talking sodas or fruit juice," I replied.

"We're not."

"Then, yeah, I'd like a drink." I was thirsty, and I'm rarely one to turn down alcohol. It's one of the very few vices from my old life that still does the trick.

"I'm afraid all I have is Scotch and beer," she said. "But it's good Scotch. Glenfiddich, twenty-one-year-old single malt."

"Beer's fine," I told her, glancing over my shoulder at one of the goons. "These guys really necessary?"

Berenice had dispatched a sullen Lenore to get my beer (and had also told her to wash the blood off her face; neither of us had been asked *how* her face had gotten that way). She seemed to consider my question, and then slowly nodded her head.

"Sure. We're all friends here," she said, and smiled that disarming smile. A few words of French, and Lurch and the other two shamblers melted into the shadows.

"Better?" she asked.

"Yeah. Lots."

"Then I'll stop wasting your time and get down to business. I assume you know about Amity, and how I'd prefer to have this incident resolved without it ever coming to our family's attention."

I leaned back in my chair, one hand on the edge of the table, balancing on two legs. "That's just about all I was told. Which leaves quite a few questions I'll need answered if I'm going to be any help whatsoever. Also, there's the matter of Mr. Lashly to be resolved."

She gave me a confused look, then said, "Excuse me?"

"Shaker Lashly? B sent him before he sent me. In fact, he sent me because he can't find Shaker."

She chewed her lower lip.

"Quinn, I'm afraid I've never heard of the man, much less have I spoken with him."

"Then" I said, "someone's got their wires crossed. Do you mind if I smoke."

"No," she replied. "Please. Be my guest."

I paused to light a Camel. The smoke hung in the air between us, heavy and gray in the lamplight. There wasn't an ashtray, but I doubted she'd mind me tapping ash on the cement floor of the warehouse. I offered her a cigarette, but she declined. Said she didn't smoke. Kids these days, right? Lenore returned with my beer, a bottle of Heineken (which I fucking despise, but didn't say so).

She'd made a half-hearted effort at washing her face, which had, at least, removed most of the Death makeup. Her nose and lip were beginning to swell, and there was a Band-Aid pasted to her chin. I took a drink of the shitty beer, and Berenice pointed at Lenore's face.

"Was *that* really necessary?" she asked me, jabbing a thumb towards her "messenger." Lenore was staring at her own feet.

"Seemed like it at the time. Want me to apologize?"

Berenice Maidstone sighed and shook her head. "That won't be necessary," she said; then she shooed the girl away on some errand or another. I don't remember just what.

"You gotta understand, Ms. Maidstone, Shaker isn't someone B wants to lose track of, or just write off as an occupational hazard. The guy's a valued asset. Can't have him falling off the face of the earth."

She didn't ask me to call her Berenice.

"I understand that, Quinn. But I don't know what else to tell you. I've never met the man."

I shrugged and let the front legs of my chair bump back to the floor. Ain't no point in my putting a spin on this so I come off like some brilliant judge of character, like I can spot a lie from ten paces. I'd told B I wasn't a detective, and that's the fuck's honest truth. Near as I could make out, Berenice was telling me the truth. Which meant she could be lying her ass off. An undead polygraph machine I ain't. Mostly, I was asking and hearing her out because I had orders to do so, and because I needed to have something to tell Mean Mr. B when I checked in with him. About the only part that made me suspicious was that insistence she had no idea who Shaker was.

Then again, those of us who work for B—the few, the just shy of expendable—we had a habit of making the worst sorts of enemies. You'll recall how B told me that up front, and it was gospel. For all I knew, one or another of those folks Shaker had pissed off caught up with him before he'd had a chance to meet with Berenice. Made sense. I moved on.

"Fine. Then let's talk about your sister."

Which is what we did. We talked about Amity Maidstone for the next hour, until well after dark.

"Sure," Berenice said, "we're not angels, either one of us. But my sister, I sometimes believe she has a talent for dreaming up brand-new vices, and that she does it just to piss off Daddy."

If I wore a watch, I'd have been checking it right about then. Instead, I made of show of looking at my bare wrist. I'd heard enough to write a biography about Amity Maidstone.

I said, "Me, I'd have thought a man like your father, he'd be proud to have his offspring wreaking havoc, getting down and dirty at every possible opportunity."

Berenice had started batting the Nora Roberts paperback back and forth, sliding it from one side of the table to the other. Made me think of a cat toying with a mouse.

"People, they get ideas in their heads," she said, sounding almost like someone talking to herself. "About my family. All manner of horrible, unsavory ideas."

"You lot *do* bring dead people back to life. You get

paid to bring dead people back to life, often for pretty shady reasons. Unless I'm mistaken."

"You're dead, Quinn," she smiled. "And I expect you know we'd have done a better job with your reanimation than any vampire could have."

"I'm just unlucky that way."

"We provide a service to the community. No different, really, than your Mr. B. People come to us with their dilemmas, and we resolve those dilemmas." She continued to play table tennis with the paperback.

"I'm not judging, okay? Just saying, that's all."

"Unless I'm mistaken, you're not here to editorialize about the Maidstone éclat. You're here to help me find Amity. Correct me if I'm wrong."

Something in her voice had changed. It was a subtle shift, yeah, but enough it sent a chill up my spine all the same. That's doesn't happen very often, which, I suppose, is saying a lot. Props to creepy Miss Berenice.

"Point taken," I said, realizing I was having trouble taking my eyes off the book.

"Apology accepted," she whispered, and batted the paperback extra hard and moved both her hands away from the tabletop. But the book didn't go sailing to the floor. It simply fucking vanished.

Parlor tricks. Probably, she had it in her head I'd be impressed. I wasn't. I dropped the butt of my third Camel to the floor and ground it out with the toe of my sneaker.

"Okay, so . . . where exactly do you suggest I start?"

Berenice didn't answer me right away. She was staring at the spot where the book had winked out of existence, like maybe she expected it to come back. Then she blinked a few times, tugged absentmindedly at her braid, and said, "There's a bordello in the—"

"Old Drusneth's whorehouse?"

Berenice scowled. "I'm not personally on a first name basis with the proprietress. Not my scene."

"But it's your sister's?"

Berenice made an annoyed expression and started to answer, but I cut her off.

"Never mind. I know the place, a dump down on Cranston Street."

I'd made Drusneth's acquaintance not long after going to work for B, but before Mercy and Grumet had put the bite on me (ha-fucking-ha). For a succubus, Dru isn't such a bad sort. As demon whorehouses go, she runs a clean joint. She makes sure her customers don't get in over their heads, that they understand the cost of a lay (their souls, a memory, a firstborn, etc.) *before* a transaction takes place. I'd made friends with one of her girls, a tall violet-skinned creature with a flare for the ironic; she'd called herself Clemency Hate-evil, a good old-fashioned Puritan name. During the week or so I'd spent trying to save my skin and figure out just what the Bride of Quiet was playing at, vamping me and all, Clemency had done me a small favor. And it had gotten her . . . well, probably not killed. Probably, it had gotten her something considerably less enjoyable than killed. You won't catch me trying to hide the fact that I am what I am, but I'm still capable of feeling an ounce or two of guilt now and then. And I didn't exactly savor the idea of visiting Drusneth, who, by the way, likes to call herself Madam Calamity. Demons, as is more or less widely known, aren't so big on using real names in their dealings on this material plane.

"Are you thinking she might have made a bad bargain?" I asked. "Started thinking with her clit?"

Berenice deflected my question by making the paperback reappear a foot or so above the table. It hovered there a few seconds; then gravity did its gravity thing and the thick book landed with a thud.

"You think you're in danger, too," I said.

"I didn't say that."

"No, but you're hiding out here with zombie bodyguards. You sent that ridiculous, annoying child to meet me today so you wouldn't have to leave your bunker. B didn't say so, but I'm betting she's also the one approached him last night about working this case."

"And this is your business why?"

My phone hummed loudly from my jeans pocket, and Berenice frowned.

"You mind?" I asked her. "I ought to take this. Sometimes they're actually important."

"No," she said, and began flipping through the pages of the paperback. "Go ahead. There's nothing much left I can tell you, anyway."

I pulled out the phone, and when she saw the Hello Kitty case, all those rhinestones sparkling in the dim lamplight, she snickered.

"It was a goddamn gift, okay?"

"Well, I think it's terribly sweet," she said, then laughed again. I gave her the finger, which only made her laugh that much harder.

The call was Mean Mr. B, which really came as no

surprise whatsoever. The bastard had probably been sitting at Babe's for hours, nursing Cape Cods and waiting for me to check in.

"How's it going, kitten?"

"It's going," I replied.

"Are you playing nice?"

"Natch, Bosco. You know me."

"I do, kitten. That's why I worry so."

There was a pause, then the sound of him taking a drag on a cigarette, the soft whoosh as he exhaled.

"Our client here isn't exactly shitting useful information," I told him. "Oh, and did I neglect to mention I'm not a detective?"

"Make the most of the least," he said, and I wasn't sure if he was referring to what I'd learned from Berenice Maidstone or his need to rely on my obvious lack of acumen as a junior shamus. Whether he was speaking to me or to himself . . . or both.

"Regardless," B continued, "if you're asking after the whereabouts of Mr. Lashly, you needn't bother yourself with him any further."

"How's that? You find him?"

"No, no. I didn't. But the police did. They fished his body out of the river this afternoon, just below the Point Street Bridge. Someone decided to put a couple of bullets in the poor sod's brain. An interesting turn of events, wouldn't you say?"

"Fuck me."

Berenice, who'd just made Nora Roberts vanish for the second time, looked up at me.

"Now, dear," B said, "you know I don't swing that way. Still, it's a kindly offer."

"Okay, so what do you want me to do now?"

"I'd like to know how Shaker got himself into that dreadful fix. I rather liked the fellow. He'll be missed. And, of course, it's possible there's a party, or parties, who doesn't wish us poking about into these troubles of the sisters."

"Right," I said. "The fun never ends."

"That, love, has been my experience."

He hung up.

"Have you found her?" asked Berenice.

I just shook my head. "We'll be in touch," I said. "Meanwhile, you hiding out here might not be such a bad idea after all. And if you happen to know any wards to fortify this shithole, any abracadabras that you haven't already raised, I'd advise you do use them."

She furrowed her brow, then shouted at the zombies in French, and I got my parka and cap back.

"Just fucking sit tight," I told her. She nodded, and one of the dead guys escorted me back to the door. Outside, it had begun to snow again, and the sky was the color of a Dreamsicle. I've always hated those things.

CHAPTER THREE

QUINN'S TERRIBLE, HORRIBLE, NO-GOOD, VERY BAD DAY

You might find this strange, but I hate morgues. So, set aside the stereotypes, slam-dunk those assumptions that vamps are, by definition, morbid. Because I hate morgues. Not only are they filled with dead people—whose company I rarely enjoy—they're full of dead people in various stages of rot, mutilation, and postmortem slice and dice. Not my scene. I hate the smell, and I hate the bright fluorescent lights.

However, after I left Kinsley Avenue, I knew B expected me to swing by the city morgue and have a look at whatever was left of Shaker Lashly. No, B didn't say it in so many lines, but when talking with that cocksucker you gotta learn to read *between* the lines. And between the lines, he'd said, in no uncertain terms, "Oh, and do please drop by the municipal meat freezer and have a look see at the earthly remains of our dearly fucking departed." Which is what I did.

Mean Mr. B has contacts just about everywhere in Providence that there are contacts to be had, fingers in lots of pies, which should come as no sort of a surprise. Besides all the creepsome sort, I mean. The cops, hospitals, the fire department, the city council, the planning commission, judges, the mayor's office, newspapers, the goddamn DMV, etc. and etc. And the Office of State Medical Examiners. Coroners. Which is why no one protested my showing up after hours at the last gasp saloon, expecting access to the corpse of my choice. Doc Tillinghast was even waiting up for me. What the hell, though; he could write it up as overtime. Tillinghast, a short man in his late fifties, bald as a baby's ass, was both an inveterate necrophile and a groupie.

But he was the sort of groupie who had the smarts not to make a nuisance of himself and interfere in the doings of the nasties he admired. This, coupled with his cooperation and occasional usefulness, had kept him alive. The pathologist was waiting for me in the basement amid those tile-covered walls and stainless-steel operating tables, the bone saws, skull chisels, and rib cutters. When I came through the doors, he was watching Tex Avery cartoons on his laptop and eating a corned beef on rye.

He looked up at me, not the least bit startled by my entrance, a dab of mustard on his chin. The thick lenses of his spectacles always made his eyes look comically huge.

"Ms. Quinn," he said, actually sounding glad to see me. Hardly anyone's ever *glad* to see me, and the exceptions always throw me for a loop.

"Yeah," I replied, taking in the row of bodies tastefully hidden beneath their white sheets. I'd say I already wanted to be out of there, but, fact is, I'd wanted to be out of there before I went in. "How's it hanging."

He blinked at me with his magnified eyes, and I could tell he was disappointed I was wearing all that MAC concealer and the hazel-green contacts.

"Can't complain," he said.

"Is it bad?" I asked, and pointed towards the bodies. I didn't have any idea which one was Shaker's.

"For a floater? Nah, not really. He hadn't been in more than a few hours, and with the river mostly frozen over, helped retard the decomp."

"Small mercies."

Tillinghast shut off the cartoons and set aside what was left of his dinner. "Third down," he said, and followed me to the table. He pulled back the sheet and yep, it was Shaker Lashly, all right. There was a perfectly centered bullet hole between his eyebrows.

"Point-blank entry wound," Tillinghast said, pointing at the hole with a scalpel. "See the abrasion ring? The seared edges? And how much cordite and gunpowder residue—"

"Yeah, I see it." There was also an imprint from a pistol's barrel.

"Poor son of a bitch also took a couple to the belly,

from farther away. But *this* is the shot killed him. It's a clean through-and-through."

"The exit wound?"

"Wanna see it?" Tillinghast asked, clearly eager to do just that. "I can roll him over. Or pull up the photos on the computer."

"You've got mustard on your chin," I told him, and I put the tip of my right index finger on the hole. I pushed it a little ways inside.

The doc leaned over and used one corner of the dead man's shroud to wipe his chin. "Well, okay. It's not an especially impressive exit. A bit disappointing, really."

"Doc, you are one sick-ass dude." I removed my finger from the hole in Shaker's face. "And the gun?"

"The cartridges I took out of his gut were both nine-by-nineteen-millimeter Parabellum."

I covered Shaker's face again, and stood there, massaging my temples a few moments. I was getting a headache, and I blamed B and the fluorescents. I wasn't going to learn anything here could have learned over the telephone.

"Do the lights *have* to be so bright?"

Tillinghast glanced towards the ceiling. "I've never thought about it," he said. "It's usually the cold bugs people."

"Nine-millimeter Parabellum," I sighed. "That so does *not* narrow it down."

"*Sic vis pacem, para bellum.* 'If you seek peace, prepare for war.'"

"Listen, professor, it's been an especially shitty day, and I don't need a goddamn lesson in Greek. I need to know who killed him and why."

Tillinghast corrected. "It's Latin, Quinn. Not Greek."

I squinted at him over my shoulder. "I hit a defenseless goth chick this afternoon. So I got no problem whatsoever hitting a loud-mouth canoe maker."

He grinned. Hardly the reaction I'd expected.

"Canoe maker," he said, nodding his bald head. "You've been watching cop shows."

"Helps pass the time."

I turned back to the body beneath the sheet. I wondered if B would even pay for a decent funeral, or if the disposal of Shaker Lashly's cadaver had become the state's problem. Either way, not my goddamn problem. None of my business. For the time being, I'd done my duty. Time to go home and get some sleep, turn off my phone, and let B sit and spin until morning.

Now, right about here, someone might inquire why a gal in my position didn't just find a handy necromancer to wake the corpse up long enough to *tell* me whatever he knew about the identity of his murderer, or maybe a medium who could hold a séance and get him on the line that way. Fair enough. Another time, I might have done just that. I'm a big believer in shortcuts. Only, everyone had made it clear this mess was all hush-hush, top-secret, cloak-and-dagger shit. I start hauling in spiritualists and sorcerers and . . . did I mention how nasties and their buds gossip? Besides, the only decent necromancers in the neighborhood were the Maidstones. So, why didn't I just ask Berenice to give it a shot? Would have made sense, right? Right. Well, fuck me if I can remember. But I didn't.

"You've got B's number," I told Tillinghast.

"Maybe we'll get something useful from ballistics."

"Not gonna hold my breath. Finish your sandwich. I'm going home."

"You hold your breath?" he asked. "I mean—"

"Good-bye, Doc. I'll be sure to tell B you were lots more helpful than you were. Also, fuck that Tex Avery crap. Stick to Chuck Jones."

And then I showed myself out, same as I'd shown myself in. "I'm *not* a goddamn detective," I muttered to myself as I headed for the stairs.

Back in the apartment I shared with house centipedes and innumerable dust bunnies I couldn't be bothered to sweep up, I switched on the television. The channel didn't matter. Animal Planet and a pack of hyenas appeared on the screen, and that was fine by me. Just something, anything, for the comforting drone of background noise to keep me company. The visit to Tillinghast's morgue had left me jumpy, on edge. I went to the bathroom and removed the contacts from my aching eyes, glad to see those black amber-threaded eyes staring back at me from the medicine cabinet. A few drops of Visine took away most of the pain, and then I washed the makeup off my face, exposing the alabaster waxiness underneath. I washed the fake teeth and put them in a cup of the store-brand, overnight denture-cleaning crap I bought at Walgreens. The water fizzed and, from the front room, a pack of hyenas barked their weird, chirping bark that doesn't sound half as much like human laughter as some people seem to think it does.

Before I'd come up the stairs and through the front door, all I'd been able to think about was bed. Now I was too restless for sleep. I went to the kitchenette and got a Narragansett from the fridge, then collapsed into the recliner I'd scrounged off a sidewalk near Brown just before the holiday break. End of the semester rolls round and lots of students drop out—or get evicted—and leave all sorts of perfectly good shit behind. Since the summer, I'd scored a good mattress that way, and my dresser, too. The dresser had been painted so many times its original color was anyone's guess; the latest coat was a grody yellow, peeling to reveal patches of avocado green and carnation pink underneath. But, hey, it had drawers and held clothes and shit, which is what dressers do. No one needs them to win beauty pageants.

I sat in the recliner, drinking my beer and watching hyenas dismember a wildebeest carcass. But my head was still in the morgue, still on that hole between Shaker Lashly's eyebrows. Shaker hadn't been such a bad guy, decent enough I'd often wondered why the hell he'd ever gone to work for B. More than likely, blackmail was involved. Maybe B had paid off some debt or another and saved his skin from one of them fates worse than death. Sure, that might have been how it had gone. I never asked. None of my beeswax. Back in the '90s, he'd come up to Rhode Island from Mississippi and had carried the accent to prove it. He knew about a thousand dirty jokes. He was aces with a single-shot bolt-action rifle. I'd once seen him take down a troublesome night gaunt with a Mauser SR-93. From half a mile away. *Without* a scope.

"Fuck it," I mumbled at the TV and the squabbling

hyenas. "Dude got sloppy. Was in the wrong place at the wrong time. Probably did something stupid, and it got him killed."

Give us enough time, we *all* make that sort of fatal, final mistake. He'd stood his ground when he shoulda run, or he'd ducked right when he shoulda dodged left. Or the sorta nasty had caught up to him ain't no dodging or ducking. Some monsters get your number, that's all she wrote.

I finished my Narragansett and set the bottle on the floor beside the chair, figuring I could at least doze awhile in the chair before Mean Mr. B called and sent me back out to chase after Amity fucking Maidstone and/or Shaker's murderer.

But . . . um . . . no. Wasn't gonna happen. Fuck all forbid.

I'd just shut my eyelids when the door burst open with enough force that the wood splintered straight down the middle and the damn thing was left hanging on its rusty hinges. And there was Rizzo, brandishing a new cross bow in one hand, and a big-ass, double-barrel shotgun in the other. By the way, *all* shotguns look big ass when someone's pointing them at you. That's some sort of universal law.

"Asshole, you *broke* my fucking front door!" I growled about half a second before he squeezed the triggers on both the bow and the shotgun. Made a shitload of noise, but, you'll remember, the downstairs neighbors were out of down. A fact of which I'm sure Rizzo was more than well aware. They'd only left the day before. Still, folks probably heard that shit over in Olneyville.

The bolt caught me in the left shoulder, just south of the clavicle, but far enough north of my heart I was in the clear. I was only hit by a dozen or so pellets of buckshot, mostly in the right cheek. The rest took out the window behind the easy chair.

"*And* my goddamn window! They make me *pay* for this shit, you know?" By that point, I was operating on pure indignant adrenaline.

The buckshot stung like I'd stuck my face in a wasp's nest. Still, I'd been in lots worse pain, so it wasn't that much of a distraction. Before he could pull the second trigger on the gun or reload the bow, I'd already yanked the bolt (which had very briefly pinned me to the chair) from my shoulder. I hit the floor and rolled to the my right, towards the bedroom. I had no plan in mind. Who has time for making getaway plans when she's just been caught off her guard by some crazy motherfucker crashing through the door, intent on doing her serious bodily harm all the way unto death?

I slammed into the wall beside the closed bedroom door, leaving a sizable dent in the sheetrock, and got a hand around the knob. I tore it free (well, half of it, the half facing the living room) and flung it straight at Rizzo. Maybe I didn't have a plan, but I was still capable of thinking fast. Also, might I add, I had considerably better aim than he did, and it caught him square between the eyes. The thing was made of cut glass, and it should have killed the bastard right then and there. But you know what they say: Some people are just too mean to die. Or too dumb. Like me and Rizzo.

Instead off dropping dead, he dropped the crossbow—

but not the gun—and stumbled backwards, out onto the narrow landing.

Among my tasty assortment of vamp superpowers is the ability to pounce good and proper and fierce as any old puma or jaguar. And pounce is what I did. I easily cleared the distance between the bedroom and the ruined front door, striking Rizzo in the solar plexus, hard enough that he took out the banister behind him and tumbled down the stairwell, ass over tits. He hit the bottom like the proverbial sack of potatoes. *Bam!* Made almost as much noise as his gun, Which, by the by, happened to fire that second barrel when he hit the foyer, taking out the lower half of the front door.

Asshole.

I stood there on the landing, glaring down at Rizzo, as he rolled over and began crawling desperately towards the hole he'd made in the antique wood. I knew B would be righteously pissed if I didn't go after him and finish the job, if I let a second opportunity—its having knocked, so to speak—to conclude our Mickey Mouse holy warrior's sorry existence right then and there. But, I thought, you know, fuck it. My face was on fire, my shoulder hurt like a son of a bitch, and I plain ol' wasn't in the mood. When I murder a motherfucker, that's my prerogative, right? I could deal with Rizzo later, whenever I had a mind to do so. I promised myself that would be the *very* next time he got in my face.

"Cock stain!" I shouted down the stairs, and just before he slithered through the hole he'd blown in the door, he paused to give me the middle finger.

"Fuck you, too," I muttered.

Yippee-ki-yay. Just another Saturday night in the unlife of Siobhan Quinn Twice-Damned, Twice-Dead.
Quinn the werepire, vampwolf, "daughter" of the late
Bride of Quiet and "bitch" whelp of an equally deceased
werewolf named Jack Grumet.

I turned and went back inside, pausing to prop the
sorry excuse that remained of my apartment door back in
place as best I could. Then headed back to the bathroom,
cursing every dick that had ever spurted cum in that long
line culminating in Bertrand Rizzo. My wounds would
heal by daylight, but in the meantime, I had a bottle of
Vicodin. On the television, the hyenas played tug of war
with a blue and pink tangle of wildebeest intestine. At
least someone was having fun.

"Wake up, kitten," Mean Mr. B whispered in my ear.
"We've work to do, and I've begun to worry about you."
His voice was sticky as molasses, irrevocably insincere.

I can't remember what exactly I was dreaming, not
specifically, but I was back in those hardscrabble, smack-
cushioned days with Lily and the others. I was back before. A shitty life that had come to seem like paradise.
You never miss the water till the well runs dry.

I told the voice dragging me up from the dream to go
fuck himself with an ice pick.

"I'm not paying you people to sleep," admonished
Berenice Maidstone, impatient, privileged, the voice of
someone whose used to folks jumping when she snaps
those long fingers of hers.

"Fuck you both," I moaned, and opened my eyes to

sunlight leaking in around the edges of the black drapes that only mostly covered my bedroom window. A while back, I'd duct-taped all the way around the curtain, but the tape had soon come loose and I'd never gotten around to sticking it down again. I squinted and rolled over, away from the sun, fumbling for the sunglasses on the small nightstand beside the bed. Vamps might not combust when exposed to sunlight, but it's hell on my eyes. Otherwise, it just sort of prickles at the back of my neck, and then usually only around noon. I found the sunglasses and sat up. The merciful storm clouds of the day before had obviously moved on. The pain in my face and shoulder had gone, but I was still a little groggy from the three twenty-five milligrams of hydrocodone I'd taken after Rizzo came calling. And my mouth tasted like shit. Not literally, but goddamn close enough. I reached beneath the bed and groped around a moment or two until I located the bottle of Bacardi I kept there. There was a glass on the nightstand, and I filled it to the brim with rum. It would help scrub away the fuzz in my head—from the painkillers *and* the tatters of that dream—and it was always easiest to begin a day with a buzz.

The rum tasted sweet, scorching hot, and smooth— all three, all at once—and it wiped away the shitty taste. I drained the glass in one long swallow.

"Wakey, wakey. Eggs and ba-ky," I grumbled, and filled the glass again, then returned the bottle to the shadows under the edge of the bed. I found my pack of Camels and lit one.

Not a pretty picture, I know, but I've never been a morning person. Going vamp only made matters worse.

I sat there, drinking and smoking, slowly waking up, and stared at my feet and the Play-Doh blue carpet. I struggled to take stock, as the events the night before gradually returned to me.

Kinsley Avenue.

The meeting with Berenice.

The call from B, and then the trip to the city morgue.

My index finger poking about inside the bullet hole someone had put in Shaker Lashly's face.

That shitbird Rizzo.

I took a very deep drag on my cigarette, exhaled, and stared at my phone and Hello Kitty, perched on the edge of the table near an overflowing ashtray that should have been emptied weeks ago. I hadn't checked in with B. I knew that I should, first thing, right then and there, but that was just about the very *last* thing I had any scrap of inclination to bother with.

Better to focus on getting the answers he wanted.

All I had was the one lead. Berenice had told me her sister sometimes frequented Drusneth's brothel in the Armory. Likely, that would prove to be a dead end, but, weird as it might seem, few and far between are the times I'd rather parlay with Mean Mr. B than a ruthless succubus madam.

I finished the second glass of Bacardi and stubbed out my smoke, then staggered off to the bathroom for a hot shower. By the time I was done and had spackled on my human mask, it was almost noon. My stomach gurgled, reminding me the time to find my next meal was fast approaching. I could put it off another night, probably, but no longer.

"Creep," I said to the creature in the mirror. "Someone finishes you off today, won't no one cry. Not one single solitary soul." The creature lip-synced every word right back at me. We smiled for one another.

By that February, I'd long since had my revenge on the nasties who'd made me one of them and dumped me so rudely into their bullshit games and double dealings, and the anger had deserted me. I was also not the completely suicidal mess I had been back at the start. The desire for vengeance is a powerful motivator, and it helps if you're mostly indifferent to your continued existence. One propels you forward, and the other makes sure you're willing to do what needs to be done to accomplish that which propels you. That day, all those many months later, looking back at myself from the bathroom mirror, I wished I'd had both those things back: the drive and the furious recklessness.

Yeah, well. It is what it is.

I dressed quickly, checked the clip in the Glock, and strapped on the shoulder holster. I also grabbed the canvas bag with the other tools of my trade. After seeing Shaker's corpse, I figured better safe than sorry, better to have all that shit and not need it, than to need all that shit and not have it. Fifteen minutes later, I was out the busted doors, out on the street. Oh, I made a mental note to call the handyman about the doors. I could always chalk it up to a break in while I'd been out. I could think of a decent enough excuse as to why I hadn't called the cops.

It took me three tries to get the rattletrap gray Econoline van started. My POS Honda hadn't survived Mercy Brown's fiery end down in Exeter, and B, cheap bastard that he is, had replaced it with the equally POS van. It was missing the front fender, the passenger seat, and the roof was so rusted out there were spots where rain and snow got in. If B's connections hadn't kept me clear of the DMV inspections, no way the hulk would have been on the road.

Okay, let's not get bogged down in the details. Who the hell gives a shit about that van? Jesus H, Quinn. Anyway, like I said, I had the one lead. The one flimsy-ass lead. And I followed it. I drove west across the Point Street Bridge and the frozen Providence River, down Westminster to the Armory District. There is just one thing I can clearly recall about that drive, even all these years later: There was a sun dog hanging in the sky above the city, a mock sun of muted, overlapping oranges, yellows, and blues. It felt like an omen.

It isn't customary to show up unannounced at "Madam Calamity's" house of ill repute and unearthly pleasures expecting an audience with Drusneth. It kinda falls into a category the nasties tend to consider ill-fucking advised. But, see, she and B, they go back a ways, and he's often summoned to take care of nuisances, deceits, and miscellaneous headaches she either hasn't got the patience to attend to herself or simply can't be bothered with. More the latter. I'd say they're friends, but that's probably going on beyond too far. More like, they're a pair of cats in a bag that, out of mutual necessity, have learned to tolerate one another's company without all the hissing and spitting and bloodshed and flying fur. So, B gets special treatment, which means, by extension, his employees—and, what with the demise of Shaker Lashly, I'd become the only one of those—also get special treatment. Usually. It's the sort of special treatment that can't be counted on.

But you do what you gotta, misgivings or no misgivings, right?

Right.

Better to show up unannounced than be told she didn't have time to see me.

That day, a couple of wealthy South Korean patrons were getting the red carpet, VIP, all the frills, bells, and whistles in exchange for whatever they'd decided they could live without. In this life and/or the next. I was ushered into Drusneth's office by a surly pair of the *se'irim* bouncers she has on hand to be sure everyone stays in line. Then she kept me waiting for over an hour. I suppose I had that coming, not even having bothered to call ahead. Wasn't the first time I'd been in the room—though it was the first time I'd been in the room *alone*—but I was still amazed by the organized clutter of the place. Sort of like the attic castoffs of an antique dealer obsessed with Late Baroque and Rococo furniture, paintings, mirrors, a chandelier, and tchotchkes (yep, I, the dropout, once read a book on art and architecture; believe it or not, I don't care). An almost surreal jackstraw heap of chairs, tables, cabinets, cupboards, bookshelves, and footstools, that room, and I always got the feeling that it wouldn't be hard to drown in all those gilded acanthus leaves and mahogany seashells. Her desk seemed to go on for-fucking-ever, side to side, front to back, adding to the dizzying impression the room was somehow bigger on the inside than on the outside, all Tardis-like. I sat and tried not to look at the portraits, because the faces in them always seemed to be peering warily back at me.

I wanted a cigarette, but I knew better.

I waited.

I waited.

I waited some more.

Finally, Drusneth swept into the room and slammed the door behind her. I've never seen her shut a door any other way. I think she just *enjoys* slamming doors. That day, she was wearing the body of a pale-skinned woman. There was a scatter of freckles across the bridge of her nose and beneath her beryl-green eyes. Her eyebrows and hair were honey blonde. Drusneth changes her skin just about as often as Mean Mr. B changes names. He'd told me one of the cabinets held a few hundred stoppered vials, each containing the likeness of a person she or one of her whores had stolen over the decades, pilfered from customers with more appetite than good sense. That day, she was decked out in a ball gown that would have been fashionable during the reign of Louis XIV and that couldn't have done a better job of clashing with her office's décor. The dress was a sickly yellow color, as though it were dying of hepatitis. She trailed the odor of rotting eggs—or, if you prefer, *brimstone*, but demons hate that word.

"Sorry to have kept you waiting," she said, taking her seat behind the gigantic desk. Her voice was simultaneously soothing and terrifying, a summer breeze and an earthquake scrambled into one incongruous omelette.

"No, no. I'm the one who should be apologizing, showing up out of the blue like this."

She smiled at me. Ain't no sort of shape-shifting in all the world can hide the wickedness of a smile like that, any more than it can hide the cruel glint in the eyes of a succubus. I couldn't have stood up and left the room if I'd wanted to. Actually, I probably did want to. But she'd nailed me to the spot. I'd come of my own accord, and there I'd stay until she was done with me. It was all I could do to keep talking.

"And just what urgent wind has blown you my way, my dear Quinn?"

I could feel the sweat beading on my forehead and upper lip. "You might have heard," I said, "that B's taken on a job for Edgar Maidstone's oldest daughter, trying to help her find her sister. Supposed to be a secret, but—"

"Yes, Quinn. The news has reached me. Only just this morning, as it happens. Though I'm not certain how this involves me." Her eyes sparkled, and I wished that I could look away.

"It probably doesn't."

"And yet here you are," she said, then made a steeple of her fingers and rested her chin on the tips.

I managed a deep breath and somehow managed to exhale. "Berenice—"

"Ever her sister's keeper."

"—said that Amity is a frequent customer of yours."

"Which gives one or the both of you cause to suspect I know what's become of Maidstone's wee slut?" She paused a moment, then, before I had a chance to answer, added a second question. "Quinn, is B aware you're here?"

"No," I replied.

"I thought not. Because I know he'd have advised

against it. More probably, he'd have wisely forbidden you to disturb me and waste my time with this poppycock."

I nodded about as slowly as anyone can. I felt mired in hot tar. "No doubt," I told her.

"Which is why you didn't ask his permission."

"B has a lot on his plate just now. He put Shaker Lashly on the case before me, and Lashly turned up dead last night."

"How very unfortunate for him," she said with not the smallest trace of sincerity. Drusneth leaned back in her chair, unsteepling her hands. She flared her nostrils.

"I should go," I heard myself whisper. "I shouldn't have bothered you."

Drusneth tilted her head to one side, and her jaundiced dress rustled and twitched.

"Quinn, you are always welcome here," she said, tossing out those six words so it was clear she meant just the opposite. "If only in memory of poor departed Clemency. But I've no idea whatsoever what has befallen Amity Maidstone. True, she has visited my parlor many times. She has a reputation for exceptionally unwonted cravings, which we have been happy to sate. Alas, she's also a shrewd girl, and we've reaped far less from our transactions with her than this house would have hoped. We are unaccustomed to such acumen, but she *is* her father's daughter."

"Weird sisters," I muttered, though I hadn't meant to say anything at all. I realized the smell of sulfur was fading, and in its place I smelled lavender.

"Of a certain," Drusneth said. Her human face had begun fading away to a see-through mask I absogoddamnlutely didn't want to see through. "But I think it best, child, that you return to B and tell him to immediately desist from this imprudent search. He has better and more profitable avenues to travel, which, I would add, should prove less hazardous to his associates."

I heard the threat, plain as day, but the odor of lavender had become intoxicating, and I was having trouble concentrating. Still, I knew I wouldn't be exiting the place as easily as I'd come in.

"Yeah," I slurred. "You bet."

Drusneth's mask was no longer merely transparent. It had begun to melt and drip. I'll never know if that was only a hallucination; it didn't much seem to matter.

"But first, I insist you partake," said Drusneth. "I can't send you back into the cold without first having indulged in the warmth of my hospitality. Something exquisite, at almost no charge . . ."

There were other words, but I've never been able to recall any of them. The lavender fog closed over me, pushing me down, down, ever fucking deeper, it felt, into myself. Here was the demonic equivalent of having been slipped a Mickey Finn. The room around me dissolved as I sank, and when I bobbed back to the surface I was naked and tangled in the satin sheets of a bed on the brothel's third floor. Never did learn who or what I *had* spent that time with, or what it might have cost me. Then again, there's shit you can glady go forever without figuring out.

It was twilight—and snowing again—before I made it to Babe's. I found B in his usual booth in the back of the bar, sipping his usual Cape Cod. There was no one with him, none of the arm candy, which was a relief. Whatever had gone down at the whorehouse had left me queasy and disoriented, and I was hardly in the mood to play polite and sociable. Hell, I was hardly in the mood for B, but I knew I didn't have much choice. He'd left two messages on my phone, each one equally terse. Apparently, news of my impromptu field trip to speak with Drusneth had reached him sometime during (or maybe even before) my long blackout.

I sat down across from him, and he stopped filing his nails and gave me the sort of look you might give a pet who'd just taken a dump on your floor.

"You're playing a dangerous game," he said calmly. "And normally, love, well, that would be all your business and none of mine. However, as you're perfectly aware, in this instance you've involved me in your gamble."

He lit a baby-blue Nat Sherman and watched me expectantly through the smoke.

"It was stupid," I said, realizing I hadn't bothered to check my makeup after leaving the whorehouse, and for all I knew, my Madame Tussauds skin was on display for all to see. Then again, no one ever seemed to pay much attention to what went on in B's booth.

"No. Stupid is crossing against the light. Or drinking the tap water while vacationing in Morocco or Guadalajara. Poking around in *her* affairs—to her face—that's damn barmy. In fact, I would go so far as to say it's suicidal."

"Yeah, well. It's all I had to go on, and now it's done. Besides, I'm pretty sure I've already paid for my fuckup."

"Also," he said, wrinkling his nose distastefully, "you smell like pussy. You smell like pussy and lavender."

I was getting tired of him stating the obvious.

"B, she said you should drop this whole thing. Stop trying to find Amity Maidstone. Truth is, maybe I agree with her."

"Of course she did, and of course you do." He tapped his cigarette on the rim of the tiny glass ashtray on the table. "But it seems to me we owe poor Mr. Lashly more than that, and what's more, I'd prefer not to disappoint Ms. Maidstone."

"She's a cunt," I sighed, and glanced at the bar, wanting a beer and a shot of tequila.

"Now, now, kitten. A sage fellow once said, 'With the rich and mighty, always a little patience.'"

"That was Jimmy Stewart in *The Philadelphia Story*."

"Yes, and he said it was from an old Spanish proverb. I have met many a sage old Spaniard."

"I want a drink," I sighed, then sniffed my hands. He was right. I smelled like pussy and lavender.

"Then you're in luck. I believe that's the house specialty."

I went to the bar and ordered a Narragansett and a shot of Jose Cuervo Black. As usual, I told the bartender to put it on B's tab. When I got back to the booth, I saw he'd produced several lottery tickets and was busy rubbing at them with a quarter.

"Speaking of gambling," I said, pointing at the Powerball tickets.

"You are well aware I am sometimes seized by the inclination. Besides, I lose this game I'm only out a few dollars, not my immortal soul."

"Touché." I downed the tequila in a single gulp, then

began nursing the beer. I'd briefly considered a trip to the restroom to scrub away the stink of sex and fake flowers, but thought better of it. So long as it annoyed Mean Mr. B, it was probably worth hanging on to.

He frowned and blew a silvery cloud from the scratch cards. Some of the stuff stuck to the condensation on my beer bottle and I wiped it away.

"Okay," I said, "so you go and indulge Berenice Maidstone, even though Drusneth warns you to back off, and even though indulging her has already gotten Lashly murdered, and even though Edgar Maidstone's gonna be infuriated if—no, *when*—he discovers you've had a hand in keeping his daughter's disappearance from him."

"At least you have a firm grasp on my present intent."

"Jesus. And here you've got the fucking nerve to call me stupid?"

None of the scratch cards were winners, and he swept them off the table and into the shadows.

"Aren't you curious why the madam of a brothel is so emphatic that we cease trying to find the girl?" he asked.

"Not especially," I replied. "Besides, I'm guessing Amity's luck finally ran out, and her kinks and Drusneth got the best of her."

B brushed silver shavings from the lapels of his seersucker suit. "Possibly," he said. "Possibly, you may have hit the nail on the head. And I've never made a habit of crossing our Miss Dru or men as influential and powerful as Edgar I. Maidstone. Lashly, yes, that's a bloody shame, and would this enterprise not have been his untimely undoing. Yet I've received a curious bit of information from down New Amsterdam way."

I took a swallow of beer and set my glass down.

"Which you're going to share," I said.

"In time. When it proves more than a rumor. *If* it proves more than that and will allow me to send you on an errand less foolhardy than marching into—"

"Can you please just fucking drop that? I screwed up, and I've said I screwed up. Give me a goddamn break."

He was silent for a full minute, maybe two, and there was only the chatter from everyone else crowded into Babe's, all those voices mingling into one. A Rolling Stones song was blaring from the speakers mounted above the bar. The clink of glasses. The blat of a car horn out on Wickenden.

Then B laughed softly and smiled a strained smile I could tell was forced.

"You mean all the world to me, Quinn," he said. "Well, no, not quite as much as *that*, but I have developed an attachment, all the same."

"Ever tell Shaker the same thing?" I asked him, never mind how, saying that, I knew I might as well have punched myself in the face.

Mean Mister B's smile didn't fade, though it did become considerably more strained. He reached across the booth and seized my throat. Now, understand, here's this son of a bitch who—despite whispers that he might have a tiny dash of demonic blood somewhere back in the twigs of his family tree—is, so far as I've ever known, little more than a mundane knows how to smooth-talk and schmooze the nightmares. But in that instant, his grip was good as iron, and I knew it was nothing I could break free of, if I was stupid enough to try. I knew he could tear my head off my shoulders, if it suited his fancy. It hurt, sure, but at least I didn't need to breathe.

When he spoke, the syllables crawled out from between clenched teeth.

"It's like this, kitten. I'm a right fickle gent. Today, you're useful, which puts you in my good graces. But . . . I *am* a fickle gent, and if you fuck with me, if you tug too frequently at your leash, my good graces will turn sour. And should *that* happen, sweetheart, by hook or by crook, I'll see you take your place in Hell well in advance of my own arrival."

No way I could have nodded, what with his fingers digging into the flesh beneath my chin. But B must have seen the submission showing through my contact lenses.

"There we go," he said. "Always good to see we're on the same page." He released me and leaned back against the red Naugahyde upholstery.

I rubbed at my throat, waiting to be dismissed. Or whatever was coming next.

"I'll be in touch," he said. "Don't stray far. And, in the future, try to avoid the instinct to display too much initiative."

He didn't have to tell me to get lost.

Sometimes it feels like there's something ironic about my having had more friends when I was alive and living on the street—alive and shooting smack and eating out of dumpsters and sleeping in abandoned buildings—than I have now. Then again, I write that down and consider how I probably have the whole thing backwards. Dead girls who turn into werewolves get more friends than homeless living girls who happen to be junkies? How's that, Quinn? You think the filthy smidgen of infamy you've "earned" as a corpsified, bestial hit woman is ever gonna be rewarded with anyone's gratitude? Ha-ha and ha. The nasties mostly hate me. A handful fear me. And what passes for rules down here in Hade's little half acre in earth say I don't go mixing with the living. Leastways, not unless the living are in on the secrecy. The ones who are, mostly who'd want to spend time in *their* company? The Maidstone girls, just for an example.

Anyway, Quinn, shove the pity party up your derriere. But that afternoon, after Drusneth and the talking-to by Mean Mr. B (never did find out what his name was that day), I found myself *needing* a friend. Which put me shit outta luck. Clemency Hate-evil, she was gone, bye-bye, and so was Aloysius, a troll who'd lived under the 195 overpass at the end of Gano Street, near my old apartment. At the time, I believed he'd been murdered by a trio of vamps gunning for me, trying to draw me out. I never had figured out who they were working for, and in the end, the end of my being caught up in the Bride and Evangelista's little catfight, I'd just chalked his death up to . . .

To what, Quinn? Don't they call that being an innocent bystander? Collateral damage? Wrong place, wrong time? Knowing the wrong people, so that gets you killed? Yeah. Like the wise man from Montreal said, "Everybody knows, that's the way it goes."

Anyway.

By the time I left Babe's, it was snowing pretty hard.

I never much paid attention to weather forecasts. Who gives a shit if it's cold when the cold doesn't cause you discomfort? I'd lost my parka and sweater back at the whorehouse, so there I was, strolling along in my black Radiohead T-shirt. Loved that shirt. It read *Kicking Squealing Gucci Little Piggy*, which I'd always thought summed up an awful lot about the world. Had it until a few years back, when I lost it in a fight with . . . but that's another story for another time. If anyone I passed thought twice about the girl out in a snowstorm in nothing but a T-shirt and jeans, they were wise enough to keep it to themselves. Good little piggies. Mind your own damn business, you live longer. Or not. Sort of a crapshoot, that.

I headed over to Eastside Market and bought a few 3 Musketeers bars, 'cause Aloysius had always loved that shit with the passion of the white hot sun. Don't ask me why. It's a troll thing, I suppose. I also stopped in a liquor store and picked up a pint of Jacquin's ginger-flavored brandy . . . another of Aloysius' fave indulgences. I'd have completed the set with a stack of porno mags, but I didn't feel like trekking to a convenience store or a newsstand. I had in mind I'd set the crap up like one of those shrines you see by the side of the road, where someone's died in a car crash or a drive-by shooting. It was odd. Truthfully, I'd done a good job of not thinking about Aloysius over the past six months. No use crying over goddamn spilled milk. But that night, well . . . spilled milk suddenly seemed awfully important.

I went down to the overpass, my offerings in a brown paper bag. Not much of the snow was blowing into that sheltered place, and I sat awhile staring out at the orange sky over Providence. Then I opened the bag and lined the candy bars up along the top edge of a guardrail. I put the bottle of brandy in a scrubby brown patch of grass beneath them. Then I sat down on the frozen dirt and gravel and just stared into the shadows.

And then . . .

There was a deeper swirl of shadows among the shadows. I figured it was just Otis coming to chase me away. Otis was the albino troll took over the spot after Aloysius vanished. Otis was a son of a bitch, in every way a troll can be a son of a bitch, and, what's more, he'd blamed me for Aloysius' death. He'd repeatedly threatened me with all manner of dreadful fairy revenge. So I'd stayed far fucking away from Otis.

I watched the oily black swirl and stood, getting ready to make my exit as soon as the pale motherfucker emerged out of his portal between here and the Hollow Hills. Only . . . it wasn't Otis who stepped out. It was *Aloysius*.

"Fuck me," I whispered. "No fucking way."

Now, for those among you unfamiliar with trolls, just imagine a really big—I'm talking nine-foot-tall—Muppet designed by someone who's dropped too much acid. These huge ears with lobes that drooped all the way down to his feet, riddled with loops of metal (no iron) and fancy wooden rings and bones. Including human bones. But that should come as no sort of surprise, as it's hardly a secret trolls have a taste for the long pork. His eyes, orange and almost bright as the setting sun. A face not even his mother could have loved.

"Fuck me," I said again, and sat back down. Hard. So, maybe it's more like I fell down.

He scratched at his head and flared his cavernous nostrils. "Quinn girl," he grunted. "Been pondering when abouts you'd come around."

"But . . . but . . . ," I stammered. "You're dead."

"Not hardly yet. Sometimes dead ain't no ways dead, and you ought'a know *that* much, bein' Twice-Dead and all."

"I ought'a," I said, and then I got up, vaulted over the guardrail, and hugged one of the ugly bastard's legs. First time I'd truly hugged anyone since . . . well, I don't really remember, but it had been a while. Aloysius made a gurgling noise I think must have been half laughter, half surprise. Hard to tell with trolls.

"Now, now, Quinn lass . . ."

"Jesus, I'm glad to see you."

You might have read somewhere that vamps can't cry. Not so. And that night, hanging on to Aloysius, I cried like a fucking baby. He stroked my hair with his huge four-jointed fingers.

"Reckon I'm glad to see you, too. Even if you aren't truly you no more. Even if you *are* the Twice-Dead and Twice-Damned they made you into."

I told him to shut up, and he did. For a while, I just stood there, hugging his leg and crying, hearing the patter of the snowfall beyond the overpass. Finally, I let go and took a few steps backwards. Aloysius wasn't crying; maybe trolls don't. I've never heard one way or the other. But it at least *seemed* he was glad to see me.

"Oh, Aloysius . . . ," I blubbered, and wiped my nose,

starting to feel stupid and embarrassed for crying. "I thought you were gone forever. Otis—"

"Don't you say that name," Aloysius said, and sat down in front of me. "Not now and not ever. You brought me something? Should hope, this being a reunion and what, you'd have brought me something."

I went back to the guardrail and retrieved the 3 Musketeers bars and brandy. He grunted in a pleased sort of way and accepted the gifts.

"But Otis—"

"Did I not tell you not to speak that name? Did I not just say that?"

"Yeah, but—"

"Won't say his name, but since you're asking and won't stop, was that ginky, hing-oot scrote tried to still my bridge."

Don't ask me to translate that. Aloysius had spent time in Scotland, hundreds of years back, and still visited various Scots relations from time to time, and was a wealth of Scots insults. I could usually get the gist of it from the tone in his voice.

"Was him spread the lies about you doing me in," Aloysius continued. "Tricked me in a riddle match, what he did, and I got myself caught in a hedge maze. But he cheated, he did. And finally, though, the Court tumbled to his chicanery and set it right. Now it *his* ass in the maze."

"Oh, Aloysius, everything is such a fucking mess."

"Got worse than being dead and gone wolfish?" he asked, and raised a scabby eyebrow suspiciously.

"Shit always gets worse," I replied. "Only absolute truth in the whole wide lousy universe, I think."

And, surprise, that's the way the day ended. Me and Aloysius sitting under the interstate watching the snow, just shooting the shit like we used to do, back before my run-in with the Bride and Jack Grumet (but after I met Mean Mr. B). Aloysius did still seem as horrified at me being an undead lycanthrope as he'd been when he first heard the news. He talked about how it sucks to be lost in a hedge maze, and I talked about the Maidstone sisters. It was the last good night I'd have for a while.

CHAPTER FOUR

DEATH FROM ABOVE, TEN BULLETS, AND THE DINGUS

Sooner or later, a junkie's gotta fix, and sooner or later, a predator's gotta kill. These are words to live by, golden rules, maxims in the great, wide, uncaring shitstorm of life. And undeath. And I hadn't gotten a red delicious fix since the day I'd been sent off to my meet-and-greet with Berenice Maidstone and Lenore the Goth and their shuffling zombie entourage.

After our reunion, I'd spent the rest of the night beneath Aloysius' overpass, first listening to him relate the details of Otis' betrayal and comeuppance, then telling him how everything had turned out with the Bride of

Quiet. Finally, I'd dozed off to the sound of the predawn traffic on 195, rumbling by high overhead. It was a little past noon when I woke. The snow had stopped, and there was no sign of Aloysius. My stomach was grumbling and cramping, and I was ravenous as fuck all. Usually, I can go a couple more days between din-din, but the past two had taken their toll, bumping up mealtime. That wasn't so bad, but here it was, broad daylight, and I'd long since learned keeping my murders nocturnal was far less risky. Still, B expected results, and I wasn't going to be worth shit until I'd eaten. There wasn't time to wait for sunset. I'd just have to make the best of it, and try extra hard to be discreet. Inconspicuous, you know.

Hookers are always an easy mark. Hookers and drug dealers. Now, as I have said before, I don't like preying on the underbelly of society, having once been part of it myself. If I had my choice, there'd be nothing on the menu but upper-crust blue bloods. Newport, for example, would be a veritable buffet. But those are the very people that if they should go missing, the cops actually have to try to find out what happened. Maybe money can't buy you love, but it sure as hell makes the life of this vamp just a little more difficult to stomach (no pun intended).

Problem is, lots easier to find both hookers and pushers after dark. And that day I wasn't especially blessed with the luxury of a long and patient hunt. I was sitting there beneath the interstate, trying to ignore my belly (ever heard whale songs?) and the cramps, when that bitch fate took pity and smiled on me. A homeless woman— maybe in her twenties, maybe in her forties—showed up, as convenient as convenient ever gets. Filthy and rail thin, probably a fellow junkie herself, she had a bulging trash bag slung over one shoulder and was dressed in mismatched clothes and three sweaters, but no coat. I watched her from the cover of dead brown weeds, and she sat down on the concrete embankment and stared out at the blanket of new snow and the furrow of freshly plowed Gano Street. She talked to herself, a rambling monologue that made no sense whatsoever, branding her as one of the mentally ill who'd fallen through all the cracks. I'd told myself I'd make it quick, that she'd never know what hit her.

I lied.

I'd developed a habit a playing with my food.

"You're a cunt, Quinn," I muttered to myself as I slipped silently from the cover of the weeds.

"Yeah, well, that's why there ain't no air conditioners in Hell, ain't it?" I muttered in reply.

I hit her like a linebacker, and she went down hard. The trash bag tore open, spilling her sad-ass, hoarded belongings across the sidewalk. She tried to scream. They almost always try to scream, even the ones who've sunk so far they've pretty much lost any desire to go on living. That scream, it's hard-wired into the human psyche. Men and women been screaming like that since cavemen huddled together watching the eye shine and shadows lurking hungrily just beyond the firelight.

She tried to scream, all right, but I clamped a hand over her mouth and dragged her back across the street to my patch of weeds. Aloysius would probably be mortified to know I was doing the deed right there in his squat, but I'd just have to worry about that later.

I pushed her down into the dirt and gravel and spat out the dental prosthetics, revealing the piranha teeth that are the tools of my trade. The makeup I'd put on the day before, almost all of that had been smudged away, so she also got the waxwork complexion, to boot. I straddled her, and her blue eyes seemed wide as quarters, her pupils swollen with fear and the strain of a useless fight-or-flight response.

"Be still," I said, then slapped her hard enough to split her lip. The spray of blood was answered by a torch song from my empty belly. I quickly glanced about to be sure we were alone. I was desperate, but I wasn't suicidal.

The woman managed to drive her left knee into my ribs, and I slapped her again, harder than before. But I'd learned the hard way vamps gotta keep that crap to love taps or off come their heads (or some part thereof), which spoils the fun and leaves you with a corpse full of rapidly cooling, dead blood. I slapped her, and a tooth went sailing from her mouth. She stopped struggling, and tears welled from those terrified eyes.

"So many places you could have gone, but you had to come here," I told her. Because, you know, it's always easier to lay at least some of the blame on the victim. She mumbled something behind my hand.

I leaned in close, forcing myself to take it slow, and licked at her throat, at the warm and pulsing river of her carotid. All around us, the cold February wind rustled the dry weeds.

And right here is when the gaunt showed up.

Night gaunts are not exactly among the rogues' gallery of nasties familiar to most people. Mr. Lovecraft, he knew about them, and he wrote about them. Made up a bunch of nonsense about them having come from some island in an alternate dimension, right, but that's a load. Way I've heard it told, they're the spawn of a Persian alchemist from way the hell back in the Middle Ages. Night gaunts are ugly sons of bitches, tall and lanky bastards with rubbery skin black as sin. What with the horns and wings and long thorny tails, lots of folks not in the know mistake them for some stripe of demon. But I digress.

The gaunt came sailing in low and hit me at least twice as hard as I'd tackled the homeless woman. It got a firm grip around my shoulders with those long claws, and the two of us went tumbling ass over tits. The woman let out a screech, scrambled to her feet, and ran. Bye-bye, juicy morsel, but I did take some very dim consolation that she was crazy enough no one was gonna believe her story about two monsters duking it out beneath 195. Small goddamn mercies.

The gaunt and me came to a stop with it on top, me on bottom, and I glared furiously up into the narrow slits that passed for its eyes. It grinned.

"That was my lunch," I growled.

It chattered something unintelligible by way of a response and grinned even wider.

I head-butted it.

Which was sort of like smacking my head against an iron girder. I was left stunned, pretty lights dancing before my eyes. And the gaunt was still right there on top of me, clearly unimpressed. It clicked its teeth together. Ever seen those deep-sea fish with the crazy long needle teeth? That's the sort of teeth night gaunts have.

"Fine," I heard myself croak through the throbbing haze inside my skull. "Be like that. Don't take a hint."

Helpful tip: Witty banter never saved anyone's butt from a monster. Or much of anything else intent on doing you bodily harm. Trust me. Or don't. But I've learned this the hard way.

The gaunt stood up then, hauling me up with it, a taloned hand beneath each of my armpits. The thing was a good nine feet tall, and I was left with the toes of my sneakers dangling above the dirt. I kicked it in the gut (at least, I think night gaunts have guts), which was no more effective than the head butt had been; plus, I damn near broke an ankle. It lifted me even higher, as if offering me up to whatever gods its kind worships. I was scratching at the creature's forearms, trying to latch on to that rubbery skin. It made a squeaky noise beneath my fingers, almost the same sound a balloon makes when you rub it.

It didn't even occur to me to reach for the Glock.

"You gonna tell me what this is about?" I asked, figuring I was at least owed that much before being dismembered or devoured or ground to a pulp. "When the hell did I piss you guys off? Refresh my memory."

There was a sickly, sour glint in its eyes, and it grinned up at me. There was another burst of chatter, and then it managed a few words of mangled English.

"Who does *not* hate you, Twice-Damned?"

It had a point. I didn't argue.

Then it lifted me maybe a foot higher, and in that final second before it hurled me at one of the overpass' concrete support columns, it murmured, "Buzz, buzz, buzz."

Buzz, buzz, buzz.

Bees.

B.

Fuck me.

I sailed four or five feet and hit the column with enough force I heard the wet crack as quite a few bones snapped. So, here was justice, with an exorbitant interest rate, for slapping that homeless woman. You gonna hear the music, sooner or later you gonna have to pay the fiddler, yeah? I lay in a crumpled heap, helpless to do anything but watch as the gaunt folded its ebony wings and lunged.

Maybe someone else would have tried to shoehorn a prayer into those last few seconds. Me, I knew better.

But . . .

A fist the size of a basketball snatched the gaunt from the air in midpounce and slammed it into the ground, over and over and over again. None of this was making much sense to me, trying to see, and suss out *what* I was seeing, through all that hurt dragging me down to the nowhere place, the anterooms of dear ol' Hades.

Before long, the gaunt wasn't much more than a bag of shattered twigs inside a latex sack. The hand dropped it into the weeds. And a moment later I was being lifted again, which might have been painful if I hadn't already *been* in so much pain. I squinted through blood and twittering birds into the gnarled, misshaped face of my savior.

"Hate that numpty lot, I do," snorted Aloysius. "Worse than vampires and wolfish sorts, they are. Sleekit wee basturts, all of 'em."

I must have said something, but I'll be tucked if I can remember what.

"You rest, Quinn girl. I'll watch out until you're not so busted. Any more them basturts come round, I'll make jelly of them right quick."

I don't get a lot of opportunities to be grateful, but grateful's what I felt as I shut my eyes and did as Aloysius said, as unconsciousness washed over me. Wicked god-damn grateful, despite the gaunt's last words spinning round and round in my head: *Buzz, buzz, buzz.*

In this line of work, she who is surprised by betrayal is a moron. Like the man said, "Everybody knows the dice are loaded. Everybody rolls with their fingers crossed." Damn straight, Mr. Cohen. And Mean Mr. B, he's about as crooked and backstabbing as they come. Maybe there is honor among thieves and maybe there isn't, but there's hardly a shred among the nasties.

Though my vamp healing superpowers still had a ways to go to make me right as rain again, soon as I was awake and could hobble, I headed for Wickenden Street. It was maybe an hour past sunset (no sign of Aloysius, by the way), and I had no doubt B would be there, recum-bent on his red Naugahyde throne. And I wasn't wrong. B was looking especially dapper that night, and I'd been around just long enough to know this could be another ill portent. Guy can always be counted on to put on the ritz when he's up to something more unsavory than usual.

Also, he was alone. No arm candy.

"Surprised?" I asked. I must have looked like some-thing from a zombie film. A zombie with a gun. But, as usual, the patrons of Babe's wisely kept their eyes to themselves. I hadn't changed clothes, just grabbed the shoulder holster with my Glock.

"Well, hello," said B, ignoring the question. "Do have a seat, my dear Miss Quinn." He motioned to the chair across from him with a grand sweep of his arm, smirking like the Cheshire Cat. He lit a Nat Sherman and blew a perfect double smoke ring my way. "Christ on his bloody cross, but you look an awful sight tonight."

"You kinda noticed that, did you?"

I sat down and he ordered me a beer.

"Yes, well, I hope you gave as good as you got," he replied, and blew more smoke rings.

"You're a son of a bitch."

He raised an eyebrow and cocked his head to one side. "And to what do I owe such unexpected flattery, obvious though it may well be?"

My Narragansett arrived, and I sat staring at the beads of condensation clinging to the bottle. They gleamed like liquid diamonds. Then I took a long swallow of beer before I asked him what the B stood for on that particular night. I'd lost some teeth to the gaunt, and they were still busy growing back in; the beer burned in the empty sockets.

"B is for Bailoch. Scots Gaelic, in case you're in a curious mood this evening." He took a sip of his Cape Cod, tapped ash into the ashtray, then said, "I know *I'm* in a curious sort of mood tonight. So, tell me, precious, how'd you get so dinged up?"

I looked up at him and thought a moment about the Glock 17 9mm tucked snugly into its shoulder holster. I knew damn well B was scared to death of guns and never went near them, relying, instead, on his reputation for seeing that people would get righteously fucked up if they laid even a single finger on one hair of his head.

"Looks as though you played chicken with a lorry."

I drew the Glock and pulled back on the slide, chambering a round. I didn't say a word, just pressed the barrel hard against his forehead, about an inch above the bridge of his nose. He scowled at me.

"Now, now. I don't know what's got your nappies in such a twist. But you and I both know you're not going to pull that trigger."

"The gaunt said it was you sent him to kill me," I snarled. No, not strictly true. But I figured I'd done a decent job of putting two and two together. "So, don't you be so sure what I will and will not do."

"This may disappoint you, kitten, but I have absolutely no idea what you're on about."

I shoved the gun hard enough to leave a decent bruise there between his eyes.

"This may disappoint *you*, Mr. Bailoch, but just before Aloysius squashed it like a cockroach, the fucker let slip how you sicced it on me."

"Aloysius," said B. "So the fellow's not deceased after all. Good news, him being such a decent sort."

His voice was cool as vanilla ice cream, not the least trace of concern, taunting me. Egging me on. My hand was beginning to shake, but I pressed the 9mm still harder against his forehead.

"You're a liar," I said.

"Pot calling the kettle, sweets. Regardless, bad idea, kiddo. Trust me." And he pointed at the pistol with the index finger of his right hand. " 'But as for the cowardly, the faithless, the detestable, as for murderers, the sexually immoral, sorcerers, idolaters, and all liars, their portion will be in the lake that burns with fire and sulfur . . .' That's Revelation 21:8, kitten."

All junkies are liars. Even the dead ones.

This is the golden rule of addicts.

"Isn't there some sort of holy cosmic law against worms like you quoting scripture?"

"Haven't been struck by lightning yet," he replied, glancing at the ceiling of the bar, as if looking heavenward for confirmation. "But, Quinn, rest assured, not only did I have no hand in . . . whatever happened to you . . . if you've gone and made someone keen to kill, well, I'm the last man you want to put in his narrow house."

"I don't believe you," I said, "and your brains would look awful nice spattered all over the wall."

Bailoch sighed. "And *this* is exactly why you're not an interior decorator, if you've ever wondered." He furrowed his brow and sat up a bit straighter, so I was thinking maybe I'd at least made him a tad or so less sure of himself. He carefully balanced his Nat Sherman on the rim of the ashtray, then looked me in the eye. Have I ever mentioned that his eyes are gray? Well, they are. Still, point is, for all his associations with the nasties, B is as mortal as they come. I'd been around long enough to figure out that much.

He sighed again, a sigh that was the very essence of having come to the end of his rope. "This is getting boring." That's when I squeezed the trigger. The Glock 17 clicked, empty as fuck. B opened his left hand, and ten bullets rolled across the table. Their shiny copper-wash jackets glinted in the dim light above the booth.

He picked up one of the shells. "Commodious spot of legerdemain Ol' Drusneth taught me a few years back. Nice, yes? Tiptop. Now, please, put away the pocket rocket."

"Dirty pool," I muttered, lowering the Glock, slipping the useless gun back into its holster.

"Only sort worth playing. Though, a fact you may not know, snooker's more my style."

"You really didn't send the gaunt?"

B rubbed at the circular red indentation the Glock had left there above the bridge of his nose. "Have I not already answered that question to your satisfaction?" He retrieved his cigarette from the ashtray, and the smoke coiled into a tidy question mark above his head. "Where's the percentage, my having you killed? You're my best girl. I'm insulted, I am."

"You'll get over it."

He stopped rubbing at his face. "I was about to ring you when you came sauntering in, looking like the ragged end of a puppy's favorite chew toy. There's been an interesting new development in the Maidstone case."

I finished my beer. "Someone found Amity?" I asked. The way we'd fallen back into the usual rhythm of our frequent conversations, you'd never know I'd tried to pop him only a minute or so before.

"Alas, no. But recall the rumor I mentioned, the one came my way from Manhattan?"

"You mentioned it, yeah." My neglected stomach rumbled, reminding me of the lost meal.

"It has proven to be more than idle gossip. It has

proven to be, I think, a common motive linking disparate elements into a single—"

"You will eventually come to the point, I trust." I ran my fingers through my hair, which was sticky and matted with blood. I found something sharp and hard in my bangs. A tiny shard of bone that had been a piece of my skull before the gaunt threw me into that concrete column. I dropped it on the table, and Mean Mr. B made his disgusted face.

"Quinn," he continued, "I admit I'm playing a hunch, and you'll please keep that in mind. But I believe Berenice Maidstone coming to me has nothing to do with a missing sister. I suspect both sisters are trying to use us—first Lashly, then you—to help them recover an extraordinary artifact." He took a drag on his cigarette, which he'd smoked down to the filter, then crushed the butt out in the ashtray and lit another.

"Okay, then why not be up-front about it? Why go to the trouble to bullshit us?"

He watched me a moment, almost as though he were trying to decide whether or not I could be trusted with the answer. Asshole. "Because, precious, they're after something that individuals considerably more formidable are also after."

"And who would those more formidable individuals be?"

"Would you like another beer?" he asked, then motioned to the bartender. He held up two fingers. Peace out, V for victory.

"Sure. Now, Bailoch, kindly fucking tell me what you're talking about."

Another bottle of Narragansett arrived, along with a fresh Cape Cod for B. When we were alone again, Mean Mr. B said, "Our Grand Dame Drusneth, for one. Which explains why she made you feel less than welcome yesterday."

"For another?"

"For another, another madam of the demonic persuasion, a certain Yeksabet Harpootlian."

I picked up the bottle, but my stomach rolled at the very thought of more beer, so I set it back down again. "Harpootlian? Even for a succubus, that's a hell of a name," I said. "No pun intended."

"That it is," said B. "If my hunch is complete in all its twists and turns—and at present I suppose it is—Harpootlian was the one had poor Mr. Lashly killed. Neither she nor Drusneth would be happy about the emergence of a third interested party."

"Why would Amity and Berenice go up against heavy hitters? They're just kids. Sure, they're Edgar Maidstone's daughters, but when did being the privileged, trust-fund brats of a local necromancer make anyone believe they could get involved in a tussle between demon whorehouses and come out in one piece?"

"How often, dear, have you reminded me of the supreme stupidity of the human race?" B waved a hand at the bone shard on the table. "Will you please remove that from view," he said.

I wiped it off onto the floor.

"If I am correct, the sisters—wishing to gain greater noteworthiness and power within their family—see the object as a shortcut to ascendancy."

"So," I said, "here's my next stupid question. What the fuck is this piece of junk they're all fighting over?"

He reached for something on the booth beside him, then pushed it across the table towards me. It was a very old pulp magazine tucked inside a plastic bag, the sort comic nerds use to keep their funny books in pristine condition. *Weird Tales*, October 1935, twenty-five cents. The cover was a garish scene of human sacrifice . . . or something of the sort. It was as vague as it was garish. But there were menacing figures in red robes gathered about what appeared to be an altar, where a woman in peril lay helpless and, no surprise, completely naked. The cover promised stories by Robert E. Howard, Arthur Conan Doyle, Robert Bloch, and a fourth person I'd never heard of, someone named Mona Q. Mars.

"What's the hell's this?" I asked, turning the magazine over, like maybe the answer to my question was printed on the back.

"That's a magazine."

"Fuck you. I mean—"

"You want to know what I believe Drusneth, the Maidstone sisters, and this Harpootlian are chasing, the most efficacious response is to be found within the pages of that fine publication."

"An old issue of *Weird Tales*?"

"I'm quite sure that's what I just said." Mean Mr. B sipped his cocktail and watched me over the rim of the martini glass.

"You can't just tell me?"

"Of course I could. But this way's more fun. On page

thirty-two, you'll find a story by a woman who wrote under the nom de plume Mona Mars."

"Her name's on the cover."

My stomach made a noise like a tiny earthquake.

"Very observant, Quinn. The story's called 'The Maltese Unicorn.'"

"You're shitting me." I might have laughed. Probably not, though. I was hardly in the laughing mood.

"No. And there's a twist. That magazine wasn't produced in our reality, but in an alternate universe that occasionally bumps up against ours. Mona Mars, or I should say, the woman writing as Mona Mars, never existed in this world. Some things have counterparts, others don't. In 1935 the venerable *Weird Tales* did. Mona Mars didn't."

I didn't bother asking how he'd gotten hold of a magazine from a parallel universe. You hear enough of this bizarre crap, you stop bothering to be astounded. In only six months, I'd heard plenty enough and spare change.

"I hate homework," I told him.

"Indulge me. It's actually not such a bad tale. True, a tad purple and overwrought at times, but not such a bad tale. Also, it involves ladies of the lesbian persuasion, which will undoubtedly appeal to you."

I was tired. Most of my body throbbed to one degree or another. And I was starving. I picked up the magazine and left him sitting there. I grabbed a quick bite in an alley off Thayer Street. Then I went home, took a long scalding shower, and read the story. B was right. Much fucking easier to get a handle on the whole mess if you start off by reading the story, instead of being lazy and listening to someone attempt to sum it up. So I'm following his example (which, by the way, almost never happens). Besides, I think it's a pretty good yarn, all on its own. Now, there will, of course, be those readers who complain that by sticking Ms. Mars' story in here, I'm yanking them out of the book.

"A short story *in* a novel? What! You've got your chocolate in my peanut butter! You've got your peanut butter in my chocolate! Oh, this person thinks she's *so* clever! Also, she's talking *to* the reader! What about my sacred fourth wall! And how can a high school dropout understand the concept of 'the fourth wall'!"

Yeah, yeah. I know. I'm a bad girl. I eat people. I curse. I smoke, and drink, and have sex with other women (some of whom aren't human). I get all hairy at least once a month. I even violate readers' lazy expectations.

Blow me.

The rest of you, read on.

THE MALTESE UNICORN

by
Mona Q. Mars

New York City (May 1935)

It wasn't hard to find her. Sure, she had run. After Szabó let her walk like that, I knew Ellen would get wise that something was rotten, and she'd run like a scared rabbit with the dogs hot on its heels. She'd have it in her head to skip town, and she'd probably keep right on skipping until she was out of the country. Odds were pretty good she wouldn't stop until she was altogether free and clear of this particular plane of existence. There are plenty enough fetid little hidey-holes in the universe, if you don't mind the heat and the smell and the company you keep. You only have to know how to find them, and the way I saw it, Ellen Andrews was good as Rand and McNally when it came to knowing her way around.

But first, she'd go back to that apartment of hers, the whole eleventh floor of the Colosseum, with its bleak westward view of the Hudson River and the New Jersey Palisades. I figured there would be those two or three little things she couldn't leave the city without, even if it meant risking her skin to collect them. Only she hadn't expected me to get there before her. Word on the street was Harpootlian still had me locked up tight, so Ellen hadn't expected me to get there at all.

From the hall came the buzz of the elevator. Then I heard her key in the lock, the front door, and her footsteps as she hurried through the foyer and the dining room. Then she came dashing into that French

Rococo nightmare of a library, and stopped cold in her tracks when she saw me sitting at the reading table with al-Jaldaki's grimoire open in front of me.

For a second, she didn't say anything. She just stood there, staring at me. Then she managed a forced sort of laugh and said, "I knew they'd send someone, Nat. I just didn't think it'd be you."

"After that gip you pulled with the dingus, they didn't really leave me much choice," I told her, which was the truth, or all the truth I felt like sharing. "You shouldn't have come back here. It's the first place anyone would think to check."

Ellen sat down in the armchair by the door. She looked beat, like whatever comes after exhausted, and I could tell Szabó's gunsels had made sure all the fight was gone before they'd turned her loose. They weren't taking any chances, and we were just going through the motions now, me and her. All our lines had been written.

"You played me for a sucker," I said, and picked up the pistol that had been lying beside the grimoire. My hand was shaking, and I tried to steady it by bracing my elbow against the table. "You played me. Then you tried to play Harpootlian and Szabó both. Then you got caught. It was a bonehead move all the way round, Ellen."

"So, how's it gonna be, Natalie? You gonna shoot me for being stupid?"

"No, I'm going to shoot you because it's the only way I can square things with Auntie H, and the only thing that's gonna keep Szabó from going on the warpath. *And* because you played me."

"In my shoes, you'd have done the same thing," she said. And the way she said it, I could tell she believed what she was saying. It's the sort of self-righteous bushwa so many grifters hide behind. They might stab their own mothers in the back if they see an angle in it, but that's jake, 'cause so would anyone else.

"Is that really all you have to say for yourself?" I asked, and pulled back the slide on the Colt, chambering the first round. She didn't even flinch . . . but wait . . . I'm getting ahead of myself. Maybe I ought to begin nearer the beginning.

As it happens, I didn't go and name the place Yellow Dragon Books. It came with that moniker, and I just never saw any reason to change it. I'd only have had to pay for a new sign. Late in '28— right after Arnie "The Brain" Rothstein was shot to death during a poker game at the Park Central Hotel—I accidentally found myself on the sunny side of the proprietress of one of Manhattan's more infernal brothels. I say *accidentally* because I hadn't even heard of Madam Yeksabet Harpootlian when I began trying to dig up a buyer for an antique manuscript, a collection of necromantic erotica purportedly written by John Dee and Edward Kelley sometime in the sixteenth century. Turns out, Harpootlian had been looking to get her mitts on it for decades.

Now, just how I came into possession of said manuscript, that's another story entirely, one for some other time and place. One that, with luck, I'll never get around to putting down on paper. Let's just say a couple of years earlier, I'd been living in Paris. Truthfully, I'd been doing my best, in a sloppy, irresolute way, to *die* in Paris. I was holed up in a fleabag Montmartre boardinghouse, busy squandering the last of a dwindling inheritance. I had in mind how maybe I could drown myself in cheap wine, bad poetry, Pernod, and prostitutes before the money ran out. But somewhere along the way, I lost my nerve, failed at my slow suicide, and bought a ticket back to the States. And the manuscript in question was one of the many strange and unsavory things I brought back with me. I'd always had a nose for the macabre, and had dabbled—on and off—in the black arts since college. At Radcliffe, I'd fallen in with a circle of lesbyterians who fancied themselves witches. Mostly, I was in it for the sex . . . but I'm digressing.

A friend of a friend heard I was busted, down and out and peddling a bunch of old books, schlepping them about Manhattan in search of a buyer. This same friend, he knew one of Harpootlian's clients. One of her *human* clients, which was a pretty exclusive set (not that I knew that at the time). This friend of mine, he was the client's lover, and said client brokered the sale for Harpootlian— for a fat ten percent finder's fee, of course. I promptly sold the Dee and Kelly manuscript to this supposedly notorious madam who, near as I could tell, no one much had ever heard of. She paid me what I asked, no questions, no haggling, never mind it was a fairly exorbitant sum. And on top of that, Harpootlian was so impressed I'd gotten ahold of the damn thing, she staked me to the bookshop on Bowery, there in the shadow of the Third Avenue El, just a little ways south of Delancey Street. Only one catch: She had first dibs on everything I ferreted out, and sometimes I'd be asked to make deliveries. I should like to note that way back then, during that long-lost November of 1928, I had no idea whatsoever that her sobriquet, "the Demon Madam of the Lower East Side," was anything more than colorful hyperbole.

Anyway, jump ahead to a rainy May afternoon, more than six years later, and that's when I first laid eyes on Ellen Andrews. Well, that's what she called herself, though later on I'd find out she'd borrowed the name from Claudette Colbert's character in *It Happened One Night*. I was just back from an estate sale in Connecticut, and was busy unpacking a large crate, when I heard the bell mounted above the shop door jingle. I looked up, and there she was, carelessly shaking rainwater from her orange umbrella before folding it closed. Droplets sprayed across the welcome mat and the floor and onto the spines of several nearby books.

"Hey, be careful," I said, "unless you intend to pay for those." I jabbed a thumb at the books she'd spattered. She promptly stopped shaking the umbrella and dropped it into the stand beside the door. That umbrella stand has always been one of my favorite things about the Yellow Dragon. It's made from the taxidermied foot of a hippopotamus, and accommodates at least a dozen umbrellas, although I don't think I've ever seen even half that many people in the shop at one time.

"Are you Natalie Beaumont?" she asked, looking down at her wet shoes. Her overcoat was dripping, and a small puddle was forming about her feet.

"Usually."

"Usually," she repeated. "How about right now?"

"Depends whether or not I owe you money," I replied, and removed a battered copy of Blavatsky's *Isis Unveiled* from the crate. "Also, depends whether you happen to be *employed* by someone I owe money."

"I see," she said, as if that settled the matter, then proceeded to examine the complete twelve-volume set of *The Golden Bough* occupying a top shelf not far from the door. "Awful funny sort of neighborhood for a bookstore, if you ask me."

"You don't think bums and winos read?"

"You ask me, people down here," she said, "they panhandle a few cents, I don't imagine they spend it on books."

"I don't recall asking for your opinion," I told her.

"No," she said. "You didn't. Still, queer sort of a shop to come across in this part of town."

"If you must know," I said, "the rent's cheap," then reached for my spectacles, which were dangling from their silver chain about my neck. I set them on the bridge of my nose and watched while she feigned interest in Frazerian anthropology. It would be an understatement to say Ellen Andrews was a pretty girl. She was, in fact, a certified knockout, and I didn't get too many beautiful women in the Yellow Dragon, even when the weather was good. She wouldn't have looked out of place in Flo Ziegfeld's follies; on the Bowery, she stuck out like a sore thumb.

"Looking for anything in particular?" I asked her, and she shrugged.

"Just you," she said.

"Then I suppose you're in luck."

"I suppose I am," she said, and turned towards me again. Her eyes glinted red, just for an instant, like the eyes of a Siamese cat. I figured it for a trick of the light. "I'm a friend of Auntie H. I run errands for her, now and then. She needs you to pick up a package and see it gets safely where it's going."

So, there it was. Madam Harpootlian, or Auntie

H to those few unfortunates she called her friends. And suddenly it made a lot more sense, this choice bit of calico walking into my place, strolling in off the street like maybe she did all her shopping down on Skid Row. I'd have to finish unpacking the crate later. I stood up and dusted my hands off on the seat of my slacks.

"Sorry about the confusion," I said, even if I wasn't actually sorry, even if I was actually kind of pissed the girl hadn't told me who she was right up front. "When Aunt H wants something done, she doesn't usually bother sending her orders around in such an attractive envelope."

The girl laughed, then said, "Yeah, Auntie H warned me about you, Miss Beaumont."

"Did she, now? How so?"

"You know, your predilections. How you're not like other women."

"I'd say that depends on which other women we're discussing, don't you think?"

"*Most* other women," she said, glancing over her shoulder at the rain pelting the shop windows. It sounded like frying meat out there, the sizzle of the rain against asphalt, and concrete, and the roofs of passing automobiles.

"And what about you?" I asked her. "Are *you* like most other women?"

She looked away from the window, looking back at me, and she smiled what must have been the faintest smile possible. "Are you always this charming?"

"Not that I'm aware of," I said. "Then again, I never took a poll."

"The job, it's nothing particularly complicated,"

she said, changing the subject. "There's a Chinese apothecary not too far from here."

"That doesn't exactly narrow it down," I said, and lit a cigarette.

"Sixty-five Mott Street. The joint's run by an elderly Cantonese fellow name of Fong."

"Yeah, I know Jimmy Fong."

"That's good. Then maybe you won't get lost. Mr. Fong will be expecting you, and he'll have the package ready at five thirty this evening. He's already been paid in full, so all you have to do is be there to receive it, right? And, Miss Beaumont, please try to be on time. Auntie H said you have a problem with punctuality."

"You believe everything you hear?"

"Only if I'm hearing it from Auntie H."

"Fair enough," I told her, then offered her a Pall Mall, but she declined.

"I need to be getting back," she said, reaching for the umbrella she'd only just deposited in the stuffed hippopotamus foot.

"What's the rush? What'd you come after, anyway, a ball of fire?"

She rolled her eyes. "I got places to be. You're not the only stop on my itinerary."

"Fine. Wouldn't want you getting in Dutch with Harpootlian on my account. Don't suppose you've got a name?"

"I might," she said.

"Don't suppose you'd share?" I asked her, and took a long drag on my cigarette, wondering why in blue blazes Harpootlian had sent this smart-mouthed skirt instead of one of her usual flunkies. Of course,

Auntie H always did have a sadistic streak to put de Sade to shame, and likely as not this was her idea of a joke.

"Ellen," the girl said. "Ellen Andrews."

"So, Ellen Andrews, how is it we've never met? I mean, I've been making deliveries for your boss lady now going on seven years, and if I'd seen you, I'd remember. You're not the sort I forget."

"You got the moxie, don't you?"

"I'm just good with faces is all."

She chewed at a thumbnail, as if considering carefully what she should or shouldn't divulge. Then she said, "I'm from out of town, mostly. Just passing through, and thought I'd lend a hand. That's why you've never seen me before, Miss Beaumont. Now, I'll let you get back to work. And remember, don't be late."

"I heard you the first time, sister."

And then she left, and the brass bell above the door jingled again. I finished my cigarette and went back to unpacking the big crate of books from Connecticut. If I hurried, I could finish the job before heading for Chinatown.

She was right, of course. I did have a well-deserved reputation for not being on time. But I knew that Auntie H was of the opinion that my acumen in antiquarian and occult matters more than compensated for my not infrequent tardiness. I've never much cared for personal mottoes, but maybe if I had one it might be, *You want it on time, or you want it done right*? Still, I honestly tried to be on time for the meeting with Fong. And still, through no fault of my own, I was more than twenty minutes late. I was lucky enough to find a cab, despite the rain, but then got stuck behind some sort of brouhaha after turning onto Canal, so there you go. It's not like the old man Fong had anyplace more pressing to be, not like he was gonna get pissy and leave me high and dry.

When I got to Sixty-Five Mott, the Chinaman's apothecary was locked up tight, all the lights were off, and the "Sorry, We're Closed" sign was hung in the front window. No big surprise there. But then I went around back, to the alley, and found a door standing wide open and quite a lot of fresh blood on the cinder block steps leading into the building. Now, maybe I was the only lady bookseller in Manhattan who carried a gun, and maybe I wasn't. But times like that, I was glad to have the Colt tucked snugly inside its shoulder holster, and happier still that I knew how to use it. I took a deep breath, drew the pistol, flipped off the safety catch, and stepped inside.

The door opened onto a stockroom, and the tiny nook Jimmy Fong used as his office was a little farther in, over on my left. There was some light from a banker's lamp, but not much of it. I lingered in the shadows a moment, waiting for my heart to stop pounding, for the adrenaline high to fade. The air was close, and stank of angelica root and dust, ginger and frankincense, and fuck only knows what else. Powdered rhino horn and the pickled gallbladders of panda bears. What-the-hellever. I found the old man slumped over at his desk.

Whoever knifed him hadn't bothered to pull the shiv out of his spine, and I wondered if the poor SOB had even seen it coming. It didn't exactly add up, not after seeing all that blood drying on the steps, but I figured, hey, maybe the killer was the sort of klutz can't spread butter without cutting himself. I had a quick look-see around the cluttered office, hoping I might turn up the package Ellen Andrews had sent me there to retrieve. But no dice, and then it occurred to me, maybe whoever had murdered Fong had come looking for the same thing I was looking for. Maybe they'd found it, too, only Fong knew better than to just hand it over, and that had gotten him killed. Anyway, nobody was paying me to play junior shamus; hence the hows, whys, and wherefores of the Chinaman's death were not my problem. *My* problem would be showing up at Harpootlian's cathouse empty-handed.

I returned the gun to its holster, then started riffling through everything in sight— the great disarray of papers heaped upon the desk, Fong's accounting ledgers, sales invoices, catalogs, letters and postcards written in English, Mandarin, Wu, Cantonese, French, Spanish, and Arabic. I still had my gloves on, so it's not like I had to worry over fingerprints. A few of the desk drawers were unlocked, and I'd just started in on those when the phone perched atop the filing cabinet rang. I froze, whatever I was looking at clutched forgotten in my hands, and stared at the phone.

Sure, it wasn't every day I blundered into the immediate aftermath of this sort of foul play, but I was plenty savvy enough I knew better than to answer that call. It didn't much matter who was on the other end of the line. If I answered, I could be placed at the scene of a murder only minutes after it had gone down. The phone rang a second time, and a third, and I glanced at the dead man in the chair. The crimson halo surrounding the switchblade's inlaid mother-of-pearl handle was still spreading, blossoming like some grim rose, and now there was blood dripping to the floor, as well. The phone rang a fourth time. A fifth. And then I was seized by an overwhelming compulsion to answer it, and answer it I did. I wasn't the least bit thrown that the voice coming through the receiver was Ellen Andrews'. All at once, the pieces were falling into place. You spend enough years doing the step-and-fetch-it routine for imps like Harpootlian, you find yourself ever more jaded at the inexplicable and the uncanny.

"Beaumont," she said, "I didn't think you were going to pick up."

"I wasn't. Funny thing how I did anyway."

"Funny thing," she said, and I heard her light a cigarette and realized my hands were shaking.

"See, I'm thinking maybe I had a little push," I said. "That about the size of it?"

"Wouldn't have been necessary if you'd have just answered the damn phone in the first place."

"You already know Fong's dead, don't you?" And, I swear to fuck, nothing makes me feel like more of a jackass than asking questions I know the answers to.

"Don't you worry about Fong. I'm sure he had all his ducks in a row and was right as rain with Buddha. I need you to pay attention—"

"Harpootlian had him killed, didn't she? And you *knew* he'd be dead when I showed up."

She didn't reply straightaway, and I thought I could hear a radio playing in the background. "You knew," I said again, only this time it wasn't a query.

"Listen," she said. "You're a courier. I was told you're a courier we can trust, elsewise I never would have handed you this job."

"You didn't hand me the job. Your boss did."

"You're splitting hairs, Miss Beaumont."

"Yeah, well, there's a fucking dead celestial in the room with me. It's giving me the fidgets."

"So how about you shut up and listen, and I'll have you out of there in a jiffy?" And that's what I did, I shut up, either because I knew it was the path of least resistance, or because whatever spell she'd used to persuade me to answer the phone was still working.

"On Fong's desk, there's a funny little porcelain statue of a cat."

"You mean the Maneki Neko?"

"If that's what it's called, that's what I mean. Now break it open. There's a key inside."

I *tried* not to, just to see if I was being played as badly as I suspected I was being played. I gritted my teeth, dug in my heels, and tried *hard* not to break that damn cat.

"You're wasting time. Auntie H didn't mention you were such a crybaby."

"Auntie H and I have an agreement when it comes to free will. To *my* free will."

"Break the goddamn cat," Ellen Andrews growled, and that's exactly what I did. In fact, I slammed it down directly on top of Fong's head. Bits of brightly painted porcelain flew everywhere, and a rusty barrel key tumbled out and landed at my feet. "Now pick it up," she said. "The key fits the bottom left-hand drawer of Fong's desk. Open it."

This time, I didn't even try to resist her. I was getting a headache from the last futile attempt. I unlocked the drawer and pulled it open. Inside, there was nothing but the yellowed sheet of newspaper lining the drawer, three golf balls, a couple of old racing forms, and a finely carved wooden box lacquered almost the same shade of red as Jimmy Fong's blood. I didn't need to be told I'd been sent to retrieve the box—or, more specifically, whatever was *inside* the box.

"Yeah, I got it," I told Ellen Andrews.

"Good girl. Now, you have maybe twelve minutes before the cops show. Go out the same way you came in." Then she gave me a Riverside Drive address, and said there'd be a car waiting for me at the corner of Canal and Mulberry, a green Chevrolet coupe. "Just give the driver that address. He'll see you get where you're going."

"Yeah," I said, sliding the desk drawer shut again and locking it. I pocketed the key. "But, sister, you and me are gonna have a talk."

"Wouldn't miss it for the world, Nat," she said, and hung up. I shut my eyes, wondering if I really had twelve minutes before the bulls arrived, and if they were even on their way, wondering what would happen if I endeavored *not* to make the rendezvous with the green coupe. I stood there, trying to decide whether Harpootlian would have gone back on her word and given this bitch permission to turn her hoodoo tricks on me, and if aspirin would do anything at all for the dull throb behind my eyes. Then I looked at Fong one last time, at the knife jutting out of his back, his thin gray hair powdered with porcelain dust from the shattered "Lucky Cat." And then I stopped asking questions and did as I'd been told.

The car was there, just like she'd told me it would be. There was a young colored man behind the wheel, and when I climbed in the back, he asked me where we were headed.

"I'm guessing Hell," I said, "sooner or later."

"Got that right," he laughed, and winked at me from the rearview mirror. "But I was thinking more in terms of the immediate here and now."

So I recited the address I'd been given me over the phone, 435 Riverside.

"That's the Colosseum," he said.

"It is if you say so," I replied. "Just get me there."

The driver nodded and pulled away from the curb. As he navigated the slick, wet streets, I sat listening to the rain against the Chevy's hard top and the music coming from the Motorola. In particular, I can remember hearing the Dorsey brothers, "Chasing Shadows." I suppose you'd call that a harbinger, if you go in for that sort of thing. Me, I do my best not to. In this business, you start jumping at everything that *might* be an omen or a portent, you end up doing nothing else. Ironically, rubbing shoulders with the supernatural has made me a great believer in coincidence.

Anyway, the driver drove, the radio played, and I sat staring at the red-lacquered box I'd stolen from a dead man's locked desk drawer. I thought it might be mahogany, but it was impossible to be sure, what with all that cinnabar-tinted varnish. I know enough about Chinese mythology that I recognized the strange creature carved into the top—a *qilin*, a stout, antlered beast with cloven hooves, the scales of a dragon, and a long leonine tail. Much of its body was wreathed in flame, and its gaping jaws revealed teeth like daggers. For the Chinese, the *qilin* is a harbinger of good fortune, though it certainly hadn't worked out that way for Jimmy Fong. The box was heavier than it looked, most likely because of whatever was stashed inside. There was no latch, and as I examined

it more closely, I realized there was no sign whatsoever of hinges or even a seam to indicate it actually
had a lid.

"Unless I got it backwards," the driver said, "Miss
Andrews didn't say nothing about trying to open that
box, now, did she?"

I looked up, startled, feeling like the proverbial
kid caught with her hand in the cookie jar. He glanced
at me in the mirror; then his eyes drifted back to the
road.

"She didn't say one way or the other," I told him.

"Then how about we err on the side of caution?"

"So you didn't know where you're taking me, but
you know I shouldn't open this box? How's that
work?"

"Ain't the world just full of mysteries?" he said.

For a minute or so, I silently watched the headlights of the oncoming traffic and the metronomic
sweep of the windshield wipers. Then I asked the
driver how long he'd worked for Ellen Andrews.

"Not very," he said. "Never laid eyes on the lady
before this afternoon. Why you want to know?"

"No particular reason," I said, looking back down
at the box and the *qilin* etched in the wood. I decided
I was better off not asking any more questions, better
off getting this over and done with, and never mind
what did and didn't quite add up. "Just trying to make
conversation, that all."

Which got him to talking about the Chicago
stockyards and Cleveland and how it was he'd eventually wound up in New York City. He never told me his
name, and I didn't ask. The trip uptown seemed to
take forever, and the longer I sat with that box in my
lap, the heavier it felt. I finally moved it, putting it

down on the seat beside me. By the time we reached our destination, the rain had stopped and the setting sun was showing through the clouds, glittering off the dripping trees in Riverside Park and the waters of the wide gray Hudson. He pulled over, and I reached for my wallet.

"No, ma'am," he said, shaking his head. "Miss Andrews, she's already seen to your fare."

"Then I hope you won't mind if I see to your tip," I said, and I gave him five dollars. He thanked me, and I took the wooden box and stepped out onto the wet sidewalk.

"She's up on the eleventh," he told me, nodding towards the apartments. Then he drove off, and I turned to face the imposing brick and limestone façade of the building the driver had called the Colosseum. I rarely find myself any farther north than the Upper West Side, so this was pretty much terra incognita for me.

The doorman gave me directions, *after* giving me and Fong's box the hairy eyeball, and I quickly made my way to the elevators, hurrying through that ritzy marble sepulcher passing itself off as a lobby. When the operator asked which floor I needed, I told him the eleventh, and he shook his head and muttered something under his breath. I almost asked him to speak up, but thought better of it. Didn't I already have plenty enough on my mind without entertaining the opinions of elevator boys? Sure, I did. I had a murdered Chinaman, a mysterious box, and this pushy little sorceress calling herself Ellen Andrews. I also had an especially disagreeable feeling about this job, and the sooner it was settled, the better. I kept my eyes on the brass needle as it haltingly swung from left to right, counting off the floors, and when the doors parted, she was there waiting for me. She slipped the boy a sawbuck, and he stuffed it into his jacket pocket and left us alone.

"So nice to see you again, Nat," she said, but she was looking at the lacquered box, not me. "Would you like to come in and have a drink? Auntie H says you have a weakness for rye whiskey."

"Well, she's right about that. But just now I'd be more fond of an explanation."

"How odd," she said, glancing up at me, still smiling. "Auntie said one thing she liked about you was how you didn't ask a lot of questions. Said you were real good at minding your own business."

"Sometimes I make exceptions."

"Let me get you that drink," she said, and I followed her the short distance from the elevator to the door of her apartment. Turns out, she had the whole floor to herself, each level of the Colosseum being a single apartment. Pretty ritzy accommodations, I thought, for someone who was *mostly* from out of town. But then I've spent the last few years living in that one-bedroom cracker box above the Yellow Dragon, hot and cold running cockroaches and so forth. She locked the door behind us, then led me through the foyer to a parlor. The whole place was done up gaudy period French, Louis Quinze and the like, all floral brocade and Orientalia. The walls were decorated with damask hangings, mostly of ample-bosomed women reclining in pastoral scenes, dogs and sheep and what have you lying at their feet. Ellen told me to have a seat, so I parked myself on a récamier near a window.

"Harpootlian spring for this place?" I asked.

"No," she replied. "It belonged to my mother."

"So you come from money."

"Did I mention how you ask an awful lot of questions?"

"You might have," I said, and she inquired as to whether I liked my whiskey neat or on the rocks. I told her neat, and set the red box down on the sofa next to me.

"If you're not *too* thirsty, would you mind if I take a peek at that first?" she said, pointing at the box.

"Be my guest," I said, and Ellen smiled again. She picked up the red lacquered box, then sat next to me. She cradled it in her lap, and there was this goofy expression on her face, a mix of awe, dread, and eager expectation.

"Must be something extra damn special," I said, and she laughed. It was a nervous kind of a laugh.

I've already mentioned how I couldn't discern any evidence the box had a lid, and I supposed there was some secret to getting it open, a gentle squeeze or nudge in just the right spot. Turns out, all it needed was someone to say the magic words.

"Pain had no sting, and pleasure's wreath no flower," she said, speaking slowly and all but whispering the words. There was a sharp *click* and the top of the box suddenly slid back with enough force that it tumbled over her knees and fell to the carpet.

"Keats," I said.

"Keats," she echoed, but added nothing more. She was too busy gazing at what lay inside the box, nestled in a bed of velvet the color of poppies. She started to touch it, then hesitated, her fingertips hovering an inch or so above the object.

"You're fucking kidding me," I said, once I saw what was inside.

"Don't go jumping to conclusions, Nat."

"It's a dildo," I said, probably sounding as incredulous as I felt. "Exactly which conclusions am I not supposed to jump to? Sure, I enjoy a good rub-off as much as the next girl, but . . . you're telling me Harpootlian killed Fong over a dildo?"

"I never said Auntie H killed Fong."

"Then I suppose he stuck that knife there himself."

And that's when she told me to shut the hell up for five minutes, if I knew how. She reached into the box and lifted out the phallus, handling it as gingerly as somebody might handle a stick of dynamite. But whatever made the thing special, it wasn't anything I could see.

"*Le godemiché maudit,*" she murmured, her voice so filled with reverence you'd have thought she was holding the devil's own wang. Near as I could tell, it was cast from some sort of hard black ceramic. It glistened faintly in the light getting in through the drapes. "I'll tell you about it," she said, "if you really want to know. I don't see the harm."

"Just so long as you get to the part where it makes sense that Harpootlian bumped the Chinaman for this dingus of yours, then sure."

She took her eyes off the thing long enough to scowl at me. "Auntie H didn't kill Fong. One of Szabó's goons did that, then panicked and ran before he figured out where the box was hidden."

(Now, as for Madam Magdalena Szabó, the biggest boil on Auntie H's fanny, we'll get back to her by and by.)

"Ellen, how can you *possibly* fucking know that? Better yet, how could you've known Szabó's man would have given up and cleared out by the time I arrived?"

"Why did you answer that phone, Nat?" she asked, and that shut me up, good and proper. "As for our prize here," she continued, "it's a long story, a long story with a lot of missing pieces. The dingus, as you put it, is usually called *le Godemichet maudit*. Which doesn't necessarily mean it's actually cursed, mind you. Not literally. You *do* speak French, I assume?"

"Yeah," I told her. "I do speak French."

"That's ducky, Nat. Now, here's about as much as anyone could tell you. Though, frankly, I'd have thought a scholarly type like yourself would know all about it."

"Never said I was a scholar," I interrupted.

"But you went to college. Radcliffe, Class of 1923, right? Graduated with honors."

"Lots of people go to college. Doesn't necessarily make them scholars. I just sell books."

"My mistake," she said, carefully returning the black dildo to its velvet case. "It won't happen again." Then she told me her tale, and I sat there on the récamier and listened to what she had to say. Yeah, it was long. There *were* certainly a whole lot of missing pieces. And as a wise man once said, this might not be schoolbook history, not Mr. Wells' history, but, near as I've been able to discover since that evening at her apartment, it's history, nevertheless. She asked me whether or not I'd ever heard of a fourteenth-century Persian alchemist named al-Jaldaki, Izz al-Din Aydamir al-Jaldaki, and I had, naturally.

"He's sort of a hobby of mine, she said. "Came across his grimoire a few years back. Anyway, he's not where it begins, but that's where the written record starts. While studying in Anatolia, al-Jaldaki heard tales of a fabulous artifact that had been crafted from the horn of a unicorn at the behest of King Solomon."

"From a unicorn," I cut in. "So we believe in those now, do we?"

"Why not, Nat? I think it's safe to assume you've seen some peculiar shit in your time, that you've pierced the veil, so to speak. Surely a unicorn must be small potatoes for a worldly woman like yourself."

"So you'd think," I said.

"Anyhow," she went on, "the ivory horn was carved into the shape of a penis by the king's most skilled artisans. Supposedly, the result was so revered it was even placed in Solomon's temple, alongside the Ark of the Covenant and a slew of other sacred Hebrew relics. Records al-Jaldaki found in a mosque in the Taurus Mountains indicated that the horn had been removed from Solomon's temple when it was sacked in 587 BC by the Babylonians, and that eventually it had gone to Medina. But it was taken from Medina during, or shortly after, the siege of 627, when the Meccans invaded. And it's at this point that the horn is believed to have been given its ebony coating of porcelain enamel, possibly in an attempt to disguise it."

"Or," I said, "because someone in Medina preferred swarthy cock. You mind if I smoke?" I asked her, and she shook her head and pointed at an ashtray.

"A Medinan rabbi of the Banu Nadir tribe was entrusted with the horn's safety. He escaped, making his way west across the desert to Yanbu' al Bahr, then north along the al-Hejaz all the way to Jerusalem. But two years later, when the Sassanid army lost control of the city to the Byzantine emperor Heraclius, the horn was taken to a monastery in Malta, where it remained for centuries."

"That's quite a saga for a dildo. But you still haven't answered my question. What makes it so special? What the hell's it *do*?"

"Maybe you've heard enough," she said, and this whole time she hadn't taken her eyes off the thing in the box.

"Yeah, and maybe I haven't," I told her, tapping ash from my Pall Mall into the ashtray. "So, al-Jaldaki goes to Malta and finds the big black dingus."

She scowled again. No, it was more than a scowl; she *glowered*, and she looked away from the box just long enough to glower *at* me. "Yes," Ellen Andrews said. "At least, that's what he wrote. Al-Jaldaki found it buried in the ruins of a monastery in Malta, and then carried the horn with him to Cairo. It seems to have been in his possession until his death in 1342. After that it disappeared, and there's no word of it again until 1891."

I did the math in my head. "Five hundred and forty-nine years," I said. "So it must have gone to a good home. Must have lucked out and found itself a long-lived and appreciative keeper."

"The Freemasons might have had it," she went on, ignoring or oblivious of my sarcasm. "Maybe the Vatican. Doesn't make much difference."

"Okay. So, what happened in 1891?"

"A party in Paris, in an old house not far from the *Cimetière du Montparnasse*. Not so much a party, really, as an out-and-out orgy, the way the story goes. This was back before Montparnasse became so fashionable with painters and poets and expatriate Americans. Verlaine was there, though. At the orgy, I mean. It's not clear what happened precisely, but three women died, and afterwards there were rumors of black magic and ritual sacrifice, and tales surfaced of a cult that worshipped some sort of daemonic objet d'art that had made its way to France from Egypt. There was an official investigation, naturally, but someone saw to it that *la Préfecture de Police* came up with zilch."

"Naturally," I said. I glanced at the window. It was getting dark, and I wondered if my ride back to the Bowery had been arranged. "So, where's Black Beauty here been for the past forty-four years?"

Ellen leaned forward, reaching for the lid to the red lacquered box. When she set it back in place, covering that brazen scrap of antiquity, I heard the *click* again as the lid melded seamlessly with the rest of the box. Now there was only the etching of the *qilin*, and I remembered that the beast has sometimes been referred to as the "Chinese unicorn." It seemed odd I'd not thought of that before.

"I think we've probably had enough of a history lesson for now," she said, and I didn't disagree. Truth be told, the whole subject was beginning to bore me. It hardly mattered whether or not I believed in unicorns or enchanted dildos. I'd done my job, so there'd be no complaints from Harpootlian. I admit I felt kind of shitty about poor old Fong, who wasn't such a bad sort. But when you're an errand girl for the wicked folk, that shit comes with the territory. People get killed, and worse.

"It's getting late," I said, crushing out my cigarette in the ashtray. "I should dangle."

"Wait. Please. I promised you a drink, Nat. Don't

want you telling Auntie H I was a bad hostess, now, do I?" And Ellen Andrews stood up, the red box tucked snugly beneath her left arm.

"No worries, kiddo," I assured her. "If she ever asks, which I doubt, I'll say you were a regular Emily Post."

"I insist," she replied. "I really, truly do," and before I could say another word, she turned and rushed out of the parlor, leaving me alone with all that furniture and the buxom giantesses watching me from the walls. I wondered if there were any servants, or a live-in beau, or if possibly she had the place all to herself, that huge apartment overlooking the river. I pushed the drapes aside and stared out at twilight gathering in the park across the street. Then she was back (minus the red box) with a silver serving tray, two glasses, and a virgin bottle of Sazerac rye.

"Maybe just one," I said, and she smiled. I went back to watching Riverside Park while she poured the whiskey. No harm in a shot or two. It's not like I had some place to be, and there were still a couple of unanswered questions bugging me. Such as why Harpootlian had broken her promise, the one that was supposed to prevent her underlings from practicing their hocus-pocus on me. That is, assuming Ellen Andrews had even bothered to ask permission. Regardless, she didn't need magic or a spell book for her next dirty trick. The Mickey Finn she slipped me did the job just fine.

So, I came to, four, perhaps five hours later— sometime before midnight. By then, as I'd soon learn, the shit had already hit the fan. I woke up sick as a dog and my head pounding like there was an ape with a kettledrum loose inside my skull. I opened my eyes, but it wasn't Ellen Andrews' Baroque clutter and chintz that greeted me, and I immediately shut them again. I smelled the hookahs and the smoldering *buk-hoor*, the opium smoke and sandarac and, somewhere underneath it all, that pervasive brimstone stink that no amount of incense can mask. Besides, I'd seen the spiny ginger-skinned thing crouching not far from me, the eunuch, and I knew I was somewhere in the rat's maze labyrinth of Harpootlian's bordello. I started to sit up, but then my stomach lurched and I thought better of it. At least there were soft cushions beneath me, and the silk was cool against my feverish skin.

"You know where you are?" the eunuch asked; it had a woman's voice and the hint of a Russian accent, but I was pretty sure both were only affectations. First rule of demon brothels: Check your preconceptions of male and female at the door. Second rule: Appearances are fucking *meant* to be deceiving.

"Sure," I moaned, and tried not to think about vomiting. "I might have a notion or three."

"Good. Then you lie still and take it easy, Miss Beaumont. We've got a few questions need answering." Which made it mutual, but I kept my mouth shut on that account. The voice was beginning to sound not so much feminine as what you might hear if you scraped frozen pork back and forth across a cheese grater. "This afternoon, you were contacted by an associate of Madam Harpootlian's, yes? She told you her name was Ellen Andrews. That's not her true name, of course. Just something she heard in a motion picture—"

"Of course," I replied. "You sort never bother with your real names. Anyway, what of it?"

"She asked you to go see Jimmy Fong and bring

125

her something, yes? Something very precious. Something powerful and rare."

"The dingus," I said, rubbing at my aching head. "Right, but . . . hey . . . Fong was already dead when I got there, Scout's honor. Andrews told me one of Szabó's people did him."

"The Chinese gentleman's fate is no concern of ours," the eunuch said. "But we need to talk about Ellen Andrews. She has caused this house serious inconvenience. She's troubled us, and troubles us still."

"You and me both, bub," I said. It was just starting to dawn on me how there were some sizable holes in my memory. I clearly recalled the taste of rye, and gazing down at the park, but then nothing. Nothing at all. I asked the ginger demon, "Where is she? And how'd I get here, anyway?"

"We seem to have many of the same questions," it replied, dispassionate as a corpse. "You answer ours, maybe we shall find the answers to yours along the way."

I knew damn well I didn't have much say in the matter. After all, I'd been down this road before. When Auntie H wants answers, she doesn't usually bother with asking. Why waste your time wondering if someone's feeding you a load of baloney when all you gotta do is reach inside his brain and help yourself to whatever you need?

"Fine," I said, trying not to tense up, because tensing up only ever makes it worse. "How about let's cut the chitchat and get this over with?"

"Very well, but you should know," it said, "Madam regrets the necessity of this imposition." And then there were the usual wet, squelching noises as the relevant appendages unfurled and slithered across the floor towards me.

"Sure, no problem. Ain't no secret Madam's got a heart of gold," and maybe I shouldn't have smarted off like that, because when the stingers hit me, they hit hard. Harder than I knew was necessary to make the connection. I might have screamed. I know I pissed myself. And then it was inside me, prowling about, roughly picking its way through my conscious and unconscious mind—through my soul, if that word suits you better. All the heady sounds and smells of the brothel faded away, along with my physical discomfort. For a while I drifted nowhere and nowhen in particular, and then, then I stopped drifting . . .

. . . Ellen asked me, "You ever think you've had enough? Of the life, I mean. Don't you sometimes contemplate just up and blowing town, not even stopping long enough to look back? Doesn't that ever cross your mind, Nat?"

I sipped my whiskey and watched her, undressing her with my eyes and not especially ashamed of myself for doing so. "Not too often," I said. "I've had it worse. This gig's not perfect, but I usually get a fair shake."

"Yeah, usually," she said, her words hardly more than a sigh. "Just, now and then, I feel like I'm missing out."

I laughed, and she glared at me.

"You'd cut a swell figure in a breadline," I said, and took another swallow of the rye.

"I hate when people laugh at me."

"Then don't say funny things," I told her.

And that's when she turned and took my glass. I

thought she was about to tell me to get lost, and don't let the door hit me in the ass on the way out. Instead, she set the drink down on the silver serving tray, and she kissed me. Her mouth tasted like peaches. Peaches and cinnamon. Then she pulled back, and her eyes flashed red, the way they had in the Yellow Dragon, only now I knew it wasn't an illusion.

"You're a demon," I said, not all that surprised.

"Only a quarter. My grandmother . . . well, I'd rather not get into that, if it's all the same to you. Is it a problem?"

"No, it's not a problem," I replied, and she kissed me again. Right about here, I started to feel the first twinges of whatever she'd put into the Sazerac, but, frankly, I was too horny to heed the warning signs.

"I've got a plan," she said, whispering, as if she were afraid someone was listening in. "I have it all worked out, but I wouldn't mind some company on the road."

"I have no . . . no idea . . . what you're talking about," and there was something else I wanted to say, but I'd begun slurring my words and decided against it. I put a hand on her left breast, and she didn't stop me.

"We'll talk about it later," she said, kissing me again, and right about then, that's when the curtain came crashing down, and the ginger-colored demon in my brain turned a page . . .

. . . I opened my eyes, and I was lying in a black room. I mean, a *perfectly* black room. Every wall had been painted matte black, and the ceiling, and the floor. If there were any windows, they'd also been painted over, or boarded up. I was cold, and a moment later I realized that was because I was naked. I was naked and lying at the center of a wide white pentagram that had been chalked onto that black floor. A white pentagram held within a white circle. There was a single white candle burning at each of the five points. I looked up, and Ellen Andrews was standing above me. Like me, she was naked. Except she was wearing that dingus from the lacquered box, fitted into a leather harness strapped about her hips. The phallus drooped obscenely and glimmered in the candlelight. There were dozens of runic and Enochian symbols painted on her skin in blood and shit and charcoal. Most of them I recognized. At her feet, there was a small iron cauldron, and a black-handled dagger, and something dead. It might have been a rabbit, or a small dog. I couldn't be sure which, because she'd skinned it.

Ellen looked down, and saw me looking up at her. She frowned and tilted her head to one side. For just a second, there was something undeniably predatory in that expression, something murderous. All spite and not a jot of mercy. For that second, I was face-to-face with the one quarter of her bloodline that changed all the rules, the ancestor she hadn't wanted to talk about. But then that second passed, and she softly whispered, "I have a plan, Natalie Beaumont."

"What are you doing?" I asked her. But my mouth was so dry and numb, my throat so parched, it felt like I took forever to cajole my tongue into shaping those four simple words.

"No one will know," she said. "I promise. Not Harpootlian, not Szabó, not anyone. I've been over this a thousand times, worked all the angles." And she went down on one knee then, leaning over me. "But you're supposed to be asleep, Nat."

"Ellen, you don't cross Harpootlian," I croaked.

"Trust me," she said.

In that place, the two of us adrift on an island of light in an endless sea of blackness, she was the most beautiful woman I'd ever seen. Her hair was down now, and I reached up, brushing it back from her face. When my fingers moved across her scalp, I found two stubby horns, but it wasn't anything a girl couldn't hide with the right hairdo and a hat.

"Ellen, what are you doing?"

"I'm about to give you a gift, Nat. The most exquisite gift in all creation. A gift that even the angels might covet. You wanted to know what the unicorn does. Well, I'm not going to tell you, I'm going to *show* you."

She put a hand between my legs and found I was already wet.

I licked at my chapped lips, fumbling for words that wouldn't come. Maybe I didn't know what she was getting at, this *gift*, but I had a feeling I didn't want any part of it, no matter how exquisite it might be. I knew these things, clear as day, but I was lost in the beauty of her, and whatever protests I might have uttered, they were about as sincere as ol' Brer Rabbit begging Brer Fox not to throw him into that briar patch. I could say I was bewitched, but it would be a lie.

She mounted me then, and I didn't argue.

"What happens now?" I asked.

"Now I fuck you," she replied. "Then I'm going to talk to my grandmother." And with that, the world fell out from beneath me again. And the ginger-skinned eunuch moved along to the next tableau, that next set of memories I couldn't recollect on my own . . .

. . . Stars were tumbling from the skies. Not a few

stray shooting stars here and there. No, *all* the stars were falling. One by one, at first, and then the sky was raining pitchforks, only it *wasn't* rain, see? It was light. The whole sorry world was being born or was dying, and I saw it didn't much matter which. Go back far enough, or far enough forward, the past and future wind up holding hands, cozy as a couple of lovebirds. Ellen had thrown open a doorway, and she'd dragged me along for the ride. I was *so* cold. I couldn't understand how there could be that much fire in the sky, and me still be freezing my tits off like that. I lay there shivering as the brittle vault of heaven collapsed. I could feel her inside me. I could feel *it* inside me, and same as I'd been lost in Ellen's beauty, I was being smothered by that ecstasy. And then . . . then the eunuch showed me the gift, which I'd forgotten . . . and which I would immediately forget again.

How do you write about something, when all that remains of it is the faintest of impressions of glory? When all you can bring to mind is the empty place where a memory ought to be and isn't, and only that conspicuous absence is there to remind you of what cannot ever be recalled? Strain as you might, all that effort hardly adds up to a trip for biscuits. So, *how do you write it down?* You don't, *that's* how. You do your damnedest to think about what came next, instead, knowing your sanity hangs in the balance.

So, here's what came *after* the gift, since *le Gode-michet maudit* is a goddamn Indian giver if ever one was born. Here's the curse that rides shotgun on the gift, as impossible to obliterate from reminiscence as the other is to awaken.

There were falling stars, and that unendurable cold . . . and then the empty, aching socket to mark the countermanded gift . . . and *then* I saw the unicorn. I don't mean the dingus. I mean the *living creature*, standing in a glade of cedars, bathed in clean sunlight and radiating a light all its own. It didn't look much like what you see in storybooks or those medieval tapestries they got hanging in the Cloisters. It also didn't look much like the beast carved into the lid of Fong's wooden box. But I knew what it was, all the same.

A naked girl stood before it, and the unicorn kneeled at her feet. She sat down, and it rested its head on her lap. She whispered reassurances I couldn't hear, because they were spoken as softly as falling snow. And then she offered the unicorn one of her breasts, and I watched as it suckled. This scene of chastity and absolute peace lasted maybe a minute, maybe two, before the trap was sprung and the hunters stepped out from the shadows of the cedar boughs. They killed the unicorn, with cold iron lances and swords, but first the unicorn killed the virgin who'd betrayed it to its doom . . .

. . . and Harpootlian's ginger eunuch turned another page (a ham-fisted analogy if ever there was one, but it works for me), and we were back in the black room. Ellen and me. Only two of the candles were still burning, two guttering, halfhearted counterpoints to all that darkness. The other three had been snuffed out by a sudden gust of wind that had smelled of rust, sulfur, and slaughterhouse floors. I could hear Ellen crying, weeping somewhere in the darkness beyond the candles and the periphery of her protective circle. I rolled over onto my right side, still shivering, still so cold I couldn't imagine being warm ever again. I stared into the black, blinking and dimly amazed that my eyelids hadn't frozen shut. Then something snapped into focus, and there she was, cowering on her hands and knees, a tattered rag of a woman lost in the gloom. I could see her stunted, twitching tail, hardly as long as my middle finger, and the thing from the box was still strapped to her crotch. Only now it had a twin, clutched tightly in her left hand.

I think I must have asked her what the hell she'd done, though I had a pretty good idea. She turned towards me, and her eyes . . . well, you see that sort of pain, and you spend the rest of your life trying to forget you saw it.

"I didn't understand," she said, still sobbing. "I didn't understand she'd take so much of me away."

A bitter wave of conflicting, irreconcilable emotion surged and boiled about inside me. Yeah, I knew what she'd done to me, and I knew I'd been used for something unspeakable. I knew *violation* was too tame a word for it, and that I'd been marked forever by this gold-digging half-breed of a twist. And part of me was determined to drag her kicking and screaming to Harpootlian. Or fuck it, I could kill her myself, and take my own sweet time doing so. I could kill her the way the hunters had murdered the unicorn. But— on the other hand—the woman I saw lying there before me was shattered almost beyond recognition. There'd been a steep price for her trespass, and she'd paid it and then some. Besides, I was learning fast that when you've been to Hades' doorstep with someone, and the two of you make it back more or less alive, there's a bond, whether you want it or not. So, there we were, a cheap, latter-day parody of Orpheus and Eurydice, and all I could think about was holding her, tight as I could, until she stopped crying and I was warm again.

"She took *so much*," Ellen whispered. I didn't ask what her grandmother had taken. Maybe it was a slice of her soul, or maybe a scrap of her humanity. Maybe it was the memory of the happiest day of her life, or the ability to taste her favorite food. It didn't seem to matter. It was gone, and she'd never get it back. I reached for her, too cold and too sick to speak, but sharing her hurt and needing to offer my hollow consolation, stretching out to touch . . .

. . . and the eunuch said, "Madam wishes to speak with you now," and that's when I realized the parade down memory lane was over. I was back at Harpootlian's, and there was a clock somewhere chiming down to three a.m., the dead hour. I could feel the nasty welt the stingers had left at the base of my skull and underneath my jaw, and I still hadn't shaken off the hangover from that tainted shot of rye whiskey. But above and underneath and all about these mundane discomforts was a far more egregious pang, a portrait of that guileless white beast cut down and its blood spurting from gaping wounds. Still, I did manage to get myself upright without puking. Sure, I gagged once or twice, but I didn't puke. I pride myself on that. I sat with my head cradled in my hands, waiting for the room to stop tilting and sliding around like I'd gone for a spin on the Coney Island Wonder Wheel.

"Soon, you'll feel better, Miss Beaumont."

"Says you," I replied. "Anyway, give me half a fucking minute, will you please? Surely your employer isn't gonna cast a kitten if you let me get my bearings first, not after the work-over you just gave me. Not after—"

"I will remind you, her patience is not infinite," the ginger demon said firmly, and then it clicked its long claws together.

"Yeah?" I asked. "Well, who the hell's is?" But I'd gotten the message, plain and clear. The gloves were off, and whatever forbearance Auntie H might have granted me in the past, it was spent and now I was living on the installment plan. I took a deep breath and struggled to my feet. At least the eunuch didn't try to lend a hand.

I can't say for certain when Yeksabet Harpootlian set up shop in Manhattan, but I have it on good faith that Magdalena Szabó was here first. And anyone who knows her onions knows the two of them have been at each other's throats since the day Auntie H decided to claim a slice of the action for herself. Now, you'd think there'd be plenty enough of the hellion cock-and-tail trade to go around, what with all the netherworlders who call the Five Boroughs their home away from home. And likely as not you'd be right. Just don't try telling that to Szabó or Auntie H. Sure, they've each got their elite stable of "girls and boys," and they both have more customers than they know what to do with. Doesn't stop each of them from spending every waking hour looking for a way to banish the other once and for all—or at least find the unholy grail of competitive advantages.

Now, by the time the ginger-skinned eunuch led me through the chaos of Auntie H's stately pleasure dome, far below the subways and sewers and tenements of the Lower East Side, I already had a pretty good idea the dingus from Jimmy Fong's shiny box was meant to be Harpootlian's trump card. Only, here was Ellen Andrews, this mutt of a courier gumming up the works, playing fast and loose with the loving cup. And here was me, stuck smack in the middle, the unwilling stooge in her double cross.

As I followed the eunuch down the winding corridor that ended in Auntie H's grand salon, we passed doorway after doorway, all of them opening onto scenes of inhuman passion and madness, the most odious of perversions, and tortures that make short work of merely mortal flesh. It would be disingenuous to say I looked away. After all, this wasn't my first time. Here were the hinterlands of wanton physical delight and agony, where the two become indistinguishable in a rapturous *Totentanz*. Here were spectacles to remind me how Doré and Hieronymus Bosch never even came close, and all of it laid bare for the eyes of any passing voyeur. You see, there are no locked doors to be found at Madam Harpootlian's. There are no doors at all.

"It's a busy night," the eunuch said, though it looked like business as usual to me.

"Sure," I muttered. "You'd think the Shriners were in town. You'd think Mayor La Guardia himself had come down off his high horse to raise a little hell."

And then we reached the end of the hallway, and I was shown into the mirrored chamber where Auntie H holds court. The eunuch told me to wait, then left me alone. I'd never seen the place so empty. There was no sign of the usual retinue of rogues, ghouls, and archfiends, only all those goddamn mirrors, because no one looks directly at Madam Harpootlian and lives to tell the tale. I chose a particularly fancy looking glass, maybe ten feet high and held inside an elaborate gilded frame. When Harpootlian spoke up, the mirror rippled like it was only water, and my reflection rippled with it.

"Good evening, Natalie," she said. "I trust you've been treated well?"

"You won't hear any complaints outta me," I replied. "I always say, the Waldorf Astoria's got nothing on you."

She laughed then, or something that we'll call laughter for the sake of convenience.

"A crying shame we're not meeting under more amicable circumstances. Were it not for this unpleasantness with Miss Andrews, I'd offer you something— on the house, of course."

"Maybe another time," I said.

"So, you *know* why you're here?"

"Sure," I said. "The dingus I took off the dead Chinaman. The salami with the fancy French name."

"It has many names, Natalie. Karkadann's Brow, *El consolador sangriento*, the Horn of Malta—"

"*Le Godemichet maudit*," I said. "Ellen's cock."

Harpootlian grunted, and her reflection made an ugly dismissive gesture. "It is nothing of Miss Andrews. It is mine, bought and paid for. With the sweat of my own brow did I track down the spoils of al-Jaldaki's long search. It's *my* investment, one purchased with so grievous a forfeiture this quadroon mongrel could not begin to appreciate the severity of her crime. But you, Natalie, you know, don't you? You've been privy to the wonders of Solomon's talisman, so I think, maybe, you are cognizant of my loss."

"I can't exactly say what I'm cognizant of," I told her, doing my best to stand up straight and not flinch or look away. "I saw the murder of a creature I didn't even believe in yesterday morning. That was sort of an eye-opener, I'll grant you. And then there's the part I can't seem to conjure up, even after golden boy did that swell Roto-Rooter number on my head."

"Yes. Well, that's the catch," she said, and smiled. There's no shame in saying I looked away then. Even in a mirror, the smile of Yeksabet Harpootlian isn't something you want to see straight on.

"Isn't there always a catch?" I asked, and she chuckled.

"True, it's a fleeting boon," she purred. "The gift comes, and then it goes, and no one may ever remember it. But always, *always* they will long for it again, even hobbled by that ignorance."

"You've lost me, Auntie," I said, and she grunted again. That's when I told her I wouldn't take it as an insult to my intelligence or expertise if she laid her cards on the table and spelled it out plain and simple, like she was talking to a woman who didn't regularly have tea and crumpets with the damned. She mumbled something to the effect that maybe she gave me too much credit, and I didn't disagree.

"Consider," she said, "what it *is*, a unicorn. It is the incarnation of purity, an avatar of innocence. And here is the *power* of the talisman, for that state of grace which soon passes from us each and everyone is forever locked inside the horn, the horn become the phallus. And in the instant that it brought you, Natalie, to orgasm, you knew again that innocence, the bliss of a child before it suffers corruption."

I didn't interrupt her, but all at once I got the gist.

"Still, you are only a mortal woman, so what negligible, insignificant sins could you have possibly committed during your short life? Likewise, whatever calamities and wrongs have been visited upon your flesh *or* you soul, they are trifles. But if you survived the war in Paradise, if you refused the yoke and so are counted among the exiles, then you've persisted down all the long eons. You were already broken and despoiled billions of years before the coming of man. And your transgressions outnumber the stars.

"Now," she asked, "what would *you* pay, were you so cursed, to know even one fleeting moment of that stainless, former existence?"

Starting to feel sick to my stomach all over again, I said, "More to the point, if I *always* forgot it, immediately, but it left this emptiness I feel—"

"You would come back." Auntie H smirked. "You would come back again and again and again, because there would be no satiating that void, and always would you hope that maybe *this* time it would take and you might *keep* the memories of that immaculate condition."

"Which makes it priceless, no matter what you paid."

"Precisely. And now Miss Andrews has forged a copy—an *identical* copy, actually—meaning to sell one to me, and one to Magdalena Szabó. That's where Miss Andrews is now."

"Did you tell her she could hex me?"

"I would never do such a thing, Natalie. You're much too valuable to me."

"*But* you think I had something to do with Ellen's mystical little counterfeit scheme."

"Technically, you did. The ritual of division required a supplicant, someone to *receive* the gift granted by the unicorn, before the summoning of a succubus mighty enough to affect such a difficult twinning."

"So maybe, instead of sitting here bumping gums with me, you should send one of your torpedoes after her. And while we're on the subject of how your pick your little henchmen, maybe—"

"*Natalie,*" snarled Auntie H from some place not far behind me. "Have I failed to make myself *understood*? Might it be I need to raise my voice?" The floor rumbled, and tiny hairline cracks began to crisscross the surface of the looking glass. I shut my eyes.

"No," I told her. "I get it. It's a grift, and you're out for blood. But you *know* she used me. Your lackey, it had a good, long look around my upper story, right, and there's no way you can think I was trying to con you."

For a dozen or so heartbeats, she didn't answer me, and the mirrored room was still and silent, save all the moans and screaming leaking in through the walls. I could smell my own sour sweat, and it was making me sick to my stomach.

"There are some gray areas," she said finally. "Matters of sentiment and lust, a certain reluctant infatuation, even."

I opened my eyes and forced myself to gaze directly into that mirror, at the abomination crouched on its writhing throne. And all at once, I'd had enough, enough of Ellen Andrews and her dingus, enough of the cloak-and-dagger bullshit, and definitely enough kowtowing to the monsters.

"For fuck's sake," I said, "I only just met the woman this afternoon. She drugs and rapes me, and you think that means she's my sheba?"

"Like I told you, I think there are gray areas," Auntie H replied. She grinned, and I looked away again.

"Fine. You tell me what it's gonna take to make this right with you, and I'll do it."

"Always so eager to please," Auntie H laughed, and the mirror in front of me rippled. "But, since you've asked, and as I do not doubt your *present* sincerity, I will tell you. I want her dead, Natalie. Kill her, and all will be . . . forgiven."

"Sure," I said, because what the hell else was I going to say? "But if she's with Szabó—"

"I have spoken already with Magdalena Szabó, and we have agreed to set aside our differences long enough to deal with Miss Andrews. After all, she has attempted to cheat us both, in equal measure."

"How do I find her?"

"You're a resourceful young lady, Natalie," she said. "I have faith in you. Now . . . if you will excuse me." And before I could get in another word, the mirrored room dissolved around me. There was a flash, not of light, but a flash of the deepest abyssal darkness, and I found myself back at the Yellow Dragon, watching through the bookshop's grimy windows as the sun rose over the Bowery.

There you go, the dope on just how it is I found myself holding a gun on Ellen Andrews, and just how it is she found herself wondering if I was angry enough or scared enough or desperate enough to pull the trigger. And like I said, I chambered a round, but she just stood there. She didn't even flinch.

"I wanted to give you a gift, Nat," she said.

"Even if I believed that—and I don't—all I got to show for this *gift* of yours is a nagging yen for something I'm never going to get back. We lose our innocence, it stays lost. That's the way it works. So, all I got from you, Ellen, is a thirst can't ever be slaked. That and Harpootlian figuring me for a clip artist."

She looked hard at the gun, then looked harder at me. "So what? You thought I was gonna plead for my life? You thought maybe I was gonna get down on my knees for you and beg? Is that how you like it? Maybe you're just steamed 'cause I was on top—"

"Shut up, Ellen. You don't get to talk yourself out of this mess. It's a done deal. You tried to give Auntie H the high hat."

"And you honestly think she's on the level? You think you pop me and she lets you off the hook, like nothing happened?"

"I do," I said. And maybe it wasn't as simple as that, but I wasn't exactly lying, either. I needed to believe Harpootlian, the same way old women need to believe in the infinite compassion of the little baby Jesus and Mother Mary. Same way poor kids need to believe in the inexplicable generosity of Popeye the Sailor and Santa Claus.

"It didn't have to be this way," she said.

"I didn't dig your grave, Ellen. I'm just the sap left holding the shovel."

And she smiled that smug smile of hers, and said, "I get it now, what Auntie H sees in you. And it's not your knack for finding shit that doesn't want to be found. It's not that at all."

"Is this a guessing game," I asked, "or do you have something to say?"

"No, I think I'm finished," she replied. "In fact, I

think I'm done for. So let's get this over with. By the way, how many women *have* you killed?"

"You played me," I said again.

"Takes two to make a sucker, Nat," she smiled.

Me, I don't even remember pulling the trigger. Just the sound of the gunshot, louder than thunder. . . .

CHAPTER FIVE

FRIENDS OF MR. CAIRO

So, there you have it. The supposedly fictional account of a supposedly fictional artifact from another universe that, according to Mean Mr. B, wasn't at all fictional. An artifact that had somehow entered *this* universe and now four power-hungry bitches were scrambling to get their paws on it before one of the others did. It was a lot to take in, and mostly I thought it was bullshit. But I'd read the story, and then I'd passed out for twelve hours. I was finally awakened by the Hello goddamn Kitty iPhone on my bedside table chirping at me like a rabid canary. I sat up, glared at it, lit a cigarette, and considered tossing the thing out the window. I knew it was B, calling from one of his merry-go-round of blocked numbers. Pretty much no one else ever calls me. Finally, I answered it. If I hadn't, he'd just kept calling back. Unless I turned off the phone, and then he'd only have sent one of his boys around.

"Yeah, what do you want?"

"Well, precious, good morning to you, too. You read the tale?" he asked.

"I did. It's a load of malarkey. The Maidstone sisters, Drusneth, that Harpootlian, they're all on a wild goose chase, and you know it. And I know you know it."

"You can be very, very narrow-minded."

"I have a headache," I said. "I think whatever I ate last night didn't agree with me. So, call back later. I need a whole fucking bottle of aspirin before I have to talk to you."

There was a moment of silence. I took a drag on my Camel and stared at a water stain on the ceiling. Through the phone, I could hear another voice, faint but audible. At least to my supersensitive vamp ears. It wasn't one of B's fuck bunnies. Sounded like an older man, maybe in his sixties.

"Who the hell's that?" I asked B.

"Another interested party," he replied.

"Jesus on a pogo stick. How many people are mixed up in this foolishness?"

Another pause. More muttering in the background.

"I take it you don't believe in the unicorn."

"Or Santa Claus. Or the Tooth Fairy. Or Old Man Jehovah looking down on us sinners through his pearly goddamn gates."

The water stain was getting as boring to look at as B was tiresome.

"Dude, even if I were to buy this whole 'magazine from another world' angle—and I don't—it's *fiction*. Or did you miss that part?"

Pause. Mutter. Mutter. Mutter. I caught ". . . move very quickly or . . ."

"Will you please tell whoever that is to shut the fuck up. He's annoying me."

"Your view of existence is sadly impoverished," said Mean Mr. B. I didn't bother asking him his name that day. I didn't give two shits.

"Poor me," I said, wondering if I even had any aspirin, wondering what the hell had been in the bloodstream of that girl I'd eaten the night before.

"The story is a fictionalized account," he went on, "of events that actually transpired, over there, in their alternate 1935."

"Right, and you know this how?"

He didn't answer the question. "You can imagine, then, the influence that would be possessed by she or he or it who comes into the possession of the unicorn."

"And you want me to get to it first, which you neglected to tell me—well, you neglected to tell me anything—"

"Yes, kitten."

"—same as Shaker Lashly, and that's what got him killed—chasing after this pie-in-the-sky nonsense, and what almost got *me* killed. Which, by the way, I'm still pissed about. You put me in the crosshairs of a bunch of lunatics because you believe in a transdimensional dildo with a fancy French name, carved from the horn of a unicorn. Which, surprise, you want for your own."

"At least you have a firm grasp of the situation."

I stubbed out the half-smoked cigarette. My mouth tasted bad enough without it, like something had crawled inside and taken a big ol' dump. I could get by without the nicotine.

"B, aren't you a little old to believe in unicorns?"

"Love, you're a vampire, and a bleeding werewolf, who works for a man who runs errands for demons. Need I bother to point out the inherent inconsonance in that query?"

"I'm passing on this one. Find another sap."

Pause Numero Très. This time, I caught ". . . need I remind . . ." and ". . . of the essence . . ." from the mutterer.

"When was our arrangement amended to permit you to pick and choose your assignments?"

Since never. Be a good doggy, Quinn. Don't make me remind you what happens to bad doggies.

"You're going to get me killed."

Found my boxers. Found my jeans. Fell on my ass trying to pull them on without putting down the phone. I lay on the phone, staring at that water stain all over again.

"You're already dead, love."

"You know what I mean."

Mutter. Mutter.

"I assure you, I'm endeavoring to prevent that outcome. Meanwhile, you're to continue to play along with those two bolshie prats and try not to reveal that we're onto them."

I shut my aching eyes. I imagined B being eaten alive by giant rats. I imagined what a shotgun could make of his smug face. Neither fantasy made me feel any better.

"And when Drusneth sends another nasty after me?"

"Oh, that wasn't Drusneth. If she'd meant to kill you, you'd never have left her cathouse. That was, in all likelihood, Harpootlian. Unless there's another player who has yet to—"

"Wait. Riddle me this. If our Harpootlian bitch is from that other universe, what the fuck is she doing here?"

The mutterer laughed. It was a high, abrasive, slightly girlish laugh.

"Often," replied B, "the hands will solve a mystery that the intellect has struggled with in vain. Carl Jung said that, kitten, and he was a wise, wise bloke. Which is to say, when you find out, we shall both of us know."

"Why don't you just have me kill the Maidstones and give you two less competitors? Also, Berenice's zombie playmates give me the creeps."

"Quinn, do you genuinely wish to be the woman with Squire Edgar Maidstone's daughters' blood on her hands? Now, stop asking stupid questions, stick close to Berenice, and let's see what they'll do next. I doubt the zombies will do you mischief. I'll be in touch."

I opened my eyes again. The water stain was beginning to look ominous. And no, this isn't foreshadowing. Sometimes a water stain is just a water stain. Also, I needed something to break up all this dialogue.

"Ever seen a movie called *The Maltese Falcon*?" I asked Mean Mr. B.

"Curious matter, that," he replied. "But, as I understand it, events in one universe very often, if not usually, parallel events in another. Doppelgängers. Overlapping individuals. Counterpart theory."

"You're beginning to fucking sound like Fox Mulder," I told him.

"Who?"

"Never mind."

Mutter. Mutter. Mutter.

"Very well," B said. "Oh, and by the way. The full moon is upon us. Do take care not to dine on our clients while you're riding the crimson wave." Then he hung up.

But he was right. The next day was Valentine's Day, all hearts and flowers and the full snow moon. It would kinda put a serious kink in B's plans if I went *loup* and ate Berenice Maidstone. But it's not like, back then, I had much control over the pooch in me, any more than it came when I called. It would be years before I figured out how that worked. I finished pulling on my jeans, then got up and went to brush my teeth. Which is when it occurred to me I'd lost the porcelain grill beneath Aloysius' overpass. The day just kept getting better.

So, if B wanted me to play along with the Maidstone sisters' plot, that's what I'd do. Certainly, I desired no part whatsoever in the grand fist fuck that was inevitably to come of all the unhealthy and imbecilic intrigue looming large on the horizon. But I was over that barrel I'd signed off on all those months earlier, before the Bride and Grumet made me what I am today. Back when Mean

Mr. B was offering me protection from the nasties and all the heroin I could shoot and still be useful to him (a fine line, by the way). I was screwed, damned if I do, et cetera.

I tarted up with a fresh coat of concealer and stuck the contacts back in. Like I said, I'd lost the false teeth, but that was something I'd have to worry about later. Meanwhile, I'd keep smiling to a minimum around all those not in the know. Anyway, it was not as if I've ever been big on smiling, and got to be even less so after going vamp and *loup*. I dragged a comb through my hair, which really only made matters worse, so I grabbed the Slytherin wool cap. Fortunately, almost all the mutilation the gaunt had done was healed up by then. I grabbed my gear, pausing to pop a fresh clip in the Glock and make sure the crossbow was in working order.

Ah, and I forgot to mention this earlier, but—though I'd called the landlord—the front door of the house still had a hole in it, and the door to my apartment still had to be propped up. Thank you, Father douche bag Rizzo. I'd have worried about being robbed, if I'd had anything worth stealing. I'd have worried about being murdered in my sleep if . . . well, you know.

I called Berenice Maidstone, and she told me she'd ditched the warehouse on Kinsley for a place above a deli on Atwells Ave. She'd decided it was wisest if she kept moving, a target in motion being harder to hit and all. Probably not such a dumb idea. She gave me the address, and I told her I was on my way.

That afternoon, the Econoline decided it was a good day to be a pain in my ass, and it took me about ten minutes to get the rust bucket's engine to sputter to life. The tailpipe coughed out a puff of black smoke, and I wondered if this would be the day the PPD pulled me over for driving a vehicle that belonged in a junkyard, not on the road. I was shifting into drive when I noticed the herring gull watching me from atop a streetlight.

You gotta understand, it was a *suspicious* seagull.

I stared back at it, showed it my middle finger, and the bird gave me a dirty look, spread its wings, and flapped away. I was jumpy enough without suspicious seagulls watching me from streetlights.

I was halfway to Berenice's deli hideout when I glanced up through the dirty windshield and saw the gull again, wheeling not far above the van.

Great. I was being tailed. By a goddamn seagull.

See, it's not all that uncommon. Lots of nasties employ birds as spies. Being airborne, they're obviously perfect for the task. Plus, they work cheap. Pigeons, sparrows, crows, and especially seagulls, which are sort of the punk-ass weasels of the whole avian kingdom. There's no job too sketchy for a gull, and herring gulls are the absolute worst. Also, they have the best command of English. Anyway, I had no idea who'd sent this one to keep its beady yellow eyes on me, but whoever had done it, I had no intention of leading the gull straight to Berenice Maidstone's hidey-hole.

I turned down a side road, and the bird followed.

I drove in circles, all the way around Brown three times, and the bird followed.

This was not a terribly bright bird, even as gulls go. Clearly I'd caught on, and if it'd had half a brain, it would have given up the chase and tried to pick up my trail again later.

I drove over to India Point Park and pulled in near a giant heap of snow the plows had dumped in the lot. About five minutes later, the gull landed on the lowest limb of one of the pines between my van and the cold, dark waters of the bay. At most, the bird was five and a half feet above the ground.

Whoever had hired this gull, they should have asked for references.

It did an absolutely lousy job of pretending not to watch me. I opened the door and walked slowly towards the water and the thin rind of ice along the shore. The bird stayed put, still as a stone. Right up until the moment I reached out and snatched the creep off the limb. Then it squawked and began frantically beating its gray wings. It pecked at my hands with its hooked beak. And sure, that hurt. But after the previous day's pummeling at the hands of a night gaunt, getting pecked wasn't much more than love taps. I had a firm hold around its bony yellow legs, and in a few seconds more, I'd wrapped my right hand firmly around its neck. It screeched and squawked loud enough people could probably hear it a mile away.

"Stop that," I growled, and the bird managed to squawk even louder. So I thumped its head against the trunk of the pine tree, twice, and it shut up.

"Who you working for?"

"What!" the bird screeched.

"Who. Are. You. Working. For?" I punched each word into the chilly air.

"What!" the bird asked again, and I thumped its skull against the tree a third time.

"What do you think you're doing!" it demanded.

"Getting ready to bash your tiny brains out."

"Fuck you," it cried out, then pecked my left wrist extra hard. I shook it, and the gull stopped pecking and blinked at me stupidly.

"People lose teeth talking to me like that. But since you don't *have* any teeth, I'll have to *improvise*."

"I don't know what you're talking about," the bird squawked. "I was just flying around, looking for scraps. Yeah, right. That McDonald's over on—"

I shook him again. Harder than before. In a comic book something cute like "bopple-bopple-bopple" would have been scribbled over the gull's head.

"B knows I'd spot you," I said. "Also, not his style. And I hear Drusneth doesn't do business with any birds but crows and ravens. So the list of suspects is getting short. Kinda like my fuse."

I narrowed my eyes, wishing I wasn't wearing the hazel contacts, because I'm a whole lot scarier without them.

"Shove off," the herring gull told me, trying to sound tough, but only sounding dazed from having its head bonked against the pine.

"Fine," I said. "Let's go for a ride, Jonathan Livingston Fuckmuppet."

"Why, why . . . you can't *do* this!"

"Blow me."

Which is how I wound up driving to a deli on Atwells with a seagull in my van, its beak, wings, and legs securely bound with duct tape. Just when you think this shit can't get any weirder. . . .

. . . **S**hit inevitably gets weirder. Shit gets weirder squared. My van had just puttered over I-95 and beneath the concrete arch where Atwells Avenue begins—that vaulted concrete gateway with its huge, dangling, welcoming bronze pinecone, *La Pigna*, that most people mistake for a pine*apple*. The gull was making noises you wouldn't think a bird could make, what with its beak taped shut and all. I was noticing how the sky was growing darker, the clouds lower, and that we'd probably have more snow before sundown when I was no longer driving on Atwells. I had no fucking idea *where* I was driving.

There was nothing even the least bit familiar about the narrow single-lane strip of blacktop stretching out before me. But I wasn't in Kansas anymore. Of that much I was absolutely goddamn certain. Very tall structures rose on either side of the road. I won't call them buildings, because I have no idea what they were. The architectural love child of H. R. Giger and M. C. Escher. That's as close as I can come to any sort of accurate description. Here and there lights seemed to burn from vaguely windowlike recesses. Every now and then, the not-buildings seemed to move, which I did my best not to notice.

All right, I thought, *don't you freak. Not like this is the first time someone's pulled this sort of total skull fuck on you.*

The seagull made a muffled sound that I'm fairly certain was a laugh. I told him to shut the hell up or I'd be selling his feathery ass to the owner of a Chinese restaurant I knew who wasn't too particular about where he got his "chicken" and "duck."

I stopped in the middle of the road. The sky no longer looked like snow. Looked more like . . . never mind.

Something seemed to detach itself from one of the not-buildings, sort of rolling from the structure, and it lay in the middle of the road—a few feet in front of the Econoline—for a minute or so. It looked sort of like an oyster-colored Volkswagen Bug, only covered with spiky bristles needle thin and long as my arm. I was about to shift into reverse. Maybe whatever portal I'd driven through was still open. Total bullshit, but a girl can hope. That's when the hairy Volkswagen unfolded itself, rising on ten or so stilts that I guessed were supposed to pass as legs. It just stood there, blocking my way.

I drew the 9mm and aimed at the windshield.

"I get the message, whoever you are," I said. "I'm impressed. So let's drop the theatrics."

I want to say that bristly thing in the road looked like a spider. Because it did. Only, somehow, it truly looked nothing *at all* like a spider. Nasties love paradoxes and tend to trot them out whenever the opportunity presents itself. Show-offs.

The creature sort of leaned forward, tilting a bit towards me. No sign of eyes, a mouth, nothing. Just those crazy granddaddy long legs and spiky hairs. Then there was a high keening noise, which I assumed it was making.

I squeezed the trigger.

Click.

Okay, that was starting to get old.

Only, I was no longer on that narrow road with its

grotesque not-buildings. I wasn't even in my van. I was sitting in a simple wooden chair in a white room. And when I say that this room was white, let me be clear that the room was *goddamn* white. Walls, floor, ceiling, and all of it washed in stark-white fluorescent light. There wasn't a door, and no windows, but I assumed if there had been, they'd have been white, too. I was no longer holding the Glock. And I wasn't alone in the white room. A painfully skinny boy in a white satin evening gown, his skin the color of cocoa, was seated several yards in front of me in a chair identical to mine. He was barefoot, with a silver ring on every toe. His shoulder-length hair was at least as white as the room, and his sharp nails were polished to match. In his right hand he held a silver chalice. His eyes were red as rubies.

Jesus, I thought. *B would love to have a go at you.*

"Okay," I said. "I give up. Who the fuck are you?"

When he answered, I knew immediately I wasn't hearing the voice that boy had been born with. Well, assuming he'd been born. It was the voice of a very, very ancient woman. Maybe the most ancient voice I'd ever heard. It sure as hell put the Bride of Quiet to shame. Maybe if the granite cliffs down in Conanicut Island could talk, they might sound like that voice.

"Forgive me," he said. Or she said. Whichever. "It was presumptuous of me to assume you'd know who I am."

"Yeah, it sorta was. I see a lot of albino transvestites in my line of work."

He took a sip from the silver cup, not taking those ruby eyes off me.

"Harpootlian?" I asked.

The incongruous voice replied, "Pleased to meet you, Siobhan Quinn. Your reputation precedes you."

I glanced around the white room. The least spot of dirt would have been a big goddamn relief right about then. A person could lose her mind, locked up with all that white.

"Bet you say that to all the monsters you kidnap. But, then again, I'm wrong more than I'm right. So, here's where you tactfully attempt to dissuade me from snooping about for your magical, mystical dildo. Well, unless I'm snooping about for you."

The boy smiled and his teeth were shiny and black.

He raised his cup in a mock toast. "Well, miss, here's to plain speaking and clear understanding."

I turned back to the pretty boy. God, how I wanted a cigarette.

"Wonderful," I said. "And if I don't happen to take your advice?"

"It's rare anyone makes that . . . choice," answered the old woman speaking through the boy. "It's rare, indeed."

"Just so you know, for the record, you're not the first demon I've ever met."

"And yet you are the very first of your kind I have ever set eyes on. A vampire who is also a werewolf. In two worlds, never have I seen anything the likes of you, Miss Quinn." The boy leaned forward, still smiling.

"I get that a lot. Now, can we get to the part where you threaten me, and I admit I'm being insanely, suicidally stupid not backing off, but refuse to back off anyway?"

The boy sat back again and tapped a nail against the rim of the silver chalice. "I was warned you are not the sort of woman—assuming that word still applies—who stands on etiquette."

"Here's to plain speaking and clear understanding," I said, and refused to turn away from his gaze.

"I was told, I was, that she picks the wrong time to say all the wrong things."

"Ah, now, please don't start referring to her in the third person. She hates that."

Maybe I'd been startled when I'd first arrived in the room, and then maybe I'd been scared. But right about then, it was a simmering anger stepping to the forefront.

"A slip of the tongue," he said. "Old habits, you know. Shall we talk of the unicorn? You've read that silly woman's silly story."

"Bet that got your goat . . . so to speak. Seeing all that shit in print."

"Miss Beaumont was summarily punished for her crimes against my court," the boy, the old woman, the demon assured me. "Indeed, she will be punished for a long, long time to come, as will the half-breed she named Ellen Andrews. They earned their corners in the pit."

I stared at him. I admit, *there* was something I hadn't exactly expected.

"Natalie Beaumont, *she* was Mona Mars? And . . . she still crossed you, after killing Andrews to square things, and then she used a pseudonym, but didn't even bother to change her name when she wrote the story? Jesus."

The boy bent over and set his chalice on the floor, then sat up again and folded his hands primly in his lap.

"It was a complicated affair," he said. "Much more so than her tale would lead one to believe. To say she was biased would be the most prodigious of understatements."

"Fuck me," I said incredulously, then sat back in that uncomfortable wooden chair and laughed. "Sure, let's talk of the unicorn."

"By rights, you know that it's mine, yes?"

I didn't answer Harpootlian immediately. When you're speaking with demons, it's wise to carefully consider your words, to handle them like sweaty antique dynamite, and I'd already pushed my luck, mouthing off with my usual disregard for diplomacy.

"You know that this is true," the boy added.

"Listen. First off, if Mars'—I mean, Beaumont's— story is half true, then it ain't entirely clear who owns the thing. You might have ended up with it—"

"Miss Quinn, excuse my interrupting you, but that which I acquire and hold is mine. These are the laws of my realm, and these laws are sacrosanct."

"Possession is nine-tenths of the law," I said.

"If you wish, yes."

"And what about Szabó, and the duplicate that Andrews created?"

"A fabrication on the part of Miss Beaumont."

I took a deep breath, exhaled very slowly, measuring my breath as carefully as I was measuring my words. Like my words, any one of those breaths might have been my last. I didn't have to be told that the slightest flick of one of the boy's index fingers would have been enough to obliterate even the memory of me.

"Then I have no idea what part of that story is true and what part of it's bull."

"I believe it's best you set the tale aside," the demon said. "Best we proceed on the most unequivocal facts."

"Which means I take your word for all of this. That I trust you're telling me the truth."

Again, not the most politic of responses.

"I do believe I have already exhibited the greatest patience, considering the circumstances, and considering we *are* discussing the theft of that which, I remind you again, is mine. You walk a fine line, Miss Quinn, expecting more from me, as I'm sure you're well aware."

"Yeah. Sorry," I said. "My mouth and me, we have sort of a Tourette's problem. Especially in stressful situations, when I have cause to expect complete annihilation any second."

The boy's red eyes regarded me with a blend of curiosity and contempt, kinda the way I might examine a two-headed cockroach just before I swatted it with a shoe.

"You're working with the Maidstone sisters, yes?" he—she—oh, fuck it—Harpootlian asked me. "And also your employer, and the bogle with whom he has aligned himself."

"Er . . . wait. What bogle?"

The boy blinked. Just once. Very, very slowly. "The one you heard muttering over the phone. The one whose brother you slaughtered."

I bit the tip of my tongue a moment, and then I said, "With all due respect, I don't recall ever having killed a bogle. Probably, that's the sort of thing I'd remember."

"He was known outside the Hollow Hills as Boston Harry. I'll not speak his true name, as the names of fairies lie like bile upon my tongue."

"Boston Harry," I said, pretty fucking much stunned.

Boston Harry had been a sort of black-market dealer in every manner of occult geegaw and whatnot under the sun and moon. During the Bride of Quiet fiasco, he'd supplied a man named Doyle with a bewitched blunderbuss that . . . okay, long story. Cut to the chase. I'd eaten Boston Harry. Well, the *loup* me had eaten Boston Harry. Him being a bogle was news to me, but then I hadn't known bogles looked like a cross between a sewer rat and a Munchkin.

"He took the smallest finger from your left hand," said Harpootlian, and the boy pointed. "He took the second toe from your left foot."

It had seemed like a fair enough trade at the time.

"I didn't *mean* to eat the ugly son of a bitch. It just . . . happened."

"His death is of no interest to me. I'm merely trying to establish your allegiances. And, as I said, these are the parties with whom you are working to acquire the unicorn, yes?"

"Maybe that depends. Appearances can be deceiving. Maybe I'm working for myself."

"Could that be?" asked Harpootlian. "I am unaware of your having ever before freelanced."

All that white was beginning to make my eyes throb. I wanted to shut them. I wanted to be anywhere but in that room with the demon's marionette.

"No one ordered me to hunt down the cunt who did

this to me," I said. There was anger in my voice that I'd been better off hiding, but there you go. "B was hiding under some rock when I went after the Bride. So we could call *that* freelance, couldn't we?"

"I would call that a vendetta, Miss Quinn."

"I would say you're splitting hairs."

Like I said, Tourette's.

"If, my dear, that is the truth—and I am exceedingly hesitant to accept that it is—you have some fraction of my admiration. A woman who looks out for herself. Any other sort, I have always found it difficult to trust."

"A woman like Natalie Beaumont."

The boy sat up straight and scratched at his chin. "As I have said, that's complicated. But, assuming you are not lying, I must say that, no matter how I might admire your greed and lack of loyalty to those who believe you loyal to them, I cannot permit you to stand between me and the Horn of Malta."

"Naturally," I said. But what I was thinking was how I'd just talked myself out of the frying pan and into the fire, how I'd gone from being someone who worked for Harpootlian's competitors to being one of her competitors in her quest for the dildo. So, my having royally fucked myself over in an effort to save myself from being royally fucked over, the time had come to think royally fucking fast. Sometimes I can actually do that.

But before I could say the next stupid thing I was bound to say, there was a rustling noise behind me. I looked over my shoulder, and there was the goddamn seagull. He squinted angrily back at me. There were patches of feathers missing where the duct tape had been.

"Oh, c'mon," I said, turning back to Harpootlian. "You're kidding me. The bird works for you?"

"In this realm," the boy replied, "my resources are limited. Your Hell is not my Hell. I must make do."

"But . . . do you even *know* how stupid this bird is? I just assumed a gull this dumb, it had to be working for the Maidstones."

Harpootlian . . . the boy flared his nostrils slightly.

"I would offer you a bargain," he and she said, "and seeing as how that will leave you with only one other option, one I am inclined to believe you'd prefer to avoid, it seems a generous proposition."

"I cast my lot with you," I said, hoping—solely for the sake of buying time—I'd hit the nail on the head.

"Then you accept?"

I looked at the bird again. "Can you at least do me the courtesy of being a little more specific, what's expect—"

"Do you a courtesy?" Harpootlian . . . let's say growled. I know I use that word a lot. But there truly is an awful damn lot of growling in my day-to-day. So, yeah, she growled. She growled indignantly, and the sound hurt my ears. Those relentless white walls actually seemed to bulge outward for an instant, as though they were made of rubber. The seagull winced, and a few more feathers dropped off its sorry carcass.

"Tourette's," I reminded her, managing to remain calm, to preserve my bullshit cool-as-a-cucumber façade.

"The *only* courtesy you will receive, Twice-Damned, is that I will not drag your soul back with me when I exit this world." At least she didn't growl that part.

And right then . . . lightbulb.

"Are you actually allowed to do that?" And here is me at my most idiotically, apocalyptically ballsy. Take note, kids. Don't try this at home. "I mean, you said yourself, your Hell isn't my Hell. And the way I understand the fine print, I am sort of twice over the property of my Hell, being, as you also said, Twice-Damned. Wouldn't that be violating some sort of grand cosmic customs law?"

I had actually managed to render a demon speechless, even if her silence didn't last very long.

"But I agree, Auntie H, that is a very generous offer. And it's one I'm going to give some serious consideration. I've no love for . . . well, much of anyone. And certainly not for that lot of cocksuckers who have me chasing after your Steely Dan. Jesus, it'd be worth it just to see the look on B's face."

In a whisper as terrible as that growl had been, Harpootlian used the boy's tongue and vocal cords to whisper, "Be assured, *dog*, there are loopholes, and—"

"Also," I went on, because if you're gonna play the fuck-you-and-the-horse-you-ride-in-on card, you gotta play it all the way, "keep that goddamn, mite-infested chicken away from me while I'm thinking this over."

"—make no mistake, I shall destroy—"

"No, I'm not joking. I'll kill him. I don't like him. He makes me nervous. I swear on Mercy Brown's ashes, I'll kill him the next time I catch him following me around."

Ever happened to see a seagull seemed like it was about to explode?

"Enough!" Harpootlian howled. Yeah, that was more

of a howl than a growl. The walls bulged again and my chair actually scooted an inch or two back from the boy's. A tiny rivulet of blood trickled from the corner of his mouth, and he hoarsely whispered, "There are loopholes in all laws, Miss Quinn, and should you cross me, by all Hells that are and ever have been, I promise I shall not fail to exploit them to my fullest advantage."

The boy quickly raised his left hand then, and the air around me crackled and hummed. The white room dissolved. I might have breathed the proverbial sigh of relief, except . . .

. . . **a** split second later, I was right back where I'd been when Harpootlian had spirited me away to the surrealist city with the bristly Volkswagen monster. No more than three or four seconds had passed, just long enough for me to lose control of the van, and there I was, barreling towards the sidewalk. A couple of pedestrians saw me coming and had just enough time to get out of the way. I stomped the brake, and the pads shrieked, but it was too late. I hit a streetlight doing thirty or forty miles an hour. And since I'd never had much use for seat belts, and the Econoline dated back before airbags, I went over the steering wheel and dashboard and through the windshield at thirty or forty miles an hour. Which means I struck the icy cement out front of Joe Marzilli's at just *under* thirty or forty miles an hour.

It's almost a cliché, but I've found that time really does seem to slow down to a syrupy crawl during shit like this, so everything went nice and slow mo just for me.

Someone screamed. Flying through the air, I heard glass breaking, and I heard the crash, which is weird, since both had to have preceded my takeoff. I heard other cars squeal to a stop. Then I heard the dull thud as I plowed into the sidewalk. I rolled through dirty snow and ended up in the shrubbery out front of the restaurant.

Yeah, a mortal human probably would have been so much potted meat after that. Me, I got some pretty bad scrapes and bruises, a few cracked ribs, all of which would heal in a few hours. I lay there a moment, waiting for my head to clear, and then I staggered to my feet. The hood of the van was literally wrapped around the silver post. Steam hissed from the ruptured radiator and a blue-green stream of antifreeze was draining out into the gutter.

A woman asked if I was okay. She sounded incredulous. Because how had anyone been able to get up after that, right? I ignored her, shook my head, because it was still foggy with pain and the shock of the impact. I heard a siren, which might have been the strangest part of all. Since when are the police that goddamn on the ball? Just my luck there must have been a squad car very close by.

So I started running. Well, more like limping. But it was a fast limp. There were enough pedestrians to be inconvenient, what with lunchtime and all. I shoved the ones who got in my way aside and paid their curses and shouts no mind. The deli wasn't far. I ducked north into an alley, found a dumpster, broke the lock, lifted the heavy lid, and slipped inside. The lid clanged down, and I sat in the darkness for the better part of an hour. Until I figured the police had decided they weren't going to find the driver of the dead Econoline, until anyone they might have bothered to question had moved on. I was lucky, and there wasn't much in the dumpster but flattened cardboard boxes, so I didn't crawl out stinking of garbage.

Maybe Harpootlian had meant to kill me, flinging me back the way she did. And maybe she hadn't. Right then, it hardly mattered.

I was about an hour and a half late for my meeting with the Maidstones, and that was mostly because of the time I'd spent tailing the seagull that had been tailing me and then lying low until the ruckus over the crash came and went. The whole infernal abduction thing, that had taken hardly more than a blink of the eye.

I went around back of the deli, like I'd been instructed to do. There was a buzzer, and I rang it. I'd expected one of the shuffling zombies to answer the door, but, instead, I got the goth kid who called herself Lenore. She looked me up and down, then scrunched up her face in a look of disgust.

"What the fuck happened to you?" she asked.

"Objects in motion remain in motion," I said, pushing her aside and stepping into the shadows at the base of a steep flight of narrow stairs. "That is, until they hit concrete. That's what happened to me."

Shocked I know about Newton's First Law, what with me dropping out of school at the age of twelve? Well, don't be. It's been a while since the Bride made me what I am, most of that while boring as hell, and when I'm bored I read. Yes, even books on physics. Also, screw your narrow-minded stereotypes. Lots of smart—hell, brilliant—kids leave school for one reason or another. Same with run-aways. And . . .

Never mind.

Like I said, I pushed my way past Lenore. Then I pulled the door shut behind me, and, before she had a chance to ask any more stupid questions, I took the stairs two and three at a time. She followed me, one step at a time. The stairs ended in a short hallway, and she told me it was the second door on the left. She didn't have to tell me it would be locked. She caught up and used her knuckles to tap out some sort of code on the wood.

Berenice Maidstone opened it. Unlike last time, her mousy hair wasn't braided, but hung loose about her face and shoulders. There was impatience in her brown eyes.

"You're late," she said. "And you look like hell."

"Jesus, nothing gets past you people."

The dingy room behind her was washed with winter sunlight coming in through tattered blinds.

"Doesn't it hurt?" she asked.

"Only when I breathe. Now, are you going to let me inside or what?"

"Your boss called," she said, like that was any sort of an answer. "He sounded concerned."

"Don't let that fool you," I replied, then pushed her aside, same as I'd done with Lenore. The room smelled of mildew, salami, and sauerkraut. Pink floral wallpaper was peeling off the walls in long strips. There were a couple of chairs and a sofa, all of which looked as if they suffered years at the claws of cats. Also, there was another girl inside, her back to me, facing one of the windows.

"Amity," I said. "Nice to meet you, too."

"Close the door," the younger girl said, either to her sister or Lenore. "Why are you late, Quinn?"

I stared at the girl's shoulders a moment or two. She had a certain uncanny splendor about her. Nothing a mundane would see, but plain as day to my eyes. Whatever brand of voodoo her sister could lay claim to, Amity possessed that tenfold or more. Here was power enough to be reckoned with, talent that completely eclipsed Berenice. And, of course, she was hungry for more. Because that's how power works. Just another addiction. The powerful are only addicts. Always a little patience with the rich and mighty. Always a little patience with junkies.

"Why are you late?" she asked again.

"Yeksabet Harpootlian," I answered, and Amity crossed her arms and looked at the dusty floorboards. Berenice sat down on the ruins of the sofa. Lenore took a few steps towards me, behind me, just off to my left. I stiffened a bit at the sound of her footsteps.

"Seems," I continued, "this little business venture of yours is attracting a lot of attention from all the wrong sorts. Not the kind of people whose shit lists you wanna end up on. Or maybe that's just me."

"She came to you?" Amity asked, her voice, smooth as cream, cold as dry ice.

"Not exactly. More like she dragged *me* to *her*."

"Yes, well . . . we'll see that your employer is well compensated for his troubles, as soon as we have the unicorn."

"Listen, *child*," I said to her, trying not to lose it, quickly failing. "Fuck my employer. Fuck this wizardy sex toy has you all hot and bothered. *I'm* the one you need to be thinking about compensating for her troubles."

"Ms. Quinn," cut in Berenice, her voice soft as a bed-bug's fart. "Maybe—"

"I don't recall saying a single motherfucking word to you," I snarled back, not taking my eyes off her kid sister.

Which is when Amity finally turned to face me.

And I wished she hadn't.

She had the sort of eyes that . . . well, like they say, if looks could kill. Hers probably had, on more than one occasion. I'd have bet Mean Mr. B's life on it. The kid couldn't have been more than sixteen, but those eyes of hers seemed at least a century older. The irises were the muddy green of Spanish olives.

"Do *not* use that tone with my sister, mongrel. Hold your tongue, or I'll gladly take the liberty myself."

If my heart was still beating, it would have skipped a few beats right then. Jesus, Joseph, and Mary, ol' Edgar had spawned a monster. And I like to think if I hadn't been careening through another stellar butt plug of a day, I'd have gotten myself under control then and there. Alas, this was very much not to be.

I scraped up a bitter, amused laugh. Poke the scary girl with a pointy stick, Quinn.

"So you think you're actually the spookiest thing I've seen today? Well, I got news for you."

I heard Lenore's footsteps. She stopped just behind me. Now, once you've had the barrel of a gun pressed against the back of your head—which, by then, I had—you kinda don't ever forget the sensation. I didn't even think. I spun around and seized Lenore by the throat. The little Sig Sauer pocket pistol slipped from her fingers and clattered against the floor.

"You wanna dance with me, little girl?"

Lenore made an alarmed, strangled sound. Her black-rimmed eyes bulged, and she clawed at my forearm.

"No, no," I whispered. "I'll lead. I insist." And I hurled her across the room into the wall beside the door. There was a sickening meaty thud, then a wet snap and crunch of bone, and then she was just a limp heap below a dented plaster wall. She looked like a broken doll.

Can't say I was sorry.

Berenice jumped up, but she sat right back down when I pointed an index finger at her. And, oh, fuck, but killing that silly bitch Lenore had felt fine, almost sweet as a mouthful of warm blood, sweeter than the cozy fog of smack had felt in the back before.

"Are we quite done with the theatrics?" Amity asked, her voice still smooth and icy. Still impatient. I turned back to face those wicked green eyes. They made me want to find a deep hole to crawl inside. I knew I had to do just the opposite.

"No one puts a fucking gun to my fucking head. I don't care whose lackey they are."

"Yes, and now she knows that," said Amity, and I caught a glimpse of her teeth for the first time. They'd all been filed to points, and, gotta admit, that gave me pause. It also got me wet. Sorry, guys, but it's the truth. In my defense, I hadn't been laid since I'd died and turned *loup*. And a girl has needs.

"She's no one who'll be missed," Amity said. "Besides, it's nothing I can't fix, if I so desire. Now, about Harpootlian—"

"I got the impression she wants you two way worse

than dead," I said, finding it hard not to stare at those teeth. "Plus, you've got Drusneth, of whom I'm sure you've heard, on your ass. Then there's B, who's not so happy about Shaker Lashly. By the way, was that really necessary?"

"You think we had him killed?"

"Sure do. B, he thinks it was Harpootlian. But I'm guessing what *really* happened is the poor son of a bitch got too close to figuring out your game, yours and your sister's. That your being missing was just a cover story to suck us in. You were afraid Shaker would tattle, and B would decide to cut his losses and drop the case. Which shows how little you know about the bastard. By the way, I'm not a goddamn detective."

Amity raised an eyebrow. "You solved the mystery of your colleague's death easily enough."

"I'm also not an idiot. Though the two of you—"

"We know what we're up against, *Siobhan*."

The way Amity said my first name, the way she spun it, like cotton candy, between her tongue and lips, those jagged teeth and her palate, well . . . I didn't tell her how much I hate being called Siobhan. I sorta just wanted to hear her say it again.

I swallowed. My mouth had gone dry. I somehow managed to work up enough spit to talk.

"Really, Amity? 'Cause I saw Harpootlian up close and personal, and you're not dealing with some cut-rate succubus. We're talking archfiend, hard-core mojo, eats the likes of me for breakfast."

"You're scared of her?"

"Lady, *I'm* scared of Drusneth, and let me tell you,

even on her best days, Madam Calamity can't lay claim to as much evil as this Harpootlian character has in her left kidney. If she has kidneys. Regardless, the two of you, by my reckoning, are shit out of luck. At best."

Amity took a deep breath and glanced at her sister, then back at me. She exhaled, and her breath, it smelled like dead roses. Like something you'd find out back of a funeral parlor.

"If Yeksabet Harpootlian is everything you say she is, why'd she let you walk? If you're right, why hasn't she already simply killed us herself and eliminated the competition?"

"Frankly, I've kind of been wondering the same thing myself," I told her, and I was trying hard to concentrate through the lingering rush of murder and the siren song of Amity's voice. Because here I was, having made a deal with this Auntie H, while conspiring with Mean Mr. B and—fuck me sideways, Boston Harry's goddamn brother—to double-cross the Maidstone sisters, all the while pretending I was still in their employ. Also, B had entirely neglected to explain how he intended to keep Drusneth from discovering what he was up to, or how he planned to make nice if she did find out. Maybe Amity thought I was asking her if she fully comprehended who and what she was up against, but I was really, truly asking myself.

"Berenice, would you please leave Siobhan and me alone for a bit?"

"Amity—" Berenice began.

"Please," Amity said again, and I heard Berenice Maidstone promptly stand and walk quickly to the door. I heard her open it and slam it shut again. So, there we were, alone in that musty, garlic-scented room above the deli on Atwells, just me and this mortal teenager who'd probably make Jeffrey Dahmer shit his tidy whities. I should have followed Berenice, but that's precisely what I didn't do.

I don't think I need to explain why.

"If we work together, you and I," said Amity, "we can find the unicorn. And when we do, there will be no one we need fear, not ever again. I have faith in you."

Liar.

She kissed me, and her mouth tasted the same as her breath. Dead roses. Which actually didn't seem so bad up close, not sliding up my nostrils and down my throat. She slipped her right hand into my jeans and . . . let's just say I'd descended to that level of stupid where my clit had seized control of all my cognitive functions. Let's just say that and tastefully fade to black. The sordid details are sorta hazy anyhow.

Actually, no. Quite a few of the sordid details aren't all that hazy. And some of the "plot" to come hinges on one particular revelation—let's say a rude awakening—I gleaned from the right and proper fucking I got that afternoon from Amity Maidstone. But I don't want to bring the "story" to a grinding halt with a protracted scene of heaving bosoms and crazed supernatural monkey sex. So I'll get back to that shortly.

But first.

It was dark by the time I pulled myself together, left Amity sleeping on that trashed sofa, and left the room above the delicatessen. The afternoon had faded past twilight to dark. When I took my leave, there was no sign of

Berenice, and I did wonder what had become of her after her sister had not so subtly told her to take a powder. Lenore still lay crumpled against the wall, and maybe some small sliver of me wished I hadn't done that. Maybe. Out in the cold, the very almost full moon was almost bright as a spotlight, and I couldn't bear to look directly at it. I'd officially reached that part of the month where all of my concentration was required to avoid going *loup* and sinking into the blackout oblivion that accompanied those murderous transformations. I was too busy and everything had gotten way too complicated to risk the Beast screwing the pooch with an indiscreet rampage.

So I kept my eyes on the icy sidewalk and asphalt and the litter. I kept my eyes off the moon, and I didn't meet anyone's gaze. The *loup* was hammering at my senses, and getting banged for the first time in months hadn't helped. Sex, death, the animal in us all. Only in some of us more than others. Way more.

The Econoline was dead, you'll recall, because Harpootlian had seen fit to kill it. Which meant I was on foot, and I'd just crossed the interstate back to College Hill and decided to take a shortcut across the Brown University quad when I blundered into the next bullshit misadventure in a week of bullshit misadventures.

I wasn't far from the spot where Lenore and I had sat on the park bench three days before, not far from the redbrick monolith of Carrie Tower. Not much light—the streetlights back the way I'd come, and the white pools from the lamps spaced out along the quad. Well, and the moon. Not that I needed electric lights, not with these eyes of mine, which *loup* season had made even more sensitive than usual. So I had a perfectly clear view of the big-ass hat who stepped out from behind a tree, clearly intent upon blocking my progress. It was one of the Drusneth's *se'irim* bouncers. Skin black as the night to mortal eyes, porcupine quills, tall impala horns, and eyes like glowing crimson Christmas lights. The fucker was at least seven feet, hooves to the tips of those horns, if it was an inch. Its matted fur gleamed, vaguely iridescent.

"Twice-Damned," it grunted, "Twice-Dead, where you bound on a winter's eve?"

I stood there staring at it a few seconds. "What's it to you, goat?"

It snorted, and twin jets of steam billowed from its nostrils. "Better to ask yourself how it concerns Madam Calamity. Better to ask yourself *that*, Twice-Damned."

"I'm going home," I replied. "And you'd better get out of my way, and run back home to tell Drusneth to go fuck herself. From what I hear, she's very good at that."

I should have heard the second *se'irim* coming up behind me. But I was tired, fighting back the *loup*, and still, admittedly, stupid from the sex. First thing I knew, a razor-sharp claw was pressed against my jugular.

"How about I take her your head, instead?" asked Thing Number One. "Would you prefer that?"

"Would *she*? Is this a dead-or-alive job, or are you trying to improvise with that shriveled cranberry you call a brain?"

The claw of Thing Number Two applied just enough pressure to break the skin and draw a few drops of blood. I knew the *se'irim* knew better than to stop at slitting my throat. I knew, if it came to that, they'd take my head off, clean as a whistle, just like Thing Number One had suggested.

"What does Drusneth want?"

The *se'irim* snorted again. "She wants the unicorn."

"And she thinks I have it?"

By the way, it occurred to me right then that no one mixed up in this game of button, button, who's got the button had any idea where the dildo was. Or even could be. Or had last been seen. Presumably, someone had stolen it from Yeksabet and smuggled it from one universe to another, but then what? Why did they seem to think it was in Providence? What did they know that no one had bothered to share with me? Now, yeah, odd time to be asking myself these questions, but I was getting accustomed to impending doom, and don't our sudden realizations always come when we least expect them? Whatever.

"That's between you and her, Twice-Damned, Twice-Cursed," Thing Number Two grunted. His breath stank like a rotting skunk. "Nothing for us to know."

"Well, I don't have it, and I don't have the foggiest where it is. I don't even *want* to know where it is. And you two can tell her that just as well as I can. Now, get outta my way and get lost."

"We have not come to bargain with you," said Thing Number One. "Nor have we come to accept no for an answer. Your compliance is not optional."

Which is when the cramps hit, pretty much in every muscle I have, all at once. When my control slipped. When these two idiotic shitbirds distracted me just enough the Beast snapped the lock and came bounding out of its cage. I had, at best, a minute before my mind was no longer mine. Probably less.

Two *se'irim* against one starving, pissed-off *loup* bitch? How would that round of psycho *kaiju* throwdown turn out? Damned if I knew. But I had a feeling I'd drawn the short straw.

The pain doubled, redoubled, washing the whole world in a kaleidoscope of reds, oranges, and yellows.

"Guys, this really isn't a good time. Take my word—"

"Not for you to say, half-breed," Thing Number Two snarled into my left ear. "You'll come with us, and you'll do it now and without any further argument."

The curtain came down hard and impenetrable as a million pounds of midnight. I didn't fight it. It wasn't a battle I could have won, anyway.

CHAPTER SIX

A FINE LOT OF LOLLIPOPS

You know, sometimes it's easier to set up the next part of the story you're telling by recourse to another story. Yeah, like I did back there with "The Maltese Unicorn" (even if Harpootlian did end up telling me it wasn't all gospel). And what came next, after the two *se'irim* squared off with me that night and me going *loup* and blacking out, frankly it'll be easier to move on to what came next if I tell you another little tale first.

Those of you who find this annoying, go read another book, instead. I won't mind.

One October, a few years after all this business with

the unicorn cluster fuck had blown over and was resigned to history's trash heap—Oh, wait. Don't you dare whine or kvetch about my having just "spoiled" this story, because if I *hadn't* lived through it, I wouldn't be writing this, now, would I? Seriously. Get a clue. Anyway, once upon a time I was up in New Hampshire, bored as hell—because, hello, it was goddamn New Hampshire. I was tooling along I-202 somewhere between Peterborough and Antrim, which is to say the corner of "no" and "where." Round about twilight, I drove by one of the innumerable fruit stands that pepper New England roadsides. Only it wasn't just another fruit stand. There was a sign out front that declared in huge red letters FREAKS! NATURE'S MISTAKES! FIENDS OF HELL! Like I said, New Hampshire, boredom, so I turned around and went back to have a look-see.

Out front, there was just the usual heaps of apples, gourds, some mealy-looking corn, lopsided pumpkins, dried bundles of Indian corn, quart bottles of cider, and plastic jugs of maple syrup, presided over by a couple of swamp Yankees who gave off a serious *Harvest Home/ Wicker Man* vibe. You just knew these two sacrificed sheep and virginal maidens to Shub-Niggurath or some corn king or who the fuck ever. I asked about the sign, and one of the swamp Yankees—a woman with a hairy mole the size of a hairy Junior Mint above her left eye— jabbed a thumb at a listing wooden shed behind the fruit stand, half hidden behind a couple of huge red oaks.

"Ten dollars," she said.

"Yup. Ten dollars," said the other swamp Yankee, a fellow in overalls and a John Deere cap.

I didn't haggle with Mr. and Ms. Creepsome Back-woods. Ten bucks for Fiends of Hell. Sounded like a bar-gain to me. Speaking as a fiend myself. I paid her, and I headed for the shed. Neither of them followed me. That was sorta a relief. Little unnerving when plain old human types can unnerve me. Oh, and I bought an apple, just to keep up appearances.

There was a narrow dirt path between the trees and the weeds. The shack wasn't locked, though there was an elaborate assortment of chains, hasps, Yale padlocks, and a thick wooden plank that could be lowered to bar the door. A big pentagram and one of the hex signs you see on barns in Pennsylvania Dutch country had been neatly painted on the door with the same shade of red paint used for that sign out front. Clearly whatever was inside, the swamp Yankees wanted to stay inside. Which raises the question of why they'd left the door *unlocked*. But that's not a mystery germane to my weird little anecdote.

Inside, it was dark, and the air was close and almost chilly, dank; it smelled like straw and animal shit and dust. At first, I had no idea how anyone who wasn't a nasty with dark-adapted eyes could have seen their way around in there. Then I noticed a milking stool with three flashlights. Of course, I didn't need one, but there you go. As for what was inside the shed, mostly it was just rows of big jars filled with formalin or alcohol. They made up what is referred to in carnie slang as a "pickled punk show." They were all bleached a cheesy white, and it was pretty much impossible to make out what those dozen or so misshapen stillbirths and genetic mishaps might have been. Except the three-headed corn snake. There were a couple of shelves crammed with a random assortment of bones—including a couple of human skulls—and some examples of creative taxidermy: a pair of jackalopes, a gopher with duck feet, the shriveled marriage of monkey and fish sometimes known as a Jenny Haniver, Siamese chickens, etc., etc., etc. All of them were moth-eaten, and some had split seams leaking sawdust. And I'm thinking, *Yeah. Sure. Ten dollars for this nonsense. I ought'a go back and eat the both of them.* Or I was thinking something of the sort.

Then, past a yellowed, swaybacked moose skeleton, there was this big cage. Iron bars spaced so close together I couldn't have gotten an arm in between them. And inside the cage, crouched in a filthy scatter of straw, was a monster. Now, usually, when I use that word, I do so without much in the way of sympathy. As the years go by, my capacity for sympathy and empathy has dwindled. That's just the way it goes on this side of the fence. You can't fucking cry over every unfortunate soul you eat. But what I saw locked inside that cage, it hurt to look at. It made my stomach lurch, and it *hurt* to see. For a moment, I actually turned away. Unlike everything else in the shack, the occupant of that iron cage was alive and breathing, and whatever pain I felt at the sight of it, the agony that racked its body—and that had for fuck only knows how long—made my discomfort seem . . . well, I might just as well have complained about a mosquito bite.

It ain't easy to freeze a *loup* midway between one shape and another. Takes some big-time finesse with the black arts, and a willingness to sink to the very asshole of sadism and depravity.

But that's what was inside that cage. She had been frozen either partway to her wolfish form or partway back to a naked twenty-something girl. Hardly mattered which. She crouched there, blazing amber eyes peering hatefully out at me, eyes burning with spite and pain. The black mane along her spine bristled, and she curled mottled lips back to expose canines long and sharp as paring knives. She titled her head to one side and dug her long, clawed fingers into the straw. She uttered a low warning growl, and I took a step backwards. She rose up on her knees then, and I could see the six teats and bulging rib cage.

"You," she said, and she made a sound that was maybe supposed to be a laugh. "I know what *you* are, sister."

"How did they—?" I began, and then stopped myself, because I'd been about to ask the most idiotic question imaginable then and there. I gagged, if you can believe it.

"Ever seen a low red moon?" she asked. "Ever seen the moon fall down and bleed? Ever run wild and free beneath the wide carnivorous sky?"

The thing in the cage was insane, and she'd probably been that way since the second or third day the inbred fucks out there at the fruit stand had turned their wizard's trick against her.

"Ever talked to the night's cunt and heard it talk right back?" she asked.

Which is when I snapped the padlock. It was sort of like grabbing hold of a live electrical cable, the bright sizzle that surged up my arm as I shattered the spell preventing the *loup* woman from breaking free. For a moment or two, the bitch didn't move. She looked confused and frightened, as if she had no idea what she was supposed to do next, as if she'd been in there so long the thought of stepping out of her prison was inconceivable.

"You tear them apart," I said, "or I'll do it myself."

She went down on all fours and crawled past me and out of the shed. There was no gratitude in her eyes, and I hadn't expected any. Less than a minute later I heard Wilbur and Lavinia Whateley begin to scream. There was a gunshot, and then more screams. I smiled at the sound, then took out my Zippo and set fire to the shack. While the *loup* took her pound of flesh, I sat beneath one of the oaks, smoked a couple of cigarettes, waiting for the sirens, and watched that hellhole burn to the ground.

So, there you go. After the face-off with Drusneth's pair of *se'irim* thugs, I oh so very slowly rose up and up and up from the merciful blackout that comes when the Beast comes. Midnight became false dawn. False dawn became the violet-gray smudge of dawn. And I felt as if there was ground glass in every joint of my body, hydrochloric acid searing muscles and flesh, salt in my eyes. Bit by bit, I came back to myself. The waking from *loup* oblivion had never been slow before; it had never been any different from jolting suddenly wide awake after the deepest sleep. As consciousness returned to me by these slow degrees, I only wanted to crawl back down to that place where there was nothing at all. Because, Jesus, anything would have been better. I was a diver come to the surface much too fast, and the bends were wrapping round me like an iron fist. I would have screamed but couldn't remember how. Dawn became the goddamn scalding fire of daylight, and it should have blinded me, but it didn't. It only seared into my skull.

There were voices.

". . . that it came to this, truly am . . ."

Okay, that was Mean Mr. B. I realized I was lying on my side, my left side. I tried to sit up, tried hard, but the ground glass in my arms and legs and between every vertebra cackled and held me down.

"It wasn't a risk I was willing to take."

And that was Drusneth. Fucking Drusneth, and without being entirely sure why, I wanted to rip the whore peddler's throat out, then and there.

". . . that we'd have brought it to you, and straightaway. Surely, you never suspected any . . ."

Now, here was an unfamiliar voice, but I guessed through the pain that it was almost certainly the mutterer from B's last phone call, who had to be Boston's Harry's bogle brother.

My mouth tasted like I'd eaten roadkill. Wouldn't have surprised me. The *loup* is hardly picky. I tried to spit, but my mouth was dry as desert sand.

". . . coming to."

A fourth voice, which I had no trouble recognizing as one of the *se'irim* douche waffles. I'd left at least one of them alive.

I forced my eyes open, did my best to force them to focus. Mostly just shapes and colors. Shapes that were distorted and colors that weren't right. Wherever I was, despite the searing light scalding my brain, I could see the place was dark. I smelled mildew, mushrooms, standing water, rotting masonry. A cellar, almost certainly a cellar. Or a subcellar. Someone was squatting a couple of yards in front of me, safe on the other side of cold iron bars.

"Wake up, kitten," said Mean Mr. B.

"Have you done?" I grunted, and it was a wonder I was able to string even those three words together.

"It's only a precaution," he replied. "One that we shall dispense with as soon as possible."

And then I understood. I was in a cage somewhere, beneath a house or a street, maybe below Drusneth's sporting house in the Armory. I was in a cage. And I wasn't entirely *loup*, and I wasn't entirely the bloodsucker that could pass for human when she tried. They'd found a way to trap me in the space between.

"Kill you *all*," I snarled; then the pain crashed into me like a ton of bricks and all I could do was lie curled fetal. I pissed myself, and the air stank of urine.

"Now, now, precious. You will do no such thing."

Drusneth said, "Don't coddle the little gooch. The clock's ticking. If I lose the unicorn—"

"Madam," the bogle simpered, "haven't we assured you no such circumstance will transpire?"

She ignored him. "If Harpootlian's getting close, *she's* the one who knows, Belmont. Stop wasting my time and get her talking."

Silence. It could have been a hundred years of silence, a hundred years of torture.

Then B, apparently Belmont for the day, said, "I think she's hardly in any shape to tell us much of anything. If you removed the execration, we'd have somewhat better luck."

"Dying," I heard myself moan, though I don't think I'd meant to say anything at all.

"No, kitten," Belmont cooed, all mock sympathy and comfort. "You're not dying. But I'm bloody certain you wish that were the case."

A spasm rolled through my body, and my legs kicked, striking the bars of the cage. Only, those weren't my legs. Not my feet. Everything below my waist was still *loup*.

"Tear you *all* to ribbons," I all but howled. Five whole words in a row. I was making progress.

"Now, that's exactly the sort of talk will prolong your suffering," said Mean Mr. B. "Bad puppy."

Then, to Drusneth, he said, much more sternly, "You know, it actually is a truism that if you hurt someone enough, he or she or it will eventually tell you anything you want to hear."

Jesus. The motherfucker was actually taking up for me. Or, more likely, protecting his investment. Now that Shaker Lashly was gone, I was his one and only pit bull.

"Please," he said.

"You're in no position to ask for a boon," Drusneth replied.

He raised his voice. There was anger creeping in around the edges, sort of like sunshine peeking out around the edges of a solar eclipse. In my delirium, it was almost beautiful to hear.

"I know, my dear, that old habits do die hard, but fuck all, this is not your river Phlegethon. We don't even know what this is doing to her."

"I believe it's causing her unbearable pain," said Drusneth. "Do you not agree, Samuel?"

Who the fuck was Samuel?

Then I heard the bogle make a hemming and hawing noise, and I knew *he* was Samuel. "Most of a certain, madam," the little rat-bastard creep told the succubus.

"The curse has served its purpose," B said. "End it, or soon she'll be too far gone to ever tell you shite."

Drusneth sighed like a hurricane. She sighed like a dying man's goddamn last breath. You get the picture.

The agony dissolved quick as butter in a hot skillet, and I was left gasping, shivering, disoriented, lying naked on the metal floor of the cage. The world swam sharply into focus. Yeah, I was in a basement. Brick walls probably stacked and mortared before the Revolutionary War. A packed dirt floor. The only light a flickering orange glow from an oil lantern the bogle clutched in one ratty paw.

"There, there, now," B said to me.

Drusneth said, "You'll cooperate, girl, or I can put you right back where you were with the flick of a wrist."

Right then, I wanted to murder the whole world, resurrect it, and murder it all over again. You know the feeling.

Twenty or thirty minutes later, I was dressed, pretty much my old fucked-up vamp self again, and sitting on a hideously upholstered divan in Drusneth's office. The damn thing had enough throw cushions on it to smother half of China. I was sitting there, nursing a hangover that probably only comes with having been pounded flatter than hammered dog shit by a couple of demons, then trapped half in and half out of your wolfdom. The parts of me that didn't hurt were too few to mention. Okay, it wasn't half as bad as the pain I'd felt in the cage, but it made me miss the dear old days of smack.

"No hard feelings?" B asked. I'd heard Drusneth refer to him as Belmont, which sounded like a hotel chain.

"Fuck you," I told him.

"Play nice," he said. "Drusneth meant what she said about rescinding her spot of mercy. You know that."

I looked from B to Dru. She was sitting behind that huge desk of hers, watching me with someone else's intense, dark eyes. That day, she was wearing the skin of a young Indian woman, some unfortunate chick from maybe Bangalore or Delhi who'd strayed too near the spider's web. She was wearing a white silk suit with an oddly iridescent tie the green-brown shades of a Japanese beetle.

"In a New York minute," she assured me.

"You know me," I said. "I'm all sunshine and daisies. I shit sunshine and daisies."

"Oh, I know you," Belmont sighed, reclining in his own hideously upholstered chair.

Standing to his left was a totally horrid beast, like something that had tumbled out of the ugly tree and hit every limb on the way down. Twice. The bogle, of course. The dear, departed Boston Harry's bro. They could have been twins, except this one's hair was Play-Doh blue. Otherwise, he might have doubled for Boston Harry. Same sewer-rat-trying-to-pass-for-human good looks. Same twitchy snout and pointy teeth. Same snide demeanor. Knee high to a Doberman. It was hate at first sight. Harry, he'd been a sort of transplanar fence, a Target or Walmart for nasties in the market for occult contraband. He'd been, as I said last time out, the go-to guy. Well, until I'd eaten him. Let me tell you, that was *not* the best meal of my unlife. Anyway, as far as Harry's brother was concerned, I had no idea what his deal was.

"What's his deal?" I asked, and pointed at the blue rat man.

"Think of him as a silent partner, precious," Belmont replied. "A consultant brought aboard this enterprise for his not inconsiderable business acumen."

"That so?" And then I spoke directly to the bogle. "Your brother took one of my fingers and one of my toes." I held up my four-fingered left hand as a visual aid.

"As I understand it," the bogle said, "it was a fair exchange for sensitive intel." Jesus, what an annoying voice. Kind of like Papa Smurf on helium. Or maybe I only thought so 'cause he was blue and all.

I didn't offer him an opinion on whether or not the deal had been fair. I blinked, squinting about the dimly lit office. I'd been given my clothing, but not my Glock. I spotted it on Drusneth's desk.

"At least your gorillas were kind enough not to lose that," I said, and nodded to the weapon. By "lose" I meant "steal," but B had said play nice, and I figured I'd give that a try for three or four minutes.

"They know better," Drusneth said.

"Mind if I have it back? Sort of tends to keep me outta tight spots. Though wasn't much help against the demon Bobbsey Twins, I'll grant you that. You get props for your choice in hired muscle, I gotta give you that."

She thanked me, considered the gun a moment—still in its holster—then picked it up and tossed it to me.

"Now, as I was saying, Belmont. What exactly is the Blue Meanie's part in this folly?"

B didn't answer. The bogle did.

"I have taken over my brother's organization. He spent so long building it up, seemed a shame to let such a profitable undertaking wither."

"That would have been a shame," I said. I was surprised to find the clip had been left in the pistol. I popped it out and was even more surprised to find no one had removed the bullets. "So, now you're the one with my missing digits?" I popped the clip back into the gun.

"Actually..." The bogle paused to scratch his left ear. "Actually, those were traded—for a handsome sum—to a Santa Muerte cult in Tucson. A bevy of transsexuals, to be precise."

"No chance of getting them back?"

"Alas, no," he said, pretending to sound apologetic. "Would that I could." He stopped scratching at his ear.

"Wrong answer," I said, pulled back the slide on the Glock, and shot the son of a bitch in the face, twice. Trapped in Drusneth's office, the gunfire was loud as a Brontosaurus falling into a truckload of cymbals. He just sort of toppled over, his corpse doing a weird sort of gory tarantella on one of Drusneth's Turkish rugs. His brains and bits of skull and fur were spattered across a nearby wall. Neither B nor Drusneth said anything for almost a full minute. And me, I was briefly rendered all but deaf, thanks to my bloodsucker supereardrums.

"Damn," I said. "Don't you hate it when that happens?"

"She goes back into the cage," Drusneth snarled at last. The succubus lifted a hand, preparing to return me to my half *loup* purgatory.

"No, no," said B, also holding up a hand. "Stop and think. Though her intentions were no doubt malicious, she's just done us a favor. Now . . . we get the unicorn, and you don't have to give that piker a bloody cent. More for you, perhaps a few dollars more for me."

Through the ringing in my ears, they sounded at least half a mile away. But I could make out the words. Barely.

Drusneth smiled with those pilfered lips. "Well, more for me. Your cut, that stays the same, Belmont."

"A man can hope." Mean Mr. B shrugged.

The bogle had stopped twitching. B glowered at me with his smoky gray eyes.

"Do you think you can behave yourself for the next ten minutes?" he asked.

"I can try," I replied, hardly able to hear myself. Too bad I hadn't had the good sense to just throw something at the bogle, instead of blasting him. "Also, can you guys speak up? I can't hear for shit."

Drusneth rolled her eyes, snapped her fingers, and, presto, my ears cleared. What a sweetheart, that Madam Calamity.

"Now, can I please get a goddamn cigarette?" I asked B. "Pretty fucking please?"

B offered me one of his rainbow-colored Nat Shermans, and I decided I didn't want a smoke *that* bad. I passed. I'd already checked my own pockets, but apparently the *se'irim* had seen fit to take their pick of my personal effects, including my lighter and half a pack of Camels.

There was a long moment of tense, uncomfortable silence. You know the sort. I listened to the ticktocking of the grandfather clock in Dru's office and the muffled racket through the walls, the sort of racket one hears in a demon brothel. It was Drusneth who broke spoke first.

"So, you're in bed with Amity Maidstone, literally. Please correct me if I'm wrong."

I sat back and stared at the ceiling. "Yeah, so I was overcome by her macabre charms and suffered a lapse of character, okay? A girl's got needs. Oh, and by the way, she has a dick."

Another moment of uncomfortable silence, this one longer than the last one.

"I shit you not," I said, mostly because the ticking of that clock was beginning to get on my nerves. So was the sound of some dude having an orgasm upstairs.

Then Mean Mr. B chuckled. "Thought you were a devout tuppence licker, through and through."

"Generally, that I am. But we were already in the moment before I made the discovery."

I stopped staring at the ceiling and looked at Drusneth instead. By her expression, it was clear she wasn't amused.

"Some people," I said to her, "got no sense of humor. So I fucked her. So what? That doesn't mean anything. It's not like we're engaged."

"It gives me pause," Drusneth said. "It leads us to doubt your loyalty."

"You mean 'us,' or do you mean 'you'?"

"Kitten—" B began, that do-be-cautious, beware-thin-ice tone in his voice, but the succubus cut him off.

"Fine, I am speaking for myself," she said.

"Fine," I replied. "How about let's pause to take stock of the situation you two have gotten yourselves and me into, why don't we?"

She glanced at B, then back to me. B just shrugged and turned his eyes towards the floor.

"And by that, what do you mean?" she asked.

"I *mean*, Drusneth, that I'm beginning to wonder if the two of you have ever actually tried to steal anything before. I'm starting to doubt either of you got slightest idea just how deep the shit you're wading into is."

"Dear," said B, "your grammar is atrocious."

I ignored him.

"Unlike either of you, I've seen this Harpootlian character, okay? Up close and personal. And, Drusneth, with all due respect, she makes *you* look like Strawberry fucking Shortcake."

"Truly, precious—"

"B, just shut up and listen for once. It's time for a reality break, no matter how much you two don't want it. This bitch jumps between parallel universes. Sure, our Madam Calamity here, she's got some ferocious tricks up her sleeves. I'm not saying otherwise. But Yeksabet Harpootlian is a goddamn thermonuclear bomb ready to go off at the drop of a pin, and *that's* with her hands partway tied by not being on her home turf. Push her far enough, I'm guessing all that's gonna be left of this city is a cloud of dust and a crater that glows in the dark. Next to her, Drusneth's really is just a whoremonger. Hell, she's not even a whoremonger. She's not even a whore. Next to Harpootlian, she's the piano player in a whorehouse, and Harpootlian's about to foreclose on the dump."

Now, yeah, I was exaggerating a smidge. After all, if the bitch was that badass, why would she have wanted or needed my help? Anyway, Drusneth looked ready to blast me into next Thursday. Or the Thursday after that. Also, as I rattled off this spiel, I was beginning to have serious flashbacks to my conversation with Amity.

"And as for the younger Maidstone whelp," I continued, "she's no lightweight her own self. Her penis wasn't the only thing caught me off my guard."

"On that subject," B said, "how did you manage to locate her?"

"B, just like you thought, she was never missing, okay? That was just some lie cooked up to get you involved."

"If she's such a force to be reckoned with, this child, why would she need Belmont's services?" asked Drusneth.

"Stop and think. The last thing the Maidstones wanted was Harpootlian going after them, so they tried to hide behind you two and me and Shaker. Make us look like her competition. She didn't fall for it, of course, but the Maidstones are even more deluded than you pair And that blue rat son of a bitch lying there. Before I shot him, I mean."

"Not the shrewdest move," B said. "Samuel was rather well connected."

"Whatever. His connections can blow me."

"So, what exactly are you saying, Quinn?" Drusneth wanted to know. "That we should simply abandon our quest for the unicorn?"

I rolled my eyes and went back to staring at the ceiling. A rhythmic thump was coming from directly overhead, so I figured one of Dru's girls or boys had their bed parked right above me and was hard at work.

"And there's another thing. Has anyone even seen this doodad? Do either of you have even the foggiest idea where it might be? Seems to me you're just blundering about with blindfolds on, hoping the dick of doom will fall into your laps, easy as pie."

"And what would you have us do?" asked B.

"Honestly? Back the fuck off and let Harpootlian have her toy. No, better yet, back the fuck off after you toss her the Maidstone sisters as a peace offering. Make them, you know, fall guys."

Drusneth laughed. B didn't.

"Might be she has a point," he said to Drusneth.

"Might be you should consider hiring toadies with balls," she told him.

"Wait, you think he *hired* me? You think I get *paid*?"

"Merely a figure of speech," she assured me. "Regardless, I'm of the opinion that it isn't the province of a minion to advise her betters as to the proper course of their actions."

My turn to laugh.

"So we all go down together," I said.

"We hold the course," she replied. "You do as you're instructed, if and until you're instructed otherwise. Keep tabs on the sisters. We think they know the present whereabouts of the unicorn."

Wrong. But why bother telling the two of them? Not like they'd have bothered to listen.

"And Harpootlian?" I asked.

"Yes," Drusneth said, leaning towards me, "there is the matter of Harpootlian. It seems unlikely she went to the trouble of scooping you up just to let you walk. By your own account, she hardly seems the trap-and-release sort. So this leads me to believe a deal was struck, which brings us back around to questions of your loyalty. After all, if you're more afraid of her than you are of me . . ."

"Dru, I'd have handed over my lady parts to get out of there. And I assure you, I treasure my lady parts."

"So what did you promise her?"

"What do you *think*? Same thing I've promised Amity and Berenice Maidstone. That I'd go turncoat and betray who-the-fuck-ever I needed to betray to help her get the dildo."

"You're a crude woman," Drusneth muttered.

"And like I said, you're a piano player in a whorehouse, but that's just a figure of speech."

If you're thinking, right about now, how my demeanor towards Drusneth had changed since I showed up unannounced asking if she'd seen Amity—how I was kowtowing before and now here I was, all up in her face and talking smack—let me just remind you of the shitstorm thrill ride I'd endured between that day and waking up half *loup* in a cage in her office. That sort of foolishness can totally wreck a person's manners.

"Belmont, you'd best put a leash on your mongrel before I do it again."

"And then what?" I asked her before B had a chance to respond one way or another. "Do you think, at this late date, that you're going to get anyone else who's wormed herself into the good graces of the Maidstones and Harpootlian? You can doubt my allegiances all you please. Makes no difference to me. But you go changing horses in the middle of the stream like that, jump back to square one, and you and I both know—"

"Enough," Mean Mr. B barked. "Enough, Quinn. We do as Drusneth says. We hold to the present course."

"Even though it's suicidal," I said.

"You let us worry about that," Drusneth told me. She'd picked a long stemmed ivory pipe up off her desk and had begun packing it with a ball of black-tar opium.

I stood up, staring at the body of the dead blue bogle. A shame he hadn't lived long enough I could have shot him twice.

"You'll forgive me if I tend to consider death wishes a somewhat personal choice," I said.

"From what I understand," Drusneth said, lighting her pipe with a greenish flame that appeared at the end of her left ring finger, "you have a stubborn habit of habit of seeking out your destruction every chance you get. Or am I wrong, Belmont?"

"I have my moments," I replied, answering for Mean Mr. B, before he had a chance.

"Go back to the Maidstones," he said. "If you need to

feed, take care of that first. But then, you go back to them and when our cheeky twat Harpootlian grabs you again—"

"Yeah, got it. You'll be the first to know."

"Good little mutt." Drusneth grinned as opium smoke leaked from her mouth, coalescing into the perfect likeness of a Chinese dragon above her pretty, borrowed head.

"The unicorn is here somewhere," B all but whispered. "Were it not, she wouldn't be here."

I wanted to kick the corpse of Samuel the Rat Man. I restrained myself. "And if the dildo turns up?"

"Then you get it here, precious. Kill who you have to, but see that you—"

"Sure. I'll just whip out my trusty six-shooter and gun down Miss Thing From Another World before she knows what hit her. You betcha."

"By the way, Quinn, where are your false teeth?" asked B, and I told him I'd misplaced them somewhere or another. He hung his head and tsk-tsked.

"Go," said Drusneth, and she waved a hand at the door. So I went. I'd had ten times enough of the both of them. And yeah, after the Beast and what came after, after my ordeal behind bars, I was starving. Outside— I've neglected to mention this—it was late afternoon, almost sunset, so hunting and disposal would be easy-peasy-lemon-squeezy. And it would give me time to ponder my ever-more-sticky predicament.

You tell a story, any story, and you can spin it an infinite number of ways. Lots of people would say that's a load, that there's the lie and there's truth of the matter. Reliable narrators and unreliable ones. Black and white, no room for the infinite confusion of gray. Which just goes to show how lots of people don't know jack about truth, lies, facts, storytelling—all that and more. Anyway, all junkies lie, remember? Every word I say is a lie, and if you didn't catch the inherent fucking paradox there, you're not paying attention and should go back to the beginning, do not pass GO, do not collect two hundred dollars.

But I digress. Sort of.

Lots of people need to pretty up and romanticize the hunger, turn bloodlust into passion and a route to eternal love, so murder becomes a surrogate for sex, hot vampire love becomes socially acceptable necrophilia, and so forth. Well, fuck that noise. Death gets you wet or gives you a hard-on? That's your business, and if you want to trip the "Don't Fear the Reaper" road, cool. Just don't pretend it's something it ain't. Don't be a coward. Problem is, very few people—even the death fetishists—want to die, and thus they invent all sorts of sparkly fantasies to keep their fear at bay. Or at least make it more palatable. Some are happy enough with the Old Man in the Sky, but others, they make caring lovers of us uncaring monsters. I call it "fiend porn." And delusional. You call it what you like.

Most people are idiots.

Which makes things a lot easier for the nasties, me included.

And don't you dare take that as an insult. To me, you're food, and when's the last time *you* were impressed by the intelligence of a cabbage or a codfish?

See, what I do, as I said right back at the start of this

tale, it isn't pretty. It isn't romantic. It isn't sweet Edward Cullen concerned for the fate of Bella Swan. It isn't Louis de Pointe du Lac getting by on poodles 'cause he just can't bring himself to be the death of another human being. If you gotta have a pop culture point of reference, it's more akin to something you'd see on the National Geographic Channel or Nature or whatnot, a lion ripping apart a wildebeest, a pack of hyenas gnawing at the carcass of a baby gazelle who couldn't keep up with the herd, a crocodile pulling out the intestines of a zebra while it's still alive and kicking and trying to cross some muddy river.

Sure, I could spin this story another way.

I could summarize the next bit, for example, something like this:

I fed once, taking a homeless teenager who was sleeping in the back of an abandoned body shop near the banks of the Seekonk River. I was gentle with him, and maybe that was guilt, but maybe it was just my lingering distaste for preying on the "dregs of society," to quote Mean Mr. B. The kid had an erection the whole time, and came about four heartbeats before he died.

I might as well tell you, "Jack the Ripper, that motherfucker did what he did, but damn, he (or she) sure was a merciful sort of bastard."

Or I could find any of a hundred thousand compromises. But I'm in the mood for something more closely approximating the facts of what happened after I strolled out of the brothel on Cranston. Yeah, all junkies are liars, those who drink blood and those who shoot heroin, but . . .

Right, so, after I left Drusneth and B, I walked and walked and walked all the way back across the river to College Hill, half-consciously following one of my usual routes, slipping between the pools of streetlight along the sidewalks with only the windows of sleeping houses eye-balling me. Despite the full moon, the bitter winter night was plenty dark enough for my purposes.

I spotted the kid sort of shuffling along Prospect Street, heading south with the bitter wind at his back, the collar of his leather jacket turned up, trying to shield his ears from the worst of it. He was maybe a hundred yards ahead of me, but it wasn't hard to catch up. I'm fast, quick like a bunny, and my feet can be as wicked silent as a cat's paws if I want them to be.

"Hey, dude. You got a light?" I asked him, taking out one of the Camels I'd bought at a gas station, just before crossing the Point Street Bridge. I didn't smile. I shivered, so he'd believe I was cold as him. He had brown hair, and that's about all I remember. I do not tend to memorize the faces of my food.

The guy turned around, and at first he just stared at me, surprised. After all, he hadn't heard anyone walking along behind him, right? Then he told me no, he didn't have a light, that he didn't smoke. I laughed, and if he noticed the piranha teeth or how my breath doesn't fog, he didn't let on that he had.

"Yeah," I said. "Seems like nobody smokes anymore. Jesus, I'm freezing my ass off. What about you?"

Ah, here's another detail I remember. He was wearing glasses, horn-rimmed, fake tortoiseshell. He furrowed his brow and squinted at me from behind the lenses. My stomach rumbled and my mouth watered.

Sometimes, by the way, I like to play with my food, make a game of it all, and that night I was definitely dragging the ritual out longer than necessary.

I pretended to have a violent coughing fit.

"You all right, man?" he asked me.

"Yeah," I replied. "I mean, except for this fucking cold night, I'm fine." But, sadly, I knew the jig was up. I could see the kid knew something wasn't kosher in Denmark, even if he *didn't* know it was time to start counting off what was left of his life in seconds, what with him standing there on death's doorstep and all.

"Well," he said, "I should get going."

"Why? What's up?" I asked, and cleared my throat.

"Nothing," he said, backpedaling, and he smiled at me. "Nothing at all. Sorry again about the light. Anyway, you take it easy. That cough sounds ugly. Better get out of the cold. Get something warm inside you."

"Yeah," I agreed. "That's what I should do."

"Take it easy, man," he said.

He would have walked away, and likely as not, our paths would never have crossed again. I'm sure that's what he was thinking. But I was on him immediately, one hand clamped tight over his mouth. Can't have screamers. He made the usual futile effort at a struggle, the way they all fight before they realize how strong I am.

I didn't apologize. I didn't say anything at all. What would have been the point? And I sure as fuck wasn't gentle. There were rhododendrons growing at the edge of the sidewalk, and I hurled him through them, slamming his body down beneath the shadow of a huge oak tree. He clawed at my eyes, so I growled my scary growl and punched him in the gut hard enough I probably ruptured his spleen or liver or something else essential. He stopped fighting, and I did what I do.

There was no mercy.

If he had an erection, if he came about four heartbeats before he died, I neither knew nor cared. I crouched there in the frost, beneath that ancient tree, and I sucked and gnawed and worried at his corpse until there was nothing left to take. Then I went on about my way, my mind busy with too many other thoughts to care about his being found. I'm usually pretty good about cleaning up after myself, but, once again, I was sloppy and indifferent.

True story.

More or less.

A billion shades of gray.

But I'm emphatically *not* trying to shock. Hell, I couldn't care less if you're horrified or revolted. Just trying to keep it honest. Just trying to tell it like it was and is and will be until the end of my days.

Cross my heart and hope to die.

So, after dinner, after stopping by my apartment (door *still* propped open after Rizzo's attack, window still shot out, etc.) for a shower and a change out of my bloody clothes, I retraced my steps across the Providence River. By nine p.m., I was in the alley that led to the back of the delicatessen on Atwells. I assumed the Maidstones hadn't pulled up stakes for another safe house. They hadn't called to tell me they had, and since I figured Amity figured she had her hooks in me, I figured they'd have let me know. And Drusneth had given me back my phone after letting me out of that cage, so I'd have gotten the call. Or text. Whatever.

I was out of the alley and halfway to the door leading to the upstairs rooms when I heard someone call my name from the shadows a heap of cardboard and crusty snow. Really, it wasn't so much someone *calling* out my name, more like what, I suppose, is meant by a *sussuration*. That soft, below a whisper, like if a voice could be the rustle of wind.

I stopped and stared at the boxes.

My name again, my name as October leaves blowing across an empty parking lot. I didn't recognize the voice.

"You gonna speak up and come the hell out of there, or am I coming in after you? I'm not in the best of moods, so I'd suggest option number one."

At first no answer, only the rumble of traffic out on Atwells and the wind between the buildings.

"Patience," I said. "Not what I got just now."

The sound of those flattened boxes shifting about, and then a paler shadow stood up, rising from its bed of darker shadows. I didn't have to ask who it was, though the smell hit me just before I recognized the face. It was Lenore. Lenore, who I'd killed the day before by slamming her into a wall like a goddamn rag doll. I also didn't have to ask how she was up and moving about. But she told me anyhow.

207

"Berenice," she said, and I could tell from her voice that her tongue had begun to swell. "She's the one who cared about me. She brought me back."

Jesus Christ on a hobby horse.

"Smells like she did bang up job," I said.

The shadow stepped out into the streetlight. Her face was white as fresh mozzarella. Her eyes were vacant, rheumy, like the eyes of a dead fish. Her hair, matted and hanging in scraggly tendrils about her face. She was naked, except for a black fur coat, surely stripped from the cadavers of fake minks.

"Berenice," she said again, "she isn't half as skilled as her sister. It's the best she could do. She apologized."

"Fuck all," I said. "Did she dump you out here in the trash after turning the resurrection trick?"

"No," said Lenore, but then offered no explanation for why she *was* out there with the deli's trash. "We have to talk," she mumbled, instead.

"Dead girl, we don't have to do jack shit. I'm in league with the ladies upstairs, not you."

"You'll want to. They can't give you what you need, Siobhan Quinn."

"Do *not* call me Siobhan."

"They have no idea how to find the unicorn."

I glanced north at Spruce Street, and at the interstate and train tracks beyond. The Xmas-tree blur of headlights rushed to and fro.

"But you do? You, the zombified gofer? I should believe that why?"

I looked back at her. Her lips were like streaks of blue chalk. Berenice really wasn't much of a necromancer.

"Yes," she said. "I have it. I've had it for weeks."

I laughed. See, here we've come upon what people who spend too much time thinking about books call a deus ex machina, the god from the machine. You know, when the solution of a story's conundrum just seems to spring out of nowhere rather from the "logical" consequences of a narrative. See, not quite as ignorant as you might think. I'm not sure precisely why this particular plot device ticks off the book nerds.

Go ahead. Stop reading. Feel free to "throw the book across the room." That's your prerogative, and I say again, it sure as shit won't hurt my feelings.

Anyway, I'm straying, digressing again, and that sort of thing also pisses off more than a few readers. Point is, like a bolt from the blue, here was Lenore, who I'd killed but who hadn't stayed dead, telling me not only that she knew where the dildo was, but that she'd had it all along.

"Bullshit," I said.

"I'm telling you the truth. What do I have to gain by lying?"

I looked up at the windows. There was a light burning. "I can probably think of half a dozen things, you give me a few minutes. So you betrayed Berenice?"

She hesitated, then replied, "I'm not proud of it. But I've never really had shit, not really, and I held that much power, and—"

"Fine," I interrupted. Power corrupts, we always hurt the ones we love, et cetera. I got the picture. "You say you have it, then time we play show-and-tell, dead girl."

"I don't have it with me," she mumbled around her puffy tongue, with her already decomposing vocal cords.

"You know, Berenice didn't exactly do you a favor, hauling you back like that. Another few days—"

"I know," she said. "I know that perfectly well. But I also know she meant well."

The best goddamn intentions of mice and men and stupid women who don't have the good sense to let the dead stay dead. I wanted to punch Berenice Maidstone in the face, but not for dragging the goth chick back—just for being such a ham-fisted idiot.

"You're saying it's real."

She sorta shuffled a step nearer. "I am."

"And you got your hands on it how?"

She hesitated, let those blank fishy eyes stray to the asphalt between our feet. "Your boss' guy, Lashly, I took it off him."

Okay. Hold the goddamn presses, right?

"You *what*?"

"I know Amity led you to believe she killed him, but—"

"She didn't come right out and say it."

"She didn't deny it, either. She insinuated."

I laughed and shook my head. "Right, but by then you were already dead, so—"

"Berenice told me."

"Of course she did. Fine, okay, you're telling me that, somehow or another, Shaker Lashly found this piece of junk right off the bat, but you got wise to him—because, I guess, the Maidstones might have had you following him—and *you* shot him, took the dildo, and dumped his corpse in the river. But you didn't take it back to the dreadful duo. You kept it for yourself. This is what you're telling me."

"Yeah."

"You know," I sighed, and it was a very loud and very exasperated sigh. I took out a cigarette but didn't light it. One day, I was gonna kill that bouncer motherfucker stole my Zippo. "You know, I don't believe even the tiniest crumb of your story. I don't know what you're playing at, but I ought'a chop you up in itty-bitty fucking undead pieces just for wasting my time."

Thing is, I *was* beginning to believe her, even if I wasn't sure why.

"I can take you—"

"First, how about you tell me how you got hold of it?"

Lenore swayed, and I reached out—just instinct, I guess—and kept her from falling.

"Thank you," she said.

"How did *you* get it, Lenore?"

She licked at her cyanotic lips with the tip of her distended tongue. "Lashly, he took it off Samuel, the bogle from up in Salem, up in Marblehead."

Yeah, that's what she said: Salem Sam.

"And he got it from?"

"He's the one crossed over, stole it from Harpootlian. Well, someone works for him crossed over."

"Worked for him. Past tense. I kinda shot him in the face tonight."

She stared at me, wrinkled her forehead like I wasn't quite making sense, then went on. "Well, he stole it. Don't know how Lashly took it from him. Thought for sure your boss would know he had it."

"My boss, despite what he might think of himself and

want others to take for granted, isn't the sharpest knife in the drawer. Where is it now?"

"Now?"

"Yes, sweetie, now."

Berenice really had done a piece of hack work. Already Lenore's brain was starting to short out. Which meant, if she wasn't lying, she might not have much longer to finish her dubious tale of skullduggery.

"You know the marble drinking fountain on the sidewalk in front of the Athenaeum? On Benefit Street?"

"Sure."

"Look behind it. You'll find the unicorn. I buried it in a locked box in the ivy there behind the old drinking fountain."

She stopped looking at me and stared up at the sky.

"I miss the stars," she said. "Grew up on a farm in Massachusetts. There were always so many stars."

"You've told me all of it?"

The clock was ticking faster than I'd thought.

"Behind the old fountain? You've told me all of it? Didn't leave anything out, like the box is booby-trapped with fucking C-4 or some shit?"

"First star to the right," she mumbled, "and straight on to morning."

Which is when I did my good deed of the month. I ripped her head off and bashed it against the deli wall until there wasn't anything left but jelly speckled with bone and shards of teeth. I'd have used the Glock, but the last thing I needed was to attract attention just then, especially that of Amity and Berenice Maidstone. Her body just dropped to its knees and then keeled over on its chest, nothing left in that husk but a few twitches. I tore off the back of the fake fur coat and did a halfway decent job of wiping my hands clean.

And then I headed to Benefit Street. Because, you know, Elvis just might have been abducted by aliens the same night a woman in South Bumblefuck, Nebraska, gave birth to the two-headed love child of Bigfoot.

A long time ago, the marble fountain out front of the library used to actually *be* a water fountain, spouting water straight from the Pawtuxet River. Not sure when that stopped being the case. The thing was put up in 1873, and probably people drank from it for, like, a hundred years. Okay, maybe not that long, but still. These days, the basin below the spigot is usually filled with trash and cigarette butts. But. Getting back to the point, the ivy that grows all around the fountain, a great huge patch of the stuff between the sidewalk and the marble steps leading up to the Athenaeum.

Wouldn't have been my first place for a spot to hide a magical geegaw, but there you go.

On the walk back to College Hill and Benefit Street, I was cursing Harpootlian and her seagull for having caused me to crash the Econoline. Maybe I don't exactly get tired the way mortals do, but all that walking gets goddamn boring, and I also had a feeling that time was more and more of the essence, as they say.

Assuming Lenore hadn't lied, maybe I actually was, finally, on the trail of the object from Mona Mars' short story, the sorcerer's sex toy that had landed Natalie

Beaumont—if she did, in fact, exist in another universe—in some perdition of Harpootlian's choosing. But okay, what were the demon and Amity up to as I trudged across town? As I trudged across town *again*. Also, I had no idea whatsoever what I'd do with the dildo if it actually was there. That part, I'd decided, was a bridge I could cross when, and if, I reached it.

Benefit was deserted, only a few cars, and despite the streetlights, I had no trouble not being seen.

Behind the low marble obelisk, I brushed aside the rind of snow and pulled up handfuls of the ivy. Below it, the frozen earth had been very recently disturbed. I dug with my bare hands. Fuck a shovel or spade. Not like I needed one. Not like the ground, even in an especially frigid February is a match for my fingers. About six inches down, in a shallow grave indeed, I found the metal box Lenore had told me I'd find. It was no more than a foot wide by a foot long, and just one sharp bump against the back of the fountain was enough that it popped open.

Inside was a roll of blue velvet.

I sat down in the snow and ivy and lifted the velvet from the box. It was heavier than I'd have expected. I held it maybe a full minute before I unwound it to reveal what was hidden inside.

It was pretty much what Mona Mars had described as coming from the "finely carved wooden box," lacquered red as blood, that she'd found with the corpse of a dead Chinese man. A phallus carved from what looked like ivory, yellowed with age, since it no longer wore that misleading coat of black porcelain enamel. On the one hand, my head sort of reeled with the possibility that this thing might actually exist and that I was holding it. On the other hand, I was also thinking how it could have been carved from an elephant or mammoth tusk, or the tooth of a narwhal, or maybe from some ivory-bearing animal in that place Harpootlian had come from, an animal that doesn't exist in this world. Either way, here was a game changer. Whether or not it really was what I'd been told it was, it was real. The wild goose chase, well, it had just become the payoff at the end of a goddamn African safari.

I'll cross that bridge when I come to it.

Only, the bridge wasn't a bridge at all. It was something more like a five-way intersection. All at once, I had to make a decision, and it wasn't any sort of decision I wanted to make. I could head right back to Drusneth and Mean Mr. B and hand it over, then hope Harpootlian decided I wasn't worth the trouble when she went after the two of them. Or I could take it back to Amity and Berenice—but that would just be fucking stupid. It was plain they posed the least threat to me, and whether or not they got their way was no longer something about which I gave a shit. Or I could put it right back in the ground and pretend zombie Lenore had never told me jack shit. But the smart thing to do, that would have been finding Yeksabet and giving her what she considered was rightfully hers, then facing whatever music I'd have to face from B and Dru (and screw the Maidstones). Yeah, that's what an intelligent werevamp would have done. But, see, there was that fifth turn at my intersection.

Hang on to it for the time being. Hide it again, where no one was going to find the "dingus." Because maybe I'd just graduated from a pawn to an actual player in this game.

And I knew *where* I could hide it, where no one would be likely to go snooping about, and even if they tried, they wouldn't find squat.

Aloysius.

Sitting there, I was tired and pissed. I was sick to puking death of the ridiculous ditch B had dug and tossed me into, hoping for a fat payday. I'd spent more than six months being his bitch, too intimidated by the threats he made. How, without him, all those nasties I'd pissed off—on his account—would come swarming down on me in a great black vengeful wave if I ever dared cross him.

Fuck him. Fuck him and Drusneth, the Maidstones and Harpootlian. I had the prize. Finders keepers. Well, at least until I had time to consider the situation, my options, just a little more. I wrapped the dildo in the velvet again, then quickly put the empty lockbox back in the ground, reburied it, and covered the dirt with ivy and a few handfuls of snow. I stood up and wiped the dirt off my hands and onto my jeans.

Which is when I heard Burt Rizzo pump the slide of a shotgun, chambering a round.

'Cause *you* know how it is. The fun never ends.

"Turn around," he said, his voice sorta like the rumble of distant thunder. "I want you to see this coming."

"Dude, that's all kinds of stupid and you know it. You

got me," I said, staring across Benefit Street at the court-house, quickly trying to guess just how far behind me he was standing. Not very fucking far. Two feet at the most. The shotgun would take my head straight off my shoul-ders, and all the vamp mojo in the world wouldn't bring me back from that.

"Not like you haven't ambushed me before. Hell, twice in one week. Just pull the fucking trigger."

"Turn *around*," he said again, and now the thunder in his voice sounded a lot nearer. I reminded myself how Rizzo wasn't some Bobby Ng screwup. I reminded my-self what an idiot I'd been passing up two chances to put Rizzo down and be done with it.

"But I just cried 'uncle' and everything. C'mon, you think you'll get a chance like this again?"

It would have been a goddamn ignominious end, get-ting my brains blown out there in front of the library. On the other hand, though, let's be honest. Not like I didn't have it coming.

"Are you deaf, monster? Now, for the third time, turn *around*."

"Or what? You'll shoot me?"

I wondered how much it would hurt, decapitation by two barrels of double-aught buckshot, and I wondered for how long. I wondered how many fuckers would be waiting in Hell to settle their scores with me, the ones I'd put there. I wondered what would become of the uni-corn.

"Fine," I sighed, feeling all those muscles tensing I'd never known I had until the Bride and Jack Grumet came down on me. Feeling the blind survival instinct that drives every nasty, from pole to pole, kicking in. I very fucking slowly turned towards him.

"But don't you dare say I didn't give you—"

The shotgun roared.

The blast missed me, but not by much. I'd tumbled to the left, rolling away through the shrubbery towards that black wrought-iron fence. The back of the fountain, it wasn't so lucky.

"Stupid, stupid, stupid," I heard myself saying, over and over like some Catholic—my mother, for example—praying the Rosary. I was up and on my feet almost before I knew I was up and on my feet. Rizzo didn't have even half a chance to reload the shotgun. I hit him like a pile of bricks, and the gun sailed away into the darkness. My ears were ringing, but I heard ribs cracking, and I heard one of the bastard's lungs collapsing. And when he hit the granite steps leading up to the front door of the Athenaeum, I clearly heard a sickening crunch, and I didn't need to be some ER doc to know I'd snapped his spine. The cold air suddenly stank of piss and shit.

To his credit, he didn't scream. Just a low moan, and that much pain all at once, you can't expect anyone to take it quietly.

I crouched over him like a spider over a fly, and stared into his eyes—at so much hate and spite and self-righteous fury—and he stared back into mine. The *loup* wanted out. It was slamming itself against the bars of my fraying will, and I very almost let it out.

Almost.

"Lots of people must have heard that," I said. "So maybe the cops will be along soon."

Though, you'll recall, they hadn't shown up when Father Rizzo threw down on me at my apartment.

"So I'm gonna give you a choice, and *I'm* not gonna offer three times. I'm only gonna offer it once. Which, mind you, is one whole time more than I got."

Maybe I was holding the Beast at bay, but the hunger was filling up every crevice of my mind. Heard that phrase "seeing red"? Right then, yeah. But it was goddamn literal. Drool leaked past my teeth and lips and spattered his face. He winced, and turned his head away.

"Stupid," I hissed again. "Stupid fucking me. Should've dealt with you a long time ago."

"So do it now and shut the fuck up," he said. "Get it over with."

"There's where your choice comes in. I leave you lying here, crippled in a pool of your own filth, and you can maybe think on all those boys you raped. Maybe someone will find you, or maybe you'll die of shock or hypothermia."

That's when I slapped him. A wonder I didn't snap his neck. "You *look* at me," I growled.

He looked at me.

"So, I can do that, or here's your other choice. Door Number Two." I leaned nearer, pressing my teeth hard against the racing drumbeat of his carotid, and, oh, that's all I wanted in the world. To open up this man of a god I had no use for and take my own communion. Instead, I whispered, "You wanna live forever, Father Bertrand Rizzo? Wanna see the stars grow old with me?"

He was silent a moment, and during that moment, I ran my tongue along his throat. I could taste the blood through stubble and skin and the cloying sweetness of aftershave.

"You'd do that?" he asked.

I sat up and slapped him again. "The real question, Father, is would *you*?"

He blinked, and now there was blood on his lips, a steady trickle from his nose. He blinked a few more times.

"Yeah," he gasped. "Yeah, I would."

I stared up at the sky, briefly trying to imagine what Lenore had seen up there just before I'd put her out of the misery Berenice had doomed her to.

"You're a piece of work, you are," I laughed.

"Better than dying," he said, gasping again, clearly having trouble getting enough air to speak, what with just the one lung and all. "Isn't it better than dying?"

No, you asshole. No, it's not.

"Rizzo, you know what I hate even worse than a rapist? Cowards and hypocrites."

"But you—"

"Lied," I said. And then I broke his neck. It was a cleaner death by far than he had coming. But I still had just enough self-control to remind myself how little time I had. I had to get the dildo to Aloysius and hope he'd help. Besides, back then, I had no idea if I actually could do to someone else what had been done to me.

I did waste half an hour hauling the body away to the river, weighing it down with a gut full of stones, and tossing it to the fishes. Then I slung the cocksucker's shotgun over my shoulder and headed for the troll's underpass.

"Don't know, Quinn lass," Aloysius said, holding the unicorn between a gigantic thumb and forefinger, well back from his tangerine eyes. "Stinks of magic. Don't like it one damn bit, I don't."

I was sitting cross-legged on a ratty mattress near his feet, a mattress someone had dragged there and left in the dirt and gravel and weeds. I'd just lit a cigarette. Breathing out smoke, it's almost like watching my breath fog in the cold.

"And you don't?" I asked.

The troll stopped staring at the dildo, and he stared at me, instead. "Ain't the same. You tumble to that."

"Whatever, dude. Fairy magic. Old-time alchemist magic. Voodoo. Demon magic. Jesus fucking loaves into—"

"You're not learning nothing," he sighed.

I blew smoke rings. "Look, I don't find a way to get the upper hand in this mess, my learning days just might be over pretty goddamn soon."

"You even bring me presents?" he asked.

I had. I dropped a plastic bag with half a dozen 3 Musketeers bars on the ground in front of him.

"King-size," I said. "Big on chocolate, not on fat. Just like you love 'em."

He grinned and swept up the bag in his free hand.

"Twenty-four hours. That's all I need. At most,

twenty-four hours. No one's gonna even think of looking here."

He flared his nostrils and went back to staring skeptically at the ivory dildo. "You so sure about that Mr. B dug of yours? He's a cannie wee cunt, that one."

"He's too busy counting money he doesn't yet have and kissing Drusneth's scaly ass."

"Always ye come askin'," he grunted. "Always with your havering, lass. Asking. Thinkin' it nae danger to me nor mine, an' not even, 'Aloysius, 's'a braw bricht moonlicht nicht the nichtaye?' Think me tally?"

"I liked you better when you spoke English."

"Liked *ye* better when ye were drawing breath and not gone wolfish."

Well, yeah. I'd liked me just a little bit better then, too. But I didn't tell him that. I just sighed and took a long drag on my Camel.

"Not even a bottle in the bag," he muttered.

"Twenty-four hours, man. That is all I'm asking Take it back into your . . . wherever . . . and I'll be back for it not later than this time tomorrow night. Cross my heart and hope to—"

"Bit late to promise that much, lass."

The son of a bitch had a point.

"Twenty-four," he said, snorting again. "Not a tickytock longer, or I toss it. Grind it to dust."

"I swear."

"The word of one gone plumb dead and wolfish," he huffed, and shook his head.

I ignored the implication I was a liar, just because I was a vampire and a *loup*. It's the sort of argument I always lose. Mostly because I'm a liar. But I was a liar a long time before I joined the ranks of the nasties. Still, no use arguing about such fine distinctions.

"That's wicked nice of you, Aloysius. And I—"

"Scramble," he grunted, then disappeared in a swirl of inky black.

And I sat there below 195, smoking and listening to the late night traffic above me, trying hard to figure out what the hell I was going to do next.

CHAPTER SEVEN

BAD AS ME

Okay, so, how about another quick and dirty rundown of my situation as it stood, that cold, cold late night after Saint Valentine's Day? Partly, for the idiot kids in the back of the class who've been too busy sexting to pay attention, but also because even I'm having trouble keeping up with all the ins and outs of this kerfuffle. And, hell, I'm the one who was caught in eye of the storm, right? Don't want this tale to end up as big a mess as, say, Howard Hawks' 1948 adaptation of Raymond Chandler's *The Big Sleep.* You may recall, the screenplay was such a complete fucking discombobulation that even the directors and screenwriters—one of whom happened to be William Faulkner—finally admitted they had no idea whether a key character had been murdered or had killed himself.

True fact, so there. Film history. Don't ever say books like this are utterly devoid of educational value.

I'd found the unicorn outside the Athenaeum, right where zombie Lenore had told me I would. Then I'd been surprised by and killed Rizzo, demon slayer.

I'd spirited the dildo away to Aloysius the troll, and he'd hidden it in Faerie, where, I figured, not even Harpootlian could find the damn thing.

As for Harpootlian, she still thought I was her bitch.

Same with the Maidstones.

And Mean Mr. B and Drusneth, those two were pretty sure they also had me in their pocket.

But by this point, I realized that I'd become a free agent. Like I said not too far back, finders keepers. But, you see, what does the finder do with what she's found?

After leaving Aloysius, I'd switched off my phone and headed to a hipster dive over on Federal Hill. That crowd, I hated them like the plague, but they were a lot less prone to staring at the waxy-skinned chick with the pointy teeth. I only had to endure the inane conversation, mostly crappy music, and the ironically mismatched and anachronistic clothing of that cooler-than-thou crowd. Pull that off, and I could drink all I wanted until the sidewalks rolled up at two a.m. Which was only about forty-five minutes after I showed up.

So, there I was, sometime after three in the morning, still four hours or so until dawn, wandering along Broadway, just thinking. Trying to get my head together, come up with at least half a plan, because I sure as shit hadn't had one when I'd taken the ivory dick to the troll. I knew I could only hide from B and Drusneth and Harpootlian just so long. Fuck the Maidstones, because I was pretty sure they posed no threat to me whatsoever. They were the odd ladies out, as it were (even if Amity *did* have a cock).

Enter the wild card.

The fresh wrinkle I should have seen coming all along, except I'd gone and bought in to Auntie H's spiel that I ought to take Natalie Beaumont's (alias Mona Mars) short story with more than a grain of salt.

Call this another deus ex machina if you want. Me, I think I've established sufficient foreshadowing that this is not the case, but whatever. I don't care, cross my heart and hope to die all the hell over again.

What happened, it wasn't so different from when Harpootlian had snatched me and my Econoline off Atwells. One moment I was strolling past the Phoenix Dragon Chinese Restaurant, and the next—poof—I was standing in a very, very black room. Black as a sky that's never even heard of starlight or the moon or light pollution. I'm not gonna go to all the trouble of describing the place, because it was pretty much a photonegative of Harpootlian's *white* room.

Me, I was seated in a black wooden chair, and just like before, I wasn't alone. A painfully skinny girl in an ebony satin evening gown, her skin just about the color of milk, was seated several yards in front of me in a chair identical to mine. Yep, she was barefoot, but with a gold—not silver—ring on every toe. Her shoulder-length hair was at least as black as that room, and her sharp nails were polished to match. In her *left* hand she held a golden chalice. Her eyes were goddamn green as emeralds.

"Well, well," I sighed, not even an itty bit surprised, "what do you know? Déjà vu, all the fuck over again. I'm gonna go out on a limb and guess you're Magdalena Szabó, and you've come for the dingus."

"You're as correct as correct can be," the girl said. Okay, not the girl. Just like it had been with the avatar of Harpootlian, the child spoke with the voice of an ancient woman.

"White and black. What *is* this with the two of you, a goddamn game of chess?"

"Miss Quinn, that isn't such an inapt analogy."

I laughed and said, "Yeah, I'm on a roll. So, you're Madam Szabó, one more thing from another world, and one more pain in my ass come to claim *le godemiché maudit*."

I even managed not to mangle the French too badly.

"And you have it, Miss Quinn."

"Correction," I replied, holding up an index finger and leaning a few inches forward, all ballsy and shit. "I *had* it. Apparently your omniscient sleight of hand is a few hours behind current events."

The girl stared at me with her green eyes. "Then where is it now, Miss Quinn?"

"Gave it away to a troll. And you know how trolls are. It could be anywhere by now, assuming he didn't eat it."

Silence from the milky girl, silence and more staring.

"You find this amusing?" she finally asked.

"Bunch of you shitbirds couldn't find your asses with both hands and a flashlight? Yeah, I'm finding that pretty damn funny right about now. Right now, on the inside, I'm laughing so hard it hurts."

"Miss Quinn—"

"Thought it would be rude to actually laugh out loud."

"The unicorn is mine," the girl said, the monster using the child like a sock puppet.

"See, that's just exactly the same line your bff Harpootlian tried to sell me. One—or both—of you's gotta be wrong, and what with you both being demons, I hope you'll see why it's kinda hard for me to make heads or tails of this."

The girl leaned closer to *me* now, and she quietly snarled, baring teeth as shiny and black as the teeth of that pretty boy in the white room had been. So, here's Szabó seeing my hand and raising it. At the sight of those teeth, all the bluster kind of drained out of me. I'm ashamed to admit it, but that's the way it was.

All junkies lie—without exception—only not when they're telling you the truth. It happens.

"Don't talk yourself into a corner you can't talk yourself out of again," the girl said, then sat back again and examined her fingernails, polished the color of a ripe blackberry. "Though I admit I do admire your ambition, reckless though it may be."

I sighed and also sat back in my chair. "When opportunity knocks," I said, "make lemonade."

The girl stopped inspecting her nails. "Twice-

Damned, just how long do you believe you can keep this shell game up, playing every side against every other, before it finally blows up in your face?"

It wasn't a question I had a good answer for, so I didn't try. All at once, sitting there, the decision to keep the dildo and hand it off to Aloysius for safekeeping while I weighed my options seemed a lot less clever than it had just before I killed Rizzo.

"End this here and now," Szabó said. "Deliver the unicorn to me and walk away. Wash your hands of this affair, Miss Quinn, this conflict in which you must know you should never have been involved."

I stared at those ten perfect alabaster toes with their ten gold rings, thinking back on the days when I'd had a full complement of ten little piggies all my own.

"You want me to think it would be that easy?" I asked the sock puppet.

"I can assure you it would be."

"You can *assure* me. You can make sure Drusneth isn't gonna see I spend the next couple of centuries locked inside a cage, half *loup*? You can do that? You can promise me Harpootlian won't rain napalm locusts down on my head? You can do that, too? And the Maidstones . . . oh, fuck the Maidstones."

"If you bring me the unicorn, yes, I assure you these are, each and every one, problems I can solve."

"Out of the kindness of your wicked, sour heart."

"It's a business proposition," she replied. "Nothing more and nothing less. I am a businesswoman, and I do not pretend there is an iota of kindness in me."

Okay, so . . . possibly there *was* a slim chance my

squirreling away the dildo *hadn't* been one hundred percent moronic, after all. But, see, even in the short six months since my death, I'd been around the block enough times to know one doesn't simply take a demon's word, not no way, not no how.

"Frankly, I don't know why Yeksabet did make the same offer," said the milky girl.

"Because she's a flaming, fucking thunder cunt?"

The girl laughed, the nasty inside the girl laughed, and it would be a while before I'd hear another sound that grisly. "Let us just say that she has a weakness for theatrics, shall we?"

"Sure," I muttered, gooseflesh up and down my arms and legs and the back of my neck. "Let's just say that. And let's also give Miss Quinn here a guarantee you're not gonna live down to received wisdom and leave me to that bunch of vultures as soon as you get your paws on that unholy fucking grail."

She narrowed her emerald eyes, considering me not so differently than she had her fingernails. Only, less bored, more bemused.

"What do you have in mind, Twice-Damned, Twice-Dead, given your inherent distrust for the Fallen?"

"I asked first."

More bemused staring. More gooseflesh.

"I cannot deny, Miss Quinn, that adding so rare a creature as you to my stable is a powerful temptation. Speaking, again, as a businesswoman. But I have only come here seeking that which is rightly mine, and I will do whatever is necessary to secure it. This includes aiding you in the elimination of any perils you would incur, should we enter into an arrangement. But you will not ever trust me, and we'll not waste time debating that point."

I went back to staring at those ten toes. This little piggy went to market. "And if I don't enter into that arrangement."

"You'll not leave this room," the child said, and this time the words were spoken in the child's voice. I'd have preferred Szabó had kept up her ventriloquist act.

"Hell of a choice," I said. "Pun intended."

"It is the best I can ever extend."

"A shame that Ellen Andrews woman in the Beaumont story didn't really make a copy."

"Often have I had that selfsame thought," the girl replied, and, mercifully, Szabó had gone back to using her own voice.

"The Maidstones," I said, pretty much thinking aloud.

The girl cocked an eyebrow. "What of them? You've already indicated they're the least of your concerns, which seems a fair assessment."

In some old gangster film, this is where the protagonist of dubious morals and devilish charms, having hit upon a plan to extract himself from a tight spot, would have snapped his fingers. Me, I settled for a nervous, halfhearted excuse for a laugh.

I told Magdalena Szabó how, just maybe, I could get her what she wanted without cutting my own throat. And the girl in the chair nodded approvingly.

"Just one thing," I said. "You gotta keep Harpootlian off my ass. You let me worry about B and Drusneth and the gruesome twosome, but you keep Auntie H off me."

"Oh, my, how she hates being called that."

"I'm fucking *serious*."

"I'll do all that I can," the girl replied.

"You'll do better than that, or I promise you're never going to see your precious play pretty again. Harpootlian gets to me first, we *both* know that's a fact. I might wind up deader than I am now, and I might wind up worse than that, but *you'll* still go home empty-handed."

The girl in the black satin dress on the black wooden chair licked her pale lips and nodded again. I stood up.

"I'm not kidding around, lady. I so much as smell—"

"Is this a threat, Twice-Damned?"

"No," I told her, "it's just business. Just a contract, the wages of supply and demand."

She smiled again, like a slice of midnight.

"Do not disappoint me," Magdalena Szabó said. "My arm is long, and my vengeance against those who fail me an abyss." And then I was back on Broadway, sitting in the dirty snow and ice and slush outside a Chinese restaurant. The sun was just beginning to rise over Federal Hill.

So for the uninitiated—which I'm guessing is most of you—here's how it usually works when someone's willingly made a deal with a demon that grants it "permission" to "temporarily" possess you. First off, the whole permission part, that's sort of a joke, as the demon's gonna do it if the mood strikes, whether you consent or not. Second, "temporarily" is a total matter of faith. The demon might decide to honor the deal and vacate the premises, and it might not. You pay your money, and you take your chances. Regardless, though I may have seemed, in the preceeding pages, to have waffled on this point, I'd reached a place where I was more than a bit indifferent as to my continued existence. Still, like I said, I told that bitch Szabó how, just maybe, I could get her the goods without cutting my own throat. So I didn't have much say-so in what would follow.

Roll the bones, right?

Seven come eleven.

Commence endgame.

Soon as Magdalena Szabó had plonked me back home from whatever pocket universe she'd dragged me off to for our confab, I went directly to my apartment. To my amazement, both the downstairs door and the door to my apartment had been replaced. There was also a yellow Post-it note my cocksucker of a landlord had stuck to my door, informing me the cost would be added to my next month's rent. Anyway, I grabbed the big gym bag in which I lugged about the tools of my trade. The crossbow was already in there, along with extra clips for the Glock. I pulled my two shotguns from beneath the bed: the sawed-off double-barreled Lupara boomstick and the Mossberg 500 tricked out with a grenade launcher (oh, I always had a wicked hard-on for that bad boy). Two boxes of shells. Check. And there was still (just barely) room for a handful of M67 frag grenades, specially modified by a paranormal branch of No Such Agency for encounters with us paranormal nasties. I won't get into the technical specs on those pineapples, but they pack a fatal wallop to pretty much anything that walks, flies, hops, prances, gallops, crawls, or slithers on its belly like a reptile, no matter what nether region it might call home. I grabbed my leather duster from the closet, which was loaded with the assortment of knives. I dropped a couple of extra grenades into the pockets.

As they say, I was loaded for bear. Or at least a werepire's last stand. But if I've just painted myself as some sort of action heroine here, Sarah Conner or Alice from those *Resident Evil* movies or one of the cookie-cutter, tramp-stamped slayers from "shifter" pulp soft core . . . then I've given you the wrong impression. Half those weapons, I'd never even fired them. B kept tossing that shit my way, and I kept stashing it. Mostly, I'd used the Glock and the crossbow. The knives. Mostly. The rest? That was all goodies for the Szabó Gambit.

I called a taxi, then lugged the bag downstairs and stood on the sidewalk watching the sky until the cab arrived. The morning seemed to promise still more goddamn snow. Anyway, I gave the driver the address of Drusneth's whorehouse on Cranston. At that hour, I knew the place would be quiet as it ever gets, and that the foul skank of a succubus' guard would be as down as she ever lets it. Even demonesses gotta sleep sometime.

Now, we could do this all blow-by-blow, right? Sure we could. But, Jesus, that shit gets old fast. I'll settle for the highlights, with just enough of the gory details to tantalize those who get off on that sort of thing. There were a couple of the *se'irim* guards stationed at the back door, smoking Kools and gossiping. They had just enough time to glare disapprovingly and suspiciously at me before I vaporized them with one of the M67s, which also punched a pretty big crater in the rear foyer and made the very dramatic entrance I'd counted on.

Wouldn't it be handy, I thought, *if B's still lurking around this dump?*

Ah, Quinn, don't get your hopes up.

And before you all start worrying about the hullabaloo and racket that ensued, Drusneth had long ago cast a spell over the brothel so that no one outside could hear anything going on inside. Probably she never imagined she'd regret that particular security measure, that it could be turned against her.

I made it to the "red room"—a parlor wallpapered in crimson velvet—just off the big staircase, and I set down the bag, quickly dumped its contents into a pile on the hardwood floor. Another *se'irim* and a burly golem (real low-class sorts, golems) appeared, and I unloaded both barrels of the Lupara, ripping them apart. Didn't kill either one, but rendered them harmless.

Right about here, as Drusneth's more serious lines of defense began to kick in, Szabó took control. Both her and Harpootlian's powers were, as I'd been told, limited in this dimension, but by routing her consciousness through me, she could take advantage of a cosmic loophole and boost her signal all to hell and back.

I know. Ha, ha, fucking ha.

And here's another one: All hell broke loose.

The bitch tumbled into my skull like a bucketful of molten glass, and I went down hard. It would take her a few seconds to get the hang of my motor control. I saw two of the prostitutes, all hooves and horns and terrified eyes, appear at the foot of the stairs, and I had just enough time to warn them to run. I gotta be honest, it was nothing personal, what was going down that morning. See, most of Drusneth's girls and boys and trannies and . . . whatnot, they're decent enough sorts. For demons.

I never lost consciousness. Not for an instant. The chaos unfolded around me like one of those dreams where you're watching yourself up on a movie screen. The thing inside me didn't even bother taking cover. It crouched there on the rug and unloaded the bow and the guns on everything that dared to show its face. It brought down the house, with cacophony enough that the concealment spell was broken and I soon heard the wail of approaching sirens. Which is when Drusneth herself finally appeared, clothed only in a blue-gray silk robe and wearing no face but that she'd been created with. She was stuck somewhere between utter disbelief and the utmost reaches of beyond pissed the fuck off. Smoke and flames curled about her, licking at her flesh, and she spread her wide leathery wings and advanced on me. Me and Magdalena. Whatever. Whomever.

"How *dare* you, Twice-Damned filth?" she roared. "Abomination, you cannot *begin* to comprehend the pain and horror I will visit upon you for all eternity and a day."

"Save it for someone who gives a shit," I heard and felt Szabó say with my tongue and my voice.

Surreal.

Drusneth made a noise like a train wreck and Godzilla, all rolled up into one, and I felt my finger squeeze the trigger of the Mossberg 500. A grenade struck her square in the chest, right between her droopy tits, and hurled her backwards into the cloud of thickening smoke. Szabó cackled and howled from somewhere deep inside me. Right then, a slimy assload of tentacles that would have made the most hard-core *hentai* fan come on the spot exploded from the burning floorboards only a few feet in front of me. I watched in awe as Szabó drew my Kershaw ten-inch bush knife—pretty much a goddamn baby machete—and sliced them up like so much sashimi (no, don't know what's with three Japanese analogies in one paragraph). The oozing stubs, spurting green-black ichor, withdrew into the gloom of the basement.

Gotta admit, I was in total fucking awe.

No *way* we were getting away with this shit.

Overhead, I heard the roof begin to come apart, and some vague approximation of the fiery perdition Drusneth had promised did indeed begin to rain down upon me. Us. Around *us*, there were only the sounds of burning, the scream of fire trucks and police cars, and the moans of the wounded and dying. The air stank of burned flesh, blood, smoke, sulfur, and gunpowder. I should have been a shredded, smoldering mess from the shrapnel and flames, but I wasn't. I chalked that up to a fringe benefit of the possession, to a wee bit of evidence Szabó was playing good to her word. And, besides, a maimed host wouldn't have been much good to her, natch. Nor would a hundred and twenty-five pounds of walking hamburger been much good for Stage Two of our master plan.

Maybe it's time to make our exit, I thought as loudly as I could. She heard me.

Likely, said my mouth, *you're correct.*

We walked through an inferno, out through a sizable hole in the wall facing Wendell Street, and not so much as a hair on my head was singed. The firemen were shouting and unrolling their hoses. If they saw the waxy-skinned girl emerge from the blaze, well, they were way too busy to say anything.

Part of me just kept thinking, *Cool*, over and over again. And some other part, all it could see was the damage done and the damage yet to come. That part of me, monster or not, felt something very near regret, and it was scared to death.

Stage Two: Find Mean Mister B.

Now, I'd assumed this was going to be anything but simple. The craven son of a butt fuck would have gotten word of the big-badda-boom holocaust at Drusneth's place and gone straight to ground. And the man's a virtuoso when it comes to tucking his tail between his legs and slinking off into secret crevices from which he doesn't emerge until the coast is clear.

They say there are exceptions to every rule.

Sometimes "they" actually do know what "they're" talking about. Not often, but occasionally.

To wit: I'd walked away from Szabó's BBQ spectacle and wandered over to the park in the shadow of the turrets and yellow-glazed bricks of the Armory. If you know Providence, you know all about that great, ridiculous castle wannabe. And if you don't know Providence, use Google. Anyway, the old snow was still ankle deep in the park, and new snow was swirling down from low bayberry clouds. The only weapons I still had on me were a couple of knives in the duster. Oh, and the last of the M67 grenades that had somehow ended up in one of the jacket's deep pockets. Maybe there would be retaliation, and maybe there wouldn't. Szabó had flown the coop, leaving my head reeling, my ears ringing, my stomach rolling like a long ride on the Block Island Ferry. I was on my second cigarette when my phone buzzed.

"A little early, precious, for the Fourth of July," said B, all French-vanilla-ice-cream smooth. I flicked the stub of my cigarette at a snowbank. Werepires can be terrible litterbugs.

"Well, never let it be said you don't have some big brass balls," I replied. "Figured you'd be halfway to China by now."

There was a short pause, and then he said, "We need to talk. We need to talk right now."

"Isn't that what we're doing?"

There was a dull *whump* back towards Drusneth's as this or that mystical thingamajig blew a little more of the shithole to kingdom come. I didn't even bother to look. I kept my eyes on the snowflakes.

"I need you face-to-face, kitten."

"It wasn't me," I said.

"That's not the word on the street."

"The street ain't always the most reliable source for current events and breaking news."

Another pause, longer than the first, and when next he spoke there was an edge in his voice, the jaggedy sort comes right before anger. I could hear him straining to keep his cool. Oh, it felt good to hear that, a crazy satisfying combination of speedball and hemoglobin and the best of orgasms. Like that song by Recoil says, . . . *some soft, soft drugs*, all red delicious in my ear.

"This isn't a bloody joke, Quinn."

"Which is why you don't hear me laughing."

"Drusneth might have taken a hard hit, but—"

"Yo, B," I cut in, "you really think it's the best idea since sliced halva to be talkin' this shit on the phone? Never know who or what's eavesdropping. Also, did I mention how *I didn't do it*?"

"Where are you?" he asked.

"I got a better one, B. Where are *you*? How about we start from there? If you're camped out in that fucking booth at Babe's, you're an even bigger idiot than me. Which is saying something, brother."

"You know the place."

"Let's say I do," I said, and fished out my last Camel and crumbled the pack before tossing it towards the aforementioned snowbank.

"Get your ass over here."

"I swear, B, I *didn't* do it."

He hung up, and I sat there and finished my smoke. So, wow. Everything going more or less according to plan. You could have knocked me over with a feather. Still, a million or so ways this thing could blow up in my face, and I wasn't about to pretend that wasn't the case.

True to his word, the bastard was hiding out in The Basement. Never thought of it as a safe house or a panic room. Once upon a time, it had been a gay bar, and then some sort of goth/BDSM club, and then B had bought it and hired two or three thaumaturgy types to wrap it in every protective ward he could afford. Of course, Dru's place had been two or three times that armored, and I'd strolled in there, pretty as you please. But where the hell else did he have left to hide?

He was sitting at the counter that had once been a bar, sitting on a stool drinking a bottle of Bass. You gotta understand, Mean Mr. B only lowers himself to lowly beer when he's got trouble with two capital *T*'s.

"You know it's not secure here?" I asked him, parking myself on a stool next to him. I reached over the bar and snagged a beer from the cooler.

"And you know some place that is?" he replied, and he laughed. It struck me as the laugh of a condemned man, a death-row dude walking Spanish, a reprobate who'd accepted the inevitable and begun resigning himself to the end times and judgment.

"Not right off."

"You say it wasn't you done this deed."

"I know how it looks."

He laughed that gallows laugh again. "Do you, now? You got some clue how much shit we are currently wading in?"

I took a swallow of the cold beer, and I nodded. "More than you, I'd wager," I told him. "Yeah, it was my body holding those guns and squeezing the triggers. Tossing the grenades. Ain't gonna deny that."

"But?"

"But it was Magdalena Szabó pulling the strings. Ever known what it feels like to be a puppet?"

"This is what you say, precious."

"Listen, B. Stop and think. If it *had* just been me, if I actually could have pulled off that sort of throw-down, you think I'd be here telling you about it? Fuck, you think I'd have walked away without so much as a goddamn bruise or scratch?"

He stared at me and rubbed his stubbly chin. Looked like he hadn't shaved in a day or two, and Mean Mr. B is a fastidious man. "Szabó? So . . ."

"Yep. She's as real as Harpootlian, and she's come to cast her hat into the ring. And from what went down this morning, I'd say she's a bit more of a power to be reckoned with than Harpootlian. When all is said and done, as regards Szabó, I think the word you might be looking for is *warpath*."

The man shut his eyes, rubbed at them, then just stared at me for a while, watching me drink my Bass.

"So, we're well and righteously screwed," he said, finally. "Fucked as a hen in a roomful of roosters."

I couldn't resist a dramatic pause. I was running mostly on my own sheer terror and anger right here, and the more I saw B sweat, the clearer my head became. Those soft, soft drugs, remember?

And then I said, "I have the unicorn."

He looked at me like I'd grown a second head.

"Well, not on me. I did, but now it's hidden. Somewhere no one can get their hands on it. Frankly, I'm beginning to wonder if I can get it back. Aloysius ain't the most reliable of safekeepers."

Thunder-struck. That's the word that was on the tip of my tongue a few seconds ago, trying to describe Mean

Mr. B's expression. He looked totally fucking thunder-struck.

"You gave it to a *troll*?"

"Seemed like a good idea at the time."

"And he—"

"Stashed it somewhere in the Hollow Hills, or at least that's my best guess."

B laughed again, but it wasn't the same laugh as before. There was a note of genuine humor.

"B, it's past time to give up on whatever get-rich-quick scheme you and Dru hatched. It's almost gotten you killed."

"Might yet," he said, then finished his beer and reached for another.

"My point exactly. Time for an exit strategy, only I'm guessing the two of you—and Boston Harry's rat fink brother—were so full of hubris it never occurred to you to come up with one."

"Is Drusneth dead?" he asked, and he almost sounded like he cared. Touching.

"Fuck if I know. She took a pineapple to the chest. Last I saw of her, she—"

"Never mind, Quinn. Just never you mind. So, assuming you can get the unicorn back from that dodgy fuck, and you being all high and goddamn mighty and the dog's bollocks of tacticians, you're gonna tell me how we extract ourselves from this prickly dilemma?"

Have I mentioned how much I suck at chess? In fact, I manage to suck *and* blow at chess. Suddenly, this seemed very, very relevant, despite my deal with Magdalena Szabó and the flour-skinned girl.

"For starters," I said, "we need a patsy. A fall guy."

"And you have one of those?" he asked, and glared at me skeptically with those gray eyes of his.

"Two, actually. Though, technically, they're fall gals. Well . . . I confess I'm still trying to suss out Amity's gender, but—"

"You want to hand over Edgar Maidstone's daughters?"

"Never said I want to. Said it's what we have, and we've come to that place, B, where we gotta do what we can with what we have."

"Caught between Scylla and Charybdis," he sighed, and shook his head.

"That's about the size of it. Maidstone might be all scary, scary, but he's still just a mortal bastard, and we can deal with him later."

"You can deal with him later."

"What the fuck ever."

"So," said B, and it occurred to me right then he'd not given me his name of the day. Which I don't think had ever happened once in all the time I'd known him. That realization sent a little chill up my back, which might seem silly, given everything I'd been through. But sometimes it really *is* the small stuff.

"So," I echoed.

"Who gets the fall guys? I don't see the angle."

I so suck at chess. "We've got one dildo, two expendable sisters, and two pissed-off demons."

"Math never was my speciality," he said.

Mine, either. I suck at arithmetic almost as much as I suck (and blow) at chess. "We gotta try to make Szabó and Harpootlian both happy, or at least redirect their ire, right?"

He rolled his empty beer bottle to and fro between his hands, all thoughtful and shit. Waiting for me to tell him I'd come up with his get-out-of-jail-free card. After all, wasn't I the son of a bitch's fixer?

And I said, "Sorta robbing Peter to pay Paul. No, that's not quite right. . . ."

"Not unless you've got a plan to simultaneously nick from Paul to pay Peter. Maybe turn that swindle Ellen Andrews pulls off in the magazine tale, and shit out a spare ivory rump-splitter."

B, he's got more synonyms for "penis" than KFC's got chicken tits.

"Not exactly," I replied. "We're gonna have to choose a side, and after what went down at the whorehouse this morning, I think you'll agree that should be Szabó. If Harpootlian was packing that sort of heat, she'd have burned us by now."

He didn't disagree.

"So, Szabó gets the unicorn," I said.

"Assuming you can get it back from that troll git."

"Yeah. Assuming that. We give her the dildo, and we give Harpootlian the sisters and convince her they're the ones stole it in the first place. That they've had it all along."

"You shot the bogle who filched it," B said.

"Yeah, I know that," I told him. "Didn't know *you* knew it, though."

"Hope you won't hold it against me, thinking you're

daft, kitten. You thinking Harpootlian's going to settle for that—or any—consolation prize and sod off."

I took another swallow of my beer, which was getting warm. I wished there were a few Narragansetts in the cooler, because I fucking hate Bass.

"Look, B, you gave up the right to ask for guarantees when you got involved in this mess. So I don't want to hear you whining about the one and only option I see open to us at this late date. Not unless you've got something better, which you don't."

"You're growing balls," he said, and straightened his tie. I remember it was the banana yellow one that had tiny red stars printed on it. Ugly as a monkfish, that tie.

"Fuck or be fucked," I said. "Now, if you'll excuse me, I'm late for my own suicide."

"Hope you won't think any less of me if I just sit here on my arse and get pissed."

"B, I couldn't think any less of you if I tried."

"Fair enough," he said, and I stood up and left The Basement. When I was back out on the sidewalk, beneath the cloudy skies of that crappy winter day, I felt better, even if the cocksucker was probably right and I was likely marching off to my own doom. I took out my phone and called the Maidstone sisters. Berenice answered.

Yeah, so I took my leave of Mean Mr. B—he who on that day was ominously nameless. And then I was walking in a winter wonderland, just like the song says.

You don't need to hear the step-by-step trek (again,

again, again) across the city. But I was surprised the Maidstone sisters were still squatting in the room above the deli on Atwells. Seemed pretty goddamn dumb to me. Might as well both draw a bull's-eye on their respective foreheads and be done with it. I'd like to say their carelessness was entirely beyond my giving half of two shits, but my plan—if I may be so bold as to actually call it that—sort of depended on the two of them staying alive long enough I could hand them over to Auntie H. I had a feeling she'd be even less happy getting nothing more than two dead bitches than getting nothing more than two live bitches.

I'm coming to the end of this tale, which should be pretty damn obvious, right? I mean, if for no other reason than there aren't a whole lot of pages remaining in the book that you're holding. And, no doubt, what's to come will leave a lot of folks dissatisfied, because they like clever plots and whatnot. But life doesn't come with plots, not even the lives of the dead and unnatural. Literary conventions spawn literary expectations, a sad fucking fact, I know. Someone has an incredibly fascinating life, and you read about it, and you want an ending that offers resolution, ties everything up all neat and tidy. But then that someone dies in a plane crash, or gets run over by a bus, or shot by some asshole robbing a 7-Eleven for twelve dollars and sixteen cents. *This* is how lives go. Yeah, even the lives of dead girls who are werewolves and are all caught up in demonic, necromantic intrigues.

But, see—and I'd think this should be clear by now— I'm here to say what *happened* that February, not to make anyone happy. Not to provide a "satisfying read." So, you'll like it or you'll lump it.

Whichever. I don't care.

So, here's what happened.

I went to the sisters, and on the way, I had a long-distance chat with Harpootlian.

I found the Maidstones pretty much as last I'd seen them, setting around on their old-money asses, waiting for someone—who would be me—to do their dirty work. Amity was all decked out in claret velvet and enough antique jewelry to sink an ocean liner. Berenice apparently wasn't quite up to putting on the ritz. Don't remember exactly what she was wearing. Not that it matters.

"You killed Lenore," Berenice said. She had her back to me, parked in front of one of the windows and peering down at the snowy street.

"Wait. You talking about when I *killed* her?" I paused and pointed at the bloody dent in the wall near the door. "Or about when I put down what you made of her *after* I killed her?"

"It wasn't your place," said Berenice Maidstone. "She was nothing of yours."

"Put a sock in it. Right now my willingness to endure more of you and your sister's bullshit is down to the thin edge of a wedge. No . . . it's *not* thin. It's gone."

Amity was sitting on the old sofa. There she sat like maybe she was *Señora de las Sombras* herself, Queen of fucking Shadows, and who was *I* to have come to the end of my rope with *her*?

"Where's the unicorn?" she asked. "We're out of time, Twice-Damned."

"That mean I don't get so much as another uck-fay from you and the unexpected baloney pony?"

The handy euphemism, that came courtesy B. Like I said, he's got a million of 'em.

"You're crass," Berenice said, and, Jesus, I had to laugh.

"Gotta admit, Big Sis, it's a surprise to them what ain't in the know. None of my business, I know, but since our tumble, I do find myself wondering just how—"

"A summoning gone wrong," Amity cut in, her voice gone sharp as the point end of a switchblade.

"Wow. That's some wicked blowback."

"*Le godemiché maudit,*" Amity said. "Where is it? You've had more than enough time to discover its where-abouts."

I silently stared at her for a minute or so, and she stared right back with those murky Spanish-olive eyes of hers. Maybe she'd already gotten the drop on me, and all my problems would be over in a few more seconds, cour-tesy some snazzy dash of wizardry. Probably, I wished it'd go that way. Sure would have simplified my conundrum. You find all your electrons and protons getting suddenly scrambled and yanked apart as every atom in your body disintegrates, at least all life's little inconveniences and the burden thereof tend to go away. Silver linings, right?

"I don't have it," I told her. "I don't have it, I do not know where it is, and what's more, I don't *want* to know where it is."

Amity didn't look stunned. She just looked about a hundred shades of pissed off.

"Our agreement—" Berenice began, not turning away from her window.

I interrupted her. "Is now null and void. I've had

enough of both of you. I'm getting off this crazy train, right now, today."

"Then get out of my sight," Amity said, spitting the words from between her filed cannibal teeth the way I've read some cobras can spit venom. "Get out of my sight before I decide my desire to undo you outweighs my concerns of retaliation from your employer."

"Did you just threaten me? Did you actually have the gall to sit there on your pampered, privileged, deluded ass and *threaten* me?"

She grinned, showing me all those pointy teeth. "I've slaughtered worse than you, Siobhan Quinn."

"Wrong answer," I said, and drew the Glock from my duster. Maybe she had a deep pocketful of carnage and annihilation, but I was fast. Thank you, Mercy Brown. I put a bullet in both Amity Maidstone's pretty shoulders and two more in her kneecaps. Nothing she'd die of, or at least nothing she'd died of before she'd ceased to be of use to me.

As you can imagine, there was a lot a screaming.

It was all Amity's, though. Berenice just turned and watched her sister curled fetal on the sofa and writhing in what I suppose was some excruciating fucking pain.

"What are you doing?" Berenice asked. The words came out small and bewildered. They came out breakable.

"The two of you put me and B in Dutch with Miss Harpootlian, and I'm about to square things by honoring her with a modest blood sacrifice. Well, actually, the blood part, that'll be up to her."

"No. I don't believe it," Berenice said with a few more of those breakable words. "You'll never get away with this."

"Don't be too sure," I told her, "I'm as stupid as I'm supposed to be."

"My father—"

"The guy you and Morticia there have been trying to fuck over? The man you were out to stab in the back by getting your hands on this artifact that would unseat him as Grand Poobah of your whole crummy family? I don't think he's gonna shed too many tears when he gets the news. He made the two of you. I imagine he can make a couple more. Shit, I might even get a reward."

"You're insane," she said.

"That's the word on the street. Now shut up, or I'll shoot you, too."

Probably, Berenice had a lot more to say, but right then's when the pretty dark-skinned, red-eyed boy in the blinding white gown showed up. He wasn't there, and then he was, standing over the mess I'd made of Amity. I can't say he seemed especially happy.

"Our agreement, Twice-Damned," said Harpootlian, "was that they would be delivered unharmed."

I put the Glock back in its holster.

"Well, she's not *too* harmed," I said. "Still plenty there for you to get creative and play around with. Hours of fun and all that."

"I suppose," she said through the boy's mouth. "Though I cannot stop contemplating how much more fun I would have playing with you. You are far, far more durable than either of these women. And you did fail me, as regards the Horn of Malta."

"True on all counts," I said, hoping Harpootlian wasn't hearing more than half how freaked out I was. "But you're a businesswoman, right? Last thing you want is word to get out you welched on a deal. People talk."

"Perhaps *we'll* talk again one day, Twice-Damned."

"You never can tell."

The boy nodded, and he reached down and touched Amity's forehead with a delicate index finger. The woman just . . . well, she wasn't squirming around on the sofa anymore. She was just gone.

Berenice bolted for that window, clearly willing to take her chances with a broken neck. I drew my pistol, but by the time I'd aimed at her left knee, she'd vanished as well. Apparently, an actual laying on of hands wasn't necessary for the Demon Madam of the Lower East Side to claim her pounds of flesh and soul.

"Walk in the light, Twice-Damned, Twice-Dead," she said, "and do pray our paths never cross again."

By the time I'd turned back towards where the boy had stood, Harpootlian was gone, and I made it to my knees before I vomited.

Out into the winter wonderland again, and watching the leaden sky shitting snow, and watching the people, and the cars, a snowplow rumbling along—all this time I'm thinking, *That was too damn easy. No way, no way in hell it's gonna be that easy.*

The day had careened into late afternoon by the time

I made it to the shelter of Aloysius' underpass. I'd stopped along the way and picked up 3 Musketeers bars and a pint of Jacquin's ginger-flavored brandy. Hobo booze, that's the way I always think of it. Old man liquor. Vile stuff. But it's what the troll likes to suck down with his chocolate, and who am I to judge another nasty's tastes?

Usually I have to call him out, but this time he was sitting way back from the road, nibbling on the carcass of a run-over skunk. Smelled just about like what you'd imagine it smelled like. Only worse. I made my way over the guardrail, through the dry brown weeds and gravel. He stopped eating the roadkill and frowned at my approach.

"What you got there?" he asked, dropping the skunk and jabbing a finger at the plastic bag I was carrying. "Might it be for me?"

"It certainly isn't for me," I replied, and set the bag down at his enormous feet, not far from the dead skunk. He snatched it up and peered inside.

"Well, it's hoora good, you thinkin' a' me like that, Quinn lass."

"Sure," I said, kicking at the gravel. "Sure, but I don't have much time, Aloysius. That thing I gave you, I need it back now."

He sighed, exhaling the comingled reek of skunk rot and troll breath. His frown became frownier. He scratched at that warty chin. "Be a toaty spot of trouble there. Fear I cannae do so easy a thing as—"

"You *lost* it?" I probably sounded a whole lot more surprised than I should have. After all, hadn't I, just a few hours earlier, admitted to Mean Mr. B there was a chance I might not be able to get the dingus back from Aloysius, that you can't exactly consider trolls the same as safe-deposit boxes?

"Naw," he grunted. "Weren't like that. But the Court got wind I was roamin' 'bout with your doddle-case French-tickler, an' when Lady Mab Underhill decides ''Ah'm gantin' my paws on it.' Don't say no to the Queen of the Daoine Sidhe, oh, no, Quinn lass."

Next stupid question:

"What the fuck does the Queen of the Faeries want with a damn dildo? Don't you people have unicorns practically falling out your asses?"

"Not no yooycarns, nay. Not in the Hollow Hills."

"But what the fuck does she want with it?"

Because, see, maybe if you ask a stupid question twice, it stops being stupid. I don't know. Words were just coming out of my mouth.

"The Tithe, be on her heels, an' Mab, she got to fancyin', 'stead of givin' over her mortal loves this round, why, she'll gan geez Hell that fine, fine wang you gan me."

And then he belted out a few lines of "Tam Lin," so astoundingly off-key it's a miracle the interstate didn't come toppling down on us:

> At the end of seven years,
> She pays a tithe to Hell.
> I so fair and full of flesh,
> I fear it be myself.

"Jesus, I *know* the fucking song," I growled, and smacked him in the belly, which is about as high up as I could reach. "The dildo wasn't yours to give away!"

"Ahyacunt!" he howled, like I'd dropped a damn Acme cartoon anvil on his head. "Gonnae no *dae* that!"

"Can you at *least* speak English? You didn't *used* to talk like that!"

"Weren't my *fault*! She'd'a seen me chibbed me good and then some, had me malkied, ya mumpty boot! I was feert she'd'a counted *me* amongst the Tithe had I said no! Now gan, bolt, Quinn gone wolfish and dead fud!"

I thought about pulling out the Glock and putting a few rounds in his skull. But I had no idea if you can shoot a fairy. Well, sure, you can shoot a goddamn fairy, but I had no idea if it would even hurt the asshole. Then again, blaming Aloysius for turning over the unicorn when Mab had ordered him to, that was sort of like getting pissed at a dog for barking. So I just slapped his belly again, instead. This time he didn't protest. He only looked sort of disgusted and hurt. Not "in pain" hurt. More like, "your BFF just told you you're worthless" hurt.

"Jesus, Joseph, and Mary," I sighed, and turned my back on him. It truly had been far too easy, handing over the Maidstone sisters and thinking the worst was over, and all I had left to do was slip Szabó the loving cup to send her happily packing back to her dimension.

"No call you skelpin' me like that," Aloysius huffed. "No cause in all the worlds."

"No, there wasn't. Sorry." In the back of my mind, I hoped I meant it, that it was a sincere apology. Aloysius had always given me a fair shake—well, more often than not—and he deserved better. "Just, dude, I am so screwed."

"How? Hoot are you talkin' aboot?"

"A righteously pissed-off bitch whore of a succubus who's gonna have my head on a pike if she doesn't get that dildo sometime in the next couple of hours. The end of me, Aloysius, that's what I'm talking about. Me *and* Mr. B *and* that skank Drusneth."

"That's a sin, 'tis, Quinn lassy."

"A sin?"

"A *shame*," he said, then continued. "Eh, not such a sin for that bastirt B whose-'is-name and for no sort of hoor succubus."

"Agreed. I'd be plenty happy to be free of B, and . . . fuck Drusneth."

"*I'd* not fuck her, not even if I was pished blind."

"Don't be an idiot. You know damn well what I meant."

"Were a joke."

I glared at him; then I reached into the plastic bag and pulled out the bottle of Jacquin's brandy, unscrewed the top, and took a very long hit. Gods, it tasted sort of like hair tonic made from gingerbread and lighter fluid.

"Oh, holy motherfucking *shit*," I said, and spat in the dirt. "How in the name of Job do you drink this stuff?"

"Just tips it up to my gob—"

"Okay, whatever. Here, take it," I told him, handing over the pint. "I'm off to see Szabó and finally be done with this."

"Who's that?"

"Magdalena Szabó, my executioner, that's who she is. It was nice knowing you, Aloysius."

To tell the truth, I think I was only about half as terrified as I should have been. The soothing opiate of resignation had begun to set in, sooner than I'd have expected. He hugged me, spilling some of the brandy in the process. It was a gentler hug than he usually gave me. I didn't hear any of my bones creaking.

"Nice knowin' you, too, Quinn lass."

And I left him there. I had no idea whatsoever where I was going, but I left. Maybe I'd head back to The Basement, or maybe back to my apartment, or maybe I'd just walk around in the snow. It hardly seemed to matter. When the time came—which I knew would be sooner, rather than later—Szabó would snatch me up wherever I was.

Remember the ending of *Jaws*? If so, it might help prepare you for where this story is headed. And if not, well, no big deal. Me, I loved that movie, but I love almost all movies about predators—natural and supernatural— devouring humans. Though I'm inevitably disappointed that the humans usually emerge triumphant in The End. Guess it truly *is* rare that we can have our cake and eat it, too.

Anyway, so, yeah, Aloysius "lost" the dingus.

And, turns out, there was even less time than I'd expected before I had to confess this unfortunate turn of events to Magdalena Szabó. Like, maybe, I don't know— fifteen or twenty minutes after I left the underpass. I was contemplating one final meal, scoping out the people passing me by, looking for a juicy mark, when I wasn't on Gano Street anymore and there wasn't any snow. I was, instead, back in that very black room, that photonegative of Harpootlian's very white room, sitting in that very black chair, and the painfully skinny girl in her ebony satin evening gown, that painfully skinny girl with skin just about the color of milk, was, once again, seated only several yards in front of me in that very black chair identical to mine. The ten gold rings on her bare toes glinted dully, and she was watching me with her emerald eyes. She smiled, revealing those teeth black as coal.

"You don't have it," the girl said, and she said it so matter-of-factly that, gotta admit, it sent a shiver down my spine.

"Word travels fast," I said.

"You've failed."

"True, that," I admitted. "But, hey, at least your archenemy didn't get it, either. Which means, you know, you sort of broke even."

The milky girl licked her lips in a hungry sort of way. She clicked her long, sharp nails together. They sounded like castanets, which is, yeah, a pretty cliché analogy. But work with me here. I'm not goddamn Tolstoy or Nabokov. I'm not even a bestseller hack like Stephen King.

I'm just some dead bitch putting words down on paper.

"You've failed," the girl said again. "Nothing else is of any consequence."

"Well, maybe you could get it back from Faerie," I ventured. "I mean, badass demon versus flitty Tinkerbell nobility, how hard can that be? Especially after what you pulled off back at Drusneth's."

"You're a fool," the pale girl sighed, and clicked her nail together again. "My strength in this world—"

"Harpootlian didn't have any trouble whisking the Maidstones away. So, maybe you're stronger than you—"

"You acted as her focus. Without your hatred for the sisters, she would have been helpless."

You learn something new every day.

I pulled my duster tighter about me. Of course, I wasn't cold. The duster was, I think, sort of like Linus and his blanket, something comforting to cling to in the last moments of my existence.

"Well, so, I go into Faerie. We team up for that possession maneuver of yours again, punch old Underhill in the box before she even sees us coming."

"You truly *are* a fool," the girl said, shook her head in a sort of disappointed way, and licked her lips again.

"What?"

"I would be even weaker in the domain of the Daoine Sidhe. I have already been greatly weakened jumping between two worlds. To jump into a third, I would be almost paralyzed. You've lost the unicorn to a witless troll."

Now, Aloysius isn't the brightest bulb in the pack, but I wouldn't exactly call him witless. I wanted to take up for him, but I kept my mouth shut.

"I have tried," said Szabó through the proxy of her living marionette, "to conceive of a punishment to suit this outrage, but it's no simple task. However, we shall have eons, you and I, to devise an appropriate penance."

I pulled the leather duster still tighter. Forget Linus

van Pelt. Think, instead, about a flying fox folding its fuzzy wings about itself before bedtime.

"You know, I'm not the one who went and lost your pervy knickknack. If you ever even *had* the thing."

"And your employer, he'll join you," Szabó went on. "I cannot take this Drusneth, as she belongs to the domain of another Hell, beyond my reach."

"Poor you," I said. "Lucky Dru."

When you're as fucked as I seemed to be, well, you might as well mouth off and get in a few parting shots. I stuffed my hands into the pocket of the duster. Right then, hearing that girl's voice, they genuinely *did* feel cold.

"Enough of this," she said, and lifted one hand. A whirl of oily blackness appeared, twining itself around and between her fingers. It reminded me of the inky shadows Aloysius uses to travel between here and the Hollow Hills. *Tenebrous.* How's that for a ten-dollar word? The blackness was *tenebrous.* It began to crackle, spilling bursts of *tenebrous* electricity.

My left hand closed around something round and solid in the pocket of my duster.

Shit a brick and fuck me sideways with it. Twice.

Back at Drusneth's, I apparently hadn't used all the M67s. An earth-shattering, ball-crushing mind fuck of the faintest third cousin of hope swept over me. And then, constant reader, our complete moron of a heroine at least had the kamikaze satisfaction of going out with a bang. All at once, I was practically standing before the grand and glorious pearly gates of Fucktopia.

"Fine," I said, "let's get this show on the road." I was

doing my best to reveal not one damn iota of the joy coursing through me. But my poker face sort of sucks.

The girl made a fist, and the intensity of that crackling blackness coiling about her hand doubled, tripled. Her eyes narrowed. "Your first lesson, Twice-Damned, will be futility."

"A whole lotta motherfuckers already beat you to it," I said, and I flipped the black chair over and rolled across the black floor. Not a chance I was gonna come out of this fracas alive . . . undead . . . whatever. But I might as well add a dash of style to that aforementioned satisfaction. Nothing to lose. Nothing whatsofuckingever.

I rolled fifteen, maybe twenty feet, and by then the grenade was out of my pocket. The painfully skinny girl, Szabó had ripped her apart and made a screaming harpy of a cyclone outta the leftovers.

I got to my knees and pulled the pin.

"Lady," I said, "I got your unicorn right here."

The demon shrieked bloody goddamn murder. In the whole history of the cosmos, probably nothing has ever sounded that thoroughly unhappy.

Words fail me.

But then, they often do.

Boom. Roy Scheider, wherever you are in that great beyond, eat your heart out.

No, I have no idea how I survived. That's an uncertainty you're just going to have to deal with, same as me. Maybe it had something to do with all that interdimensional, straddling-here-and-there gobbledygook. But there was light so bright it must have put the big bang to shame, and then I was lying in the snow on Gano, not far from my old apartment. The only sound was the wind.

I lay there a long, long time. It was almost an hour past twilight before I moved.

ASHES TO ASHES

Two days later.

I'd spent most of those two days sleeping. I'd made a messy, thirst-quenching kill the night of my escape from Szabó and the black room. I had no idea if Szabó had survived the blast, same as I had no idea how I had. For the time being, I didn't give a shit. Like I said, I went back to my apartment, took a very long shower, and passed out naked on the bed. Surely, I'd earned a long winter's nap.

Two days later, my phone woke me up. Mean Mr. B. Of course it was B. Now that Shaker Lashly was dead and gone, no one else had the number. Well, except for that geek Cutter. Anyhow . . .

"Time to rise and shine, sunshine. Meet me at the club." See, B's always called Babe's "the club," even though it ain't nothing but a bar. It was dark outside. The clock by the bed told me it was a quarter past ten.

"We have some catching up to do," he said.

I told him to go fuck himself. Then I told him to give me thirty minutes or so.

I wore my duster. Ever since that February, I've worn that duster. In the instant it had taken me to pull the safety pin of that M67, it had become my rabbit's foot.

I didn't bother with makeup or the contacts. Just a pair of wraparound shades. For one night, let the looky-loos gawk their beating hearts out.

I found B in the back, where I always found B. He sipped on a Cape Cod, probably his fourth or fifth of the evening, and told me to have a seat. I didn't.

I said, "I figure you've got the lowdown by now. The highlights, at least."

"I am not one to be kept in the dark, kitten."

"Which is ironic," I said. "Can think of no place better suited for you."

He grinned and tapped his right index finger against his right temple.

"You've not lost your sense of humor," he said. "Well, such as it is. Good, that."

"Yeah, I'm a barrel of laughs."

I was starving. The place smelled like an all-you-can-eat buffet. My stomach rumbled eagerly.

"Also, you'll be pleased to know Drusneth's decided

to let bygones be bygones, so you needn't worry your pretty little head over that."

"It never even crossed my mind," I said, and then I turned my back to him and stared towards the door and snowy Wickenden Street beyond.

"Anyway, love," he said. "We can talk of your misadventures another time. Happens your return, your timing, it's most fortuitious. Have an especially delicate job out in Tiverton I wouldn't trust to anyone else."

"That so?" I asked him, and glanced over my shoulder, then back to the door. It opened, and a guy came in. The door jingled shut behind him.

"That is *very, very* so. Before he died, that wanker Rizzo up and tangled with these other wankers who found at a bleedin' *yard sale*—get this, kitten—a copy of the *Dhol Chunts* and—"

"Not my problem," I said.

You could have heard a pin drop. I mean, even if you weren't a vamp.

"And how is that, Quinn?"

"I ain't your bitch anymore, that's how. Find someone else. You're a resourceful sort. Shouldn't be too hard."

"Not a bright move," he said. "Not a bright move at all. You've made a lot of people very unhappy."

"B—"

"Bergman, sweetness. Tonight it's Bergman."

I began again. "Bergman, I'm starting to think I don't need your protection half as much as you'd like me to believe I do. That I'll do just fine on my own. But if that ain't so, it ain't so."

I heard him light a Nat Sherman.

"It isn't any better anywhere else," he sighed. "What you are, what that means, it isn't a predicament you can run from. It's the sort that follows you."

"I know," I replied.

He sighed again, louder than the first time.

"And where do you think you'll go?" he asked calmly, without the slightest hint of exasperation or irritation or even disappointment in his voice.

"I haven't thought that far ahead. Maybe Brooklyn. Maybe Boston. Fuck, Miami sounds kind of nice."

A song came on the radio, loud through the bar's stereo speakers; Patti Smith singing about Johnny and horses. A song for my funeral.

"Well, if you've made up your mind."

I told him I had.

"Then walk in the light, precious," he said, and I imagine he raised his glass to me. "Until we meet again."

"Yeah, until that day," I said, and I left Babe's for the last time ever.

I stood awhile on the sidewalk, staring up past the streetlights at the waning moon, the moon staring back down at me. Some eyes pry, no matter how much you try to hide your monster's face. Some eyes, they know the truth of truths, and they watch you every goddamn place you go, and you just have to live with knowing how they always will.

AUTHOR'S BIOGRAPHY

Kathleen Rory Tierney, despite her very Irish name, has never once left her home state of Mississippi. She is a five-time recipient of the Howling Poughkeepsie Prize for Fictionalized Biographies of Dubious Reliability, and her haiku has been collected in three volumes—*Severed Shrews and Other Perambulations, The Lives and Times of a Russion Entomologist,* and *I Wrote This While You Were Writing Reviews for Amazon.com.* She currently resides in a shotgun shack in Bird in the Hand, Pennsylvania, where she whiles away the time polishing antique sex toys. *Red Delicious* is her second novel, written shortly after her untimely demise during a stampede of guinea fowl.